W9-CFQ-024

Dear Readers,

They say March comes in like a lion, and on a blustery day, there's nothing better than four sizzling Bouquet romances to warm you from head to toe.

Legendary, award-winning author Leigh Greenwood sets the pace this month with **Love on the Run,** as a woman desperate to clear her name discovers that the P.I. hired to help her may be a danger himself—to her heart. In **Little White Lies,** from favorite Harlequin and Loveswept author Judy Gill, a contented bachelor who needs a fiancée for a month only learns that his "intended" is the one woman he could love forever.

When two stubborn people collide, it's a sure thing that sparks will fly. In Harlequin author Valerie Kirkwood's **Looking for Perfection,** a small Kentucky town is the setting for a story about two single parents who find love in a surprising place. Finally, Silhouette author Mary Schramski takes us on a search for **The Last True Cowboy,** the story of a hard-living rodeo rider—and the woman who's stolen his renegade heart.

So curl up with your favorite quilt, a cup of tea, four breathtaking, brand-new Bouquet romances and dream of spring!

Kate Duffy
Editorial Director

TWO KINDS OF KISSES . . .

Without warning, Eric put his hand under Claire's chin and lifted her head until he was looking right into her eyes. Then he kissed her.

For a moment, the world faded. Then she came to her senses. "Is this how you seduce all those women you bring home with you?" she asked.

"Can't you tell the difference," Eric asked, kissing her again, "between seduction and friendship?"

"I've never been kissed like that before," Claire said. "How is a woman supposed to know the difference?"

"Like this."

Eric put his arm around her and crushed her body to his. His mouth captured her lips in a ragged, hungry kiss. His lips covered her whole mouth, devouring her like some starving animal. She could feel the power of his arms as they encircled her, the strength of his legs as he pressed them against her thighs.

Claire was certain she would faint.

Then, just as suddenly as Eric embraced her, he released her. "There," he said, sounding nearly as breathless as she felt. "Now you know the difference."

LOVE ON
THE RUN

LEIGH GREENWOOD

Zebra Books
Kensington Publishing Corp.
http://www.zebrabooks.com

ZEBRA BOOKS are published by

Kensington Publishing Corp.
850 Third Avenue
New York, NY 10022

Copyright © 2000 by Leigh Greenwood

Zebra and the Z logo Reg. U.S. Pat. & TM Off.

First Printing: March, 2000
10 9 8 7 6 5 4 3 2 1

Printed in the United States of America

ONE

"I'm not taking any more clients," Eric Sterling said with a scowl. "I've retired."

Claire Dalton felt her stomach clench into a hard knot. The sense of panic that had been chasing her all week threatened to overtake her. But desperation got there first. Eric Sterling had to help her. If he didn't, she would go to jail.

"Everybody says you're the best in the business," she said, struggling to keep the hysteria from her voice. "You can't retire yet."

"Why not?"

They were sitting in the living room of a houseboat anchored at a private dock in Lake Wylie just southwest of Charlotte, North Carolina. Claire had never seen a houseboat before, much less been inside one. She could hardly believe how much stuff could be crammed into such a small space. Kitchen, dining, and living areas all merged into one. She assumed one of the two doors led to the bedroom. Sliding glass doors separated the interior from a deck furnished with several canvas-back chairs. The houseboats were docked side-by-side under a huge shed within a few feet of each other. The owners could visit back and forth without leaving their own boats.

"You've got to help me," Claire said.

"There's no sign on my door that says I have to help

every woman who comes in here wanting some dirt on her husband so she can divorce him," Eric shot back, his stare hard and indifferent.

"I'm not married, and I don't want a divorce."

He looked surprised. "Then what are you doing here? That was my speciality—finding dirt."

"I'm accused of stealing secrets from my company and selling them to the competition."

"Look, lady—"

"Claire. My name is Claire Dalton."

"Okay, Ms. Dalton. You've come to the wrong man," he said, impatient now. "I don't do computer espionage. I'm retired."

"You're not fully retired," Claire said. "You're testifying in a divorce case next week. You could be through with my case by then."

"Why have you been checking me out?"

She could tell he didn't like that. "They told me you were always busy, that you didn't take cases that didn't involve a lot of money. I'm not rich, but I thought since you weren't particularly busy right now . . ."

"I might be desperate enough to take your case," he finished for her.

"Not desperate, just that you would have time."

"What else did they tell you about me?"

He growled at her rather than talked to her. He was trying to scare her off. If she hadn't been so desperate, he would have succeeded.

"That you might not take me, but that if anybody could help me, you could."

"Enough with the soft soap. What did they really tell you?"

"They said you were the best," Claire repeated.

"They didn't mention my sunny disposition?"

"No."

"That's because I don't have one."

"Neither do the men I work with. They're tyrannical, overbearing, conceited, and completely insensitive to, or unconcerned about, the wants and needs of anybody but themselves."

"Then why did you come to me?"

"Because I couldn't find a female detective."

"You're in luck. I can direct you to one. Marsha Afflick."

"I've already seen her. She's the one who told me to see you."

"She should have told you my clients *never* come see me. We stay in contact by phone."

"She did, but I had to come. You wouldn't return my calls."

"Because I'm retired."

"You can't retire. I need you."

She was begging. When she left college, she'd promised herself she'd never beg or demean herself in any way. But as much as she hated herself for doing it, she didn't have any choice now. Nothing else had worked.

"And what makes you think I could care enough about you to change my plans?"

He had her there. She was a stranger. He had no reason to want to help her, to care if she went to jail. For all he knew, she could be the most notorious criminal in the rapidly growing arena of computer theft.

"You're a professional. Everybody says this job is too difficult for them, that you're the only one who can tackle it." That wasn't exactly true. They'd said the job was impossible, that the evidence against her was airtight. They'd said the only person who could possibly help her—and they didn't seem hopeful about that—was Eric Sterling.

"Look, lady, don't try to con me. My being a professional—if you can even call what I do a *profession*—has nothing to do with it."

His irritation, his obvious distaste for what he did, his whole attitude toward his work, surprised her. She'd expected him to be proud of his reputation.

"I'm not trying to con you."

"Yes, you are. You're trying to corral me with your little-miss-Sunday-school attitude, make me feel guilty. It's a waste of time. I don't have a sense of guilt. What little bit I had—and I'm not sure I ever had any at all—disappeared long ago. I don't have a conscience, either. It would have gotten in the way in this business."

"How can you feel apologetic about being the best in your field?"

He looked like he felt sorry for anyone naive enough to ask such a question.

"If that's the way you think, I'm surprised your company let you near anything worth stealing."

"I am a vice president in charge of investment banking in Charlotte. I am—was—the highest ranking woman in the bank."

"They fired you?"

"Yes."

"Then sue them."

She felt the weight of defeat coming back, the heavy sense of futility she'd kept at bay as long as she could hope Eric Sterling would take her case.

"They and the police agree they have proof I'm guilty."

"Then you're wasting your time here."

"I'm not guilty. I don't even know what computer secrets they're talking about."

"I thought you said you were intelligent."

"I'm being framed for something someone else did."

He looked disgusted, exasperated, annoyed.

"That's the oldest excuse in the book, a guilty person's last, desperate attempt to throw the blame on somebody else."

"But I didn't do it," Claire insisted. "I don't even know what was stolen. They won't tell me."

"This sounds more and more ridiculous," he said. "I'm sorry if you've done something stupid and gotten caught. I'm sorry if your partner is trying to throw all the blame on you. I am not, however, interested in helping you beat the rap."

The sound of the buzzer on the microwave oven broke into the tension between them.

"That's my dinner," Eric said. "I want you out of here. I want to eat."

"But you haven't heard my story," Claire said.

"Since I'm not taking your case, I don't need to. In fact, you shouldn't tell me anything about it."

"But you can't turn me down without listening to me."

"I just have."

Claire couldn't turn and walk off this boat. It would be the end of everything she'd fought for since she was a girl. Twenty years of careful planning, grinding work, rising above snubs, fighting against being passed over in favor of less-deserving males. All of it would go down the drain. She couldn't let that happen.

She sat down in the nearest chair, a canvas-back chair he'd probably brought in from the deck. It wasn't comfortable, but it was probably more comfortable than anything she'd find in jail.

"I'm not leaving until you hear what I have to say." She didn't know where she'd found the courage to tell this fierce man she wasn't going to leave his boat. She supposed it was desperation. He couldn't do anything worse to her than would happen if she walked away.

She observed the hardening of his expression, but the cold blue eyes continued to watch her with the unflinching intensity of an eagle following its prey. As long as she was going to be destroyed, it didn't much matter who did it.

"Do you make a habit of entering men's apartments

and refusing to leave until you get what you want?" he asked.

"This is a houseboat, not an apartment," she said, wondering why she bothered to make the distinction, "and I've never done anything like this before. I'm desperate."

He continued to watch her in that cold, calculating way that was nearly as bad as the cold, beady look of satisfaction the police investigator had had when he told her they had incontrovertible proof she'd stolen information, sold it to a competitor, and deposited the money in an account she'd never heard of.

"I believe you about being desperate, but don't get your hopes up," he said before she could speak. "It's pure gut instinct. You look too young, too intense, too driven to waste your time popping into one man's bed after another. I imagine you could be a pretty hot number if you ever got revved up, but right now your engine's choked way down."

"I'm not here to discuss my personal life." She'd been told he was a man who appreciated women, in the plural rather than the singular sense. She supposed she couldn't blame him for being what he was. Still, she didn't have to like it.

"If I were to take your case, that's exactly what I'd have to do," he said. "I don't know anyone who can completely separate their public and private lives. If they cheat and steal in one, they'll cheat and steal in the other."

"I haven't cheated or stolen in either, and that's what I want you to prove."

He studied her a little longer.

"Your dinner's getting cold," she reminded him.

"I've eaten cold food before."

"There's no need to now. I can wait."

"I don't want you to wait."

"I'm going to." She wondered if he'd try to force her to leave. He had every right.

He was also big enough. He looked to be well over six feet with well-muscled shoulders. She wondered how he got them, how he kept them. She thought private detectives spent most of their time sitting in cars or searching through files. The other two she'd interviewed had well-developed paunches, not shoulders.

"What if I throw you out?"

"I'll come back. You're my last hope."

"Great. Now you're trying guilt. I've spent most of my career helping women. I used to think they had a pretty rough deal, that they deserved a helping hand. Not anymore. Not only do they have Nature and the law on their side, they've got all the psychological advantages, too."

"How do you figure that?"

"Babies, motherhood, the little woman taking care of her man, being smaller and more helpless, having to sacrifice their bodies and pride so the crass, insensitive male can satisfy his base instincts. A few dozen other things, too, but just about the biggest is guilt. And every one of you wields it with championship skill. It must be part of your DNA."

"That's a very chauvinistic attitude."

"Maybe so, but it's one I got working for women."

"Maybe you shouldn't limit yourself to women wanting divorces from wealthy husbands. Not all of us are looking for million-dollar settlements. Maybe you ought to take a couple of cases for ordinary women who're just looking for a fair shot. All I want is my freedom."

"You're bound to have money if you're a vice president."

"I'm out on bail. I've got to hire a lawyer and a private investigator. I'll be lucky if I come out of this without being in debt."

"You're sticking to it that you're innocent."

"There's no *sticking* about it. I am innocent."

"What do the police say?"

"They say they have incontrovertible proof."

"What does your lawyer say?"

"I don't have one. They don't believe me any more than you do. Everyone I interviewed advised me to plead guilty. They said the judge would probably go easy on me since I'm a woman and this is my first offense."

"So why don't you take their advice?"

"First, I'm not guilty. And second, I'm not going to hide behind my sex. I refuse to do it in my work. I won't let it happen to me in this, either."

"Even if it means a longer jail sentence?"

"Look, I have only one thing keeping me sane in this business, the knowledge I'm innocent. Even if they send me to jail, I can go with a clear conscience. If I plead guilty just to get a shorter sentence, that's the same as confessing I've been lying, the same as telling everybody I'm guilty twice. I may have done something very stupid—I won't know until I know what actually happened—but I'm not a thief. If I can't clear my name, there won't be any point in staying out of jail. No one will ever hire me."

He was studying her again. She could see why his clients kept in touch with him by phone. She didn't know how anybody could face down his stare day after day.

"Look, I'm going to eat my dinner. That usually takes about ten minutes. Longer if I decide to linger over a glass of wine. So let's say you've got fifteen minutes to tell me your story. After that I want you out of here."

She tried not to look triumphant. She didn't want to do anything that would irritate him.

"But don't think this means I'm going to take your case," he warned as he turned toward the microwave. "You've succeeded in making me feel sorry for you; so I'll listen to your sad tale."

"Thank you."

"Don't. I'm not feeling too friendly toward you just now. Like I said, you used this psychological guilt thing on me, and I'm mad I'm still dumb enough to fall for it."

She was glad he still had at least one soft spot in his armor. She had begun to believe he was impervious.

She watched him take his dinner out of the oven and remove its plastic covering. It was lasagna made with lots of meat and cheese. She wondered who had made it for him. It obviously wasn't a store-bought meal. She started to tell him it wasn't healthy to eat so much meat and cheese, then thought better of it. She'd be a fool to stretch his patience now. He might have agreed to listen to her, but he hadn't agreed to take her case.

"Go ahead," he said. "Talk."

"I was waiting until you'd gotten everything ready to eat."

"I can listen while I move around. Besides, if you start now, maybe you'll be gone before I'm through eating. Then I can enjoy my glass of wine in peace."

Not a very promising attitude, but she still had a chance. "Quite frankly, I'm not sure what happened," she began.

"Great. You expect me to prove your innocence, some lawyer to represent you in court, but you don't know what happened. Look, lady, I'm not going to waste my time listening to you edit a story to make yourself sound better. One thing you need to learn about detectives and lawyers. We don't deal only with innocent people. We help the guilty as well. But we have to know the truth, especially if you're guilty. Now why don't you save us both a lot of time and just leave."

"You said you'd listen to my story."

"Sure, but—"

"Then you have to listen to it the way I tell it. I can't tell you what I don't know."

He'd collected silverware, a napkin, and a glass of water, which he set on the table next to his meal. He didn't take out a wine glass. Claire figured that gave her no more than ten minutes.

"Okay, have it your way. But the minute the last mouthful goes into my mouth—"

"If you don't gobble your food, I'll be finished before you are."

"I don't gobble."

"Good. It's bad for your digestion."

"Lady, *you're* bad for my digestion."

"My name is Claire."

"I don't expect you to be around long enough for me to need to know it."

"How like a man to have made up his mind before he knows all the facts."

"If you deal with the men at your company the way you've dealt with me, I wouldn't be surprised if they stole that stuff just to get rid of you."

"I have an excellent working relationship with my co-workers."

"Now that you're fired, I guess you do."

Her boss, Mr. Deter, had been apologetic about having to fire her. He'd said he couldn't believe she'd stolen the information or that she would sell it to a competitor. He said it hurt him personally because he was so fond of her, had supported her in her climb up the corporate ladder.

He was trying to be nice, to comfort her, but he had ended up making her feel that she'd let him down, let herself down. She gave him credit for supporting her, but she wasn't a fool. He wasn't altruistic. She'd worked her butt off to make him look good. He'd gotten at least one promotion because of it. He supported her because of what she had done for him. She had worked late and on weekends. She had done twice as much work as anybody else in the office. And she had done it well.

Eric looked as though he were on the verge of losing his temper, but he sat down. "Talk, but don't tell me what you think happened or what you guess. Just the facts."

"I always deal in facts," she said. "I wouldn't be a successful investment banker if I didn't."

He took a mouthful of his lasagna. She could just imagine the oil in all that cheese and sauce. He'd be lucky if he lived to forty. He ought to get married and let his wife fix decent meals.

"I was working late," she began. "One of the quickest ways to get ahead is to do more work than anybody else around you."

"How often do you work late?"

He talked with food in his mouth, something else a good wife would change.

"All the time. Weekends, too."

"Don't you date, hang out with friends, go shopping?"

"My social life isn't at issue here."

"I'm just trying to get a picture of the landscape."

"You're trying to criticize me."

"That, too."

"Why?"

"Because you irritate me. You've forced your way in here, and now I'm having to listen to this endless story."

"It wouldn't be endless if you'd stop interrupting. And you might not be so irritated if you had a glass of red wine. It would also help you digest that lasagna."

He fixed her with a frosty gaze. "So now you want to improve my eating habits."

"I'm not trying to improve anything. Your interruptions are making it impossible for me to tell you what happened."

"I think I will have that wine. I expect I'm going to need it."

TWO

Claire bit her tongue to keep from making a hasty retort. "I was working late."

"You already said that."

"I had just received a big promotion," she said, determined she wasn't going to let him get her off the topic again. "I had an old project to finish up and a lot of new material to get familiar with. I'd been in the office until nearly eleven o'clock every night the previous week. Plus spending most of my weekend there."

"You ought to be on a first name basis with the cleaning crew."

"I am, as a matter of fact. They keep my office cleaner than any other in the building."

"It always pays to remember the little people."

"Why are you such a cynic?"

"It's called realism. Actually, I think you ought to remember the little people. They're usually worth a half dozen of the big ones. But go ahead. I don't want you complaining that I'm slowing you down again."

She had no idea how he'd gotten a reputation for being the best detective in North Carolina, but she knew exactly why he had a reputation for being the most difficult.

"Anyway, I was working very late," she said, determined to get through this without losing her temper. "I was tired

and ready to go home. I had only one more thing to do
when the hard drive on my computer crashed. There was
nothing I could do but go to another computer. I decided
to use my boss's. I grabbed everything on my desk and
hurried into his office. I was in the middle of studying
the report when the entire computer system went down.

"You were very unlucky to have both happen on the
same night."

She started up from her chair. "If you're going to dis-
believe everything I say, there's no point in continuing."

"I told you that ages ago. You're the one who insisted
I listen."

Telling herself to control her temper, Claire sat back
down. She needed his help, but she didn't have to like
even the smallest thing about him.

"I had to start work on an important report the next
day, but I needed to finish studying some documents first.
I decided to finish working at home."

"If you have a computer at home, why do you stay in
the office so much?"

"I don't like to confuse home and work environments.
I like to be able to relax when I'm home."

"It sounds to me like you're never home to relax. Do
you eat frozen dinners?"

"What do you care what I eat?" she demanded, exasperated.

"I don't. I was just wondering."

He was doing this to annoy her. No man of his type
cared about a woman's well-being. They certainly didn't
concern themselves with whether she could relax or if
she ate properly. Well, he wasn't going to get the better
of her. She'd survived a father, five brothers, four uncles,
and countless cousins. She could survive one rude detective.

"I took everything home," she said. "I finished studying the reports and went to bed. Next day I took every-

thing back to the office and started on the new report. Three days later the police came to my office to tell me I was under arrest for selling company information. I had no idea what they were talking about, but they didn't believe me. I told them there was nothing in my office worth selling. They said it was worth five hundred thousand dollars to the competition. I told them that was absurd. They could check my apartment, my credit record, my bank accounts. I didn't have fifty thousand dollars to my name, certainly not five hundred thousand."

"What did you do with the money?"

"I didn't do anything with it," she shouted. "I never sold any information."

"Just checking." He took a sip from his wine.

Fighting off a desire to throttle him, Claire forced herself to calm down and continue.

"They told me the money had been deposited in a bank account they had traced to me. I told them that was impossible, that I had only one account and could prove it had less than ten thousand dollars. They said they had the bank records, the money, a clear trail that implicated me. They started to read me my rights. I stopped them and asked where they heard about this supposed theft, who had told them and when. They wouldn't say anything except they'd received an anonymous tip."

"Why should anyone want to tip them off?" Eric asked. "I'd have thought any third party would have come to you first, wanting part of the action, trying to blackmail you."

"I didn't steal any information," she said. "I didn't sell it, and nobody tried to blackmail me."

He took a sip of his wine, watching her over the top of the glass. "Not a likely chain of events," he muttered. "So what happened after that?"

"They took me to jail and booked me. It took me all day to arrange bail."

"What did your boss do?"

"Nothing."

"Doesn't sound to me like your boss believed in you very much. If you're all that valuable as an employee, he ought to have been falling over himself to help you find a lawyer and arrange bail."

Claire had thought the same thing.

"He told me he wanted to but the president told him to fire me, tell the business office to settle all financial obligations immediately, and get me out of the building as soon as possible. The president also said Mr. Deter was to make certain I returned everything in my possession that belonged to the investment department or had anything to do with bank business."

"Making a clean sweep right fast, if you ask me."

She wondered if Mr. Sterling's attitude toward her had started to soften. He didn't sound so skeptical. He didn't even sound as if he thought every word coming out of her mouth was a lie. But his expression hadn't changed. His blue-eyed gaze still bored into her. She wondered if he'd always been this hard, this distant, so incapable—or unwilling—to feel sympathy for his clients. She wondered what he had been like when he finished college, before he became disgusted with the sordid motives of the people who hired him.

"I thought so, too," she said. But on the other hand, it seemed logical. She wouldn't have wanted an employee around who'd been convicted of stealing information and selling it to the competition. And though she hadn't actually been convicted, everybody talked as if she had.

"What's happened since then?" he asked.

"I tried to talk to Mr. Deter, to find out what had been stolen; but he told me he'd been forbidden to talk to me about the case, that it might damage the bank's position. I didn't get a chance to talk to anybody else. They sent security up to watch me clean out my desk. They brought boxes in case I didn't have any. They made Mr. Deter go through everything to make sure I wasn't taking anything that belonged to the bank. I was humiliated. It was all I could do not to burst into tears."

She knew immediately saying that was a mistake. Men never liked it when women cried. They didn't know what to do. And if the woman didn't stop, they got mad. She doubted Eric Sterling would waste the energy to get angry. He'd just add it to the list of psychological tricks women employed to get men to do what they wanted and use it as an additional reason to refuse her case.

"Of course I didn't," she added. "I don't cry. It's a waste of time and never solves anything."

"I know a lot of women who disagree with you."

"I'm sure you do, but I doubt any of them are corporate vice presidents."

She wasn't about to let him lump her with all the women who hired him to help them dump their husbands for money. If she wanted wealth, she wouldn't stoop so low as to marry a man and divorce him to get it. She meant to earn everything she had, to deserve it.

But if she didn't convince Eric Sterling to take her case, she wouldn't have a career . . . or much of anything else.

"Go on," he said.

"That's it. There's nothing else to tell. The police won't tell me anything, and the people at the office won't talk to me or return my calls. I feel like an outcast."

"Most thieves are."

"I'm not a thief!"

"Okay, have it your way."

"You don't believe me."

"What I believe doesn't matter. It's what the judge and jury believe. If the police have the money, the account, and a trail directly to you, they're going to believe you're guilty. You ought to take the lawyer's advice and cop a plea. Go to court dressed like a young girl getting ready for church. Cry, plead, promise never to do it again, claim you were abused by your father, your uncle, the priest, anybody. Put the blame anywhere you can. If you're as clever as I think you are, you can get their sympathy. If you're really good, you probably won't spend more than a few months in jail."

Claire could hear the door slam, see her last chance fade. Until now, she had still had hopes Eric Sterling would take her case, that he would somehow figure out what had happened and prove her innocence. But now that wouldn't happen. He was about to refuse to help her. A feeling of total devastation swept over her.

"So that's your advice, that I throw myself on the mercy of the court."

"I don't see that you have any other choice."

"That I sacrifice any remaining dignity I might have by playing on the credulity of the jurors. That I try to make them believe somebody else—*anybody else*—is responsible for my being a thief."

"I wouldn't like to do it myself, but it works. A good lawyer can tell you how it's done. You can read up on the cases, see what the defendants said, and work out your own plan."

Claire got to her feet. He didn't believe her any more than the other private detectives she'd interviewed—or the lawyers she'd contacted.

She was alone.

"Thank you for taking the time to listen to me," she said. Only fierce pride enabled her to keep her voice steady. "I'll even thank you for your advice. I wouldn't have three days ago; but since it agrees with what everyone else tells me, I suppose it's good advice, the kind people pay a lot of money for.

"But I'm not going to take it. I'm innocent. I know you don't believe that, but somewhere out there, somebody knows the truth. I'm going to keep trying to find it. But if I don't, I'm not going to plead insanity, that I was molested, or that my childhood warped my sense of values. I may have to go to jail, but I won't sacrifice my pride. It's all I've got left."

"Look, lady—"

"My name is Claire, but you don't have to remember it because you won't be seeing me again. Now I'll leave you to your wine."

Eric watched Claire turn to leave. He had to give her credit. She had stuck to her story despite admitting the police felt they had overwhelming evidence of her guilt. That didn't surprise him. People accused of crimes usually stuck to their story, no matter how flimsy, in the beginning. Only later, when they became convinced their case was hopeless, when they saw their only chance was for a plea bargain, did they come round to telling the truth. Or as much of the truth as was necessary. Little Miss Claire would do the same thing when her time came.

But when she turned around as she reached the door and gave him one last look, he started to wonder. She looked exactly like the kind of woman to stick to her story even if it meant going down with the ship. He hated that. Useless nobility infuriated him. Take a critical, unemotional look at the situation, work out all the possible options, then choose the one most likely to give you the results you wanted. It was a simple philosophy, one that didn't take a lot of brains. In fact, it ought to have been imprinted in DNA. Self-preservation. Every person, male or female, ought to go straight to it.

But he had a gut feeling Claire Dalton would stick with her story, even if it meant going to jail for a longer term. The door clicked shut, and he heard her steps on the deck.

Why would she do something stupid like that? She was an intelligent woman. She had to be to become a vice president in the investment arm of one of the biggest banks in the country. She also had to have a large amount of common sense, an ability to weigh pertinent factors, figure how they'd play out, and make her move accordingly. So why was she sticking to her story?

The most obvious answer was that she was innocent. But if the police had an open-and-shut case against her, that couldn't be true. So what was she after? She couldn't sue her employer for firing her if she were convicted of theft. She couldn't sue for discrimination. She'd advanced a long way up the corporate ladder to still be on the green side of thirty.

Pride? Pride in what . . . being able to stick to a story in the face of overwhelming evidence? That didn't make any sense, either. She apparently hadn't let pride get in the way of her advancement in a world dominated by men.

No, the only thing that made sense was that she was innocent, that she had been framed.

But why would anyone frame a junior executive? They might want to get rid of her, but putting five hundred thousand into an account in her name was a very expensive way to do it. And what about that competition? Apparently they'd admitted to buying the information, so *someone* obviously had stolen it. If the money was in Claire Dalton's account, then it was obvious Claire Dalton had stolen it.

She had to be guilty.

But as Eric watched her standing on the dock just off his boat, not moving, seeming to be reassessing what to do, possibly bucking up her courage to face what must come next, he couldn't get rid of the gut feeling that, as unreasonable as it seemed, as implausible as her story sounded, as contrary to facts as it appeared to be, she was telling the truth. That somebody *had* framed her.

No sooner had that thought occurred to him than he told himself not to be a fool, not to let the fact she was a woman influence him.

He knew he had a weakness there. He'd always liked women. His mother's suffering had made him want to protect them, so he had become a divorce law attorney. His first few clients had wanted divorces from abusive husbands. They couldn't get one, or couldn't get a reasonable settlement, because they didn't have proof their husbands were cheating on them, hiding assets, transferring property out of their names. He'd had to turn investigator in order to win the kind of settlement the women deserved.

After that he slid away from the courtroom in favor of gathering information. It soon became clear he was better at it than most, and lawyers started coming to him, offering large fees if he'd find the information they needed. Only recently had he come to realize that he'd completely left the practice of law, the thing that had drawn him into this work in the first place, and that he didn't really like prying into the sleazy affairs of married men. But what was like a slap in the face was realizing his clients were no longer the wronged, defenseless women he had started out to help. Now he was dealing with women who used marriage as a means of becoming wealthy, women who were just as ready to play around as their husbands.

That's why he only talked to his clients over the phone or through their lawyers. He'd let his sympathy for them seduce him one time too many. Much more and he wouldn't have any pride at all. He'd always known that was important. Claire Dalton's stubborn insistence on her innocence reminded him a man could stand a lot, endure a lot, give up a lot as long as he had his pride. Once that was gone, he was usually for sale to the highest bidder.

Claire still stood on the dock. She hadn't moved since she had gotten off his boat. He wondered what was going through her mind. She could try to leave the country. He'd forgotten to mention that. Maybe the bank wouldn't push things hard enough to have her extradited. It could work. A couple of the husbands he'd investigated had taken up permanent residence abroad. They had kept their careers and most of their wealth.

Maybe he ought to tell her.

He started toward the door, then stopped. He'd refused her case. He'd offered his best advice. She must have other people who could advise her. He was out of it, and he ought to keep it that way. He wouldn't have any problem if she'd just leave. Her standing there, immobile, mute, seemed a silent indictment against him.

Damn his conscience. Damn his weakness for people with pride, especially women who wouldn't bend no matter what they faced. He'd never been able to resist them. He wanted to. He just couldn't help himself. People shouldn't be programmed to do precisely what they didn't want to do.

He turned away from the window. He refused to look at her any longer. He would clear away the leavings of his dinner. He'd fix himself a stiff scotch, get a book, and sit out on the deck. If that didn't take his mind off Claire, he'd visit with the Stricklands next door, a delightful old couple from Rhode Island who spent most of the year on their houseboat in Lake Wylie. They had a daughter in Charlotte. They went to Florida for two months after Christmas and back to New England in August.

Eric put his dishes in the sink and poured himself a straight scotch. A second thought caused him to add several ice cubes. He tended to drink straight scotch at room temperature too fast. Ice slowed him down. He liked his scotch, but he also liked a clear head.

Now if he could just manage a clear conscience.

Dammit! He had no reason to feel guilty. He was retired. If he needed any investigating done in the future, he'd hire someone else. He didn't understand why Claire Dalton's case should bother him so much. It was pointless to take the job. The woman was guilty. Her only hope was a plea bargain.

He couldn't stand it any longer. He turned and looked out the window.

She was leaving. Finally, he wouldn't have her standing there, accusing him without even looking in his direction. How did women do that? A man couldn't do it unless he was down and bleeding. Even then he'd have to make eye contact.

It wasn't her looks or her body. He'd seen a lot better of both. Well, maybe not a lot better, but Claire Dalton couldn't claim to be the most beautiful woman he'd ever seen. Still, she was very attractive.

He was drawn to the door. He couldn't help it. He had to know Claire was gone. He couldn't get rid of the nagging suspicion she might have stopped a few paces down the walkway that served the twenty houseboats at this docking shed. He wondered if her pride would cause her to do something foolish. She didn't appear to be a woman given to melodrama, but you could never tell what a person would do when they were driven against the wall. And people with great amounts of pride were the most unpredictable.

He stepped out onto the deck of his boat. His was the last docking slip on his side. Claire had to walk between eighteen houseboats before she would make a left turn that would take her to the shore. The water at that end of the shed was only ten feet deep, but you could drown in a lot less if you wanted to.

She walked slowly but steadily. She didn't look back. Just kept going.

"Another client?" Mr. Strickland asked. He and his wife were sitting outside until their favorite television show came on the educational channel.

"I told you I'm retired," he said.

"She looks like a nice woman," Mrs. Strickland said. "Maybe you ought to take just one more case."

"If I kept taking *one more case,* I'd never retire."

"Mildred is a softie for women in trouble," Aubrey Strickland said.

"You bet I am," Mildred said. "We have to watch out for each other. You men don't always do it right."

"So you keep telling me," her husband said, smiling fondly.

"You do fine. You just need a little prodding occasionally."

Eric grinned as he watched Claire walk away. They were a delightful couple, very much in love after more than fifty years of marriage. If that kind of love and devotion hadn't been so rare, Eric might have considered marriage; but they were the only example he knew. He didn't figure that suggested good odds.

"What are you going do to with your free time?" Aubrey asked.

"Nothing for a few weeks." Eric didn't turn toward Aubrey. A man had just emerged from between two boats after Claire passed. Eric couldn't see the man's face and didn't recognize his outline. He was too big, too well-muscled to be any of the retired men who lived on these boats.

"You'd better not sit around doing nothing for too long," Aubrey said. "You might start to like it."

"What you need is a wife." Mildred said that frequently. "Someone to give your life a sense of direction."

Something about the man's movement caused Eric to tense. He was following Claire, getting closer. He had done nothing overtly threatening, but Eric set down his drink, stepped toward the dock.

"Did you hear what I said?" Mildred Strickland asked.

"Claire!" The shout tore from his throat even before he saw the man take something from his pocket and lunge forward. Claire had stopped, started to turn, when the man hit her over the head. Claire's turning caused it to be a glancing blow. If it had hit her squarely, as the man had apparently intended, it could have killed her. Eric was off the boat and running down the dock as the man pushed Claire's slumping body into the water.

"Eric, what's—"

Eric didn't stop. He didn't know how badly the blow might have injured Claire; but even if it had only knocked her unconscious, she could drown. It was bingo night up at the marina. Everybody was gone except him and the Stricklands.

Eric could hear the man's footsteps on the wooden slats of the walkway as he made his escape. Claire's body floated just below the surface of the water. She was slowly sinking to the bottom.

He dived into the water.

The sudden cold shocked his body, caused his muscles to tighten. The water in the lake was always cold in April, even in the shallows; but he couldn't afford to give in to the tightening, the beginning of a cramp. He forced himself through the water until he reached Claire's limp body, managed to get his arm around her chest. He kicked with all his strength until he broke the surface of the water. He didn't know how much water she might have swallowed or breathed into her lungs. He had to get her to the dock as quickly as possible.

"What happened?" Aubrey asked. He and Mildred

were standing at the end of the dock, watching Eric tow Claire's unresponsive body to the dock.

"Somebody hit her over the head and shoved her into the water. Help me get her on the dock. We've got to get the water out of her lungs."

He was fortunate Aubrey and Mildred hated bingo. He didn't know if he could have gotten Claire onto the dock by himself. Aubrey and Mildred managed to hold Claire out of the water until Eric could climb onto the dock. He pulled her up and laid her on the dock on her stomach, her head turned to one side. He pushed hard on her back just under the shoulder blades. Water spewed out of her mouth. He lifted her arms then pushed on her shoulders again. A smaller amount of water came out this time. He had repeated the process three more times when she suddenly coughed and spit out a little remaining water.

He sank back, straddling her body. She was breathing. She would be all right.

"What's all this about?" Aubrey asked. "I've tied up at a dozen docks between Rhode Island and Florida, and I've never had to help pull a young woman from the water because some man tried to murder her."

"The police arrested her for stealing information and selling it to the opposition," Eric said between heaving breaths. "They said they had an airtight case. Claire insisted she was innocent, that somebody had framed her. I didn't believe her. I told her to find someone else."

"But you're the best," Mildred said.

"That's what she kept telling me, but she claims she has no idea what was stolen, when, where, why, or by whom. Even if I believed her, I wouldn't know where to start."

"Well, I guess you'll have to believe her now," Aubrey said.

"I guess so." He didn't know anything about computer

theft, but he couldn't imagine her employer ordinarily made a practice of hiring thugs to knock young female executives over the head and push them into the lake to drown. Maybe they thought she had still more information she could sell, but the most likely conclusion at this point was that Claire Dalton was innocent and someone was trying to make certain she didn't hire him to dig up the truth.

"I don't know why you didn't believe her from the beginning," Mildred said. "One look at her ought to tell you she couldn't do anything as awful as steal."

That was part of the problem. From the very first, he'd been pestered by the nagging feeling Claire was telling the truth, that he ought to help her. But he'd been assailed by an even stronger feeling that this woman represented danger to him, that he'd better get her off his boat and out of his life as quickly as possible.

"What are you going to do with her?" Mildred asked. "You can't leave her lying on the dock for people to step over."

"I'm not," he said, feeling a ghost of a smile curve his lips. "I'm going to take her to my boat."

THREE

"We can't leave her in those wet clothes," Mildred said.

Eric had laid Claire on a plastic sheet on his bed. She looked pale and drawn, but her breathing was steady. She would have a big lump on her head. The blow had broken the skin—she had some blood in her hair—but at least she was alive. At worst, she'd have a concussion.

"I don't have anything she can wear," Eric said.

"I could give her one of my nightgowns," Mildred offered, "but I can't undress her by myself."

"I can help," Aubrey offered.

"Not on your life," his wife replied promptly. "One glance at a body as young and shapely as hers, and you'd drop dead of a heart attack. I'd have to go live with Paul and Jean, and you know that would give me a stroke."

"One of the ladies can help you when they get back from bingo," Eric said.

"We can't wait that long," Mildred said. "Besides, none of them are strong enough to lift her. I'm afraid you're going to have to help me."

"Why won't it give *him* a heart attack?" Aubrey asked.

"Because he looks at beautiful naked women all the time," Mildred replied. "I see the ones he brings to this boat. Now go get me a nightgown. Make it the beige flannel. It won't look pretty on her, but she needs to be kept warm." She gave Eric a skeptical glance. "And he needs to be kept away from temptation."

"That beige flannel ought to do it," Aubrey muttered as the left the boat.

"Shouldn't we call the police before we undress her?" Mildred asked.

Eric had been thinking about that. He wasn't sure he was doing the right thing—he was certain he was on shaky legal ground—but he'd decided to call the police later.

"I'm not going to call them yet," he said.

Mildred favored him with a sharp look. "Why not? Someone tried to kill her."

"She's still unconscious. She can't talk to anybody, and she needs rest."

"She can get that in the hospital."

"I'm not taking her to a hospital."

"There'd better be something you're not telling me," Mildred said, her disapproval abundantly plain.

"She's been fired from her job. I don't know if anybody's going to care much what happens to her. She didn't mention any family, and she works too much to have friends. I'm not even sure the police will believe she didn't do this to herself to support her contention that someone is trying to frame her."

"She still needs to go to a hospital."

"I'll call a doctor, but I don't want anybody to know she's here. Somebody tried to kill her. If they know she's still alive, they might try again."

"I suppose this means her story is correct."

"It has to be."

"It sounds like something a lot bigger than stolen information."

"I think she stumbled into something really big without knowing it. Somebody is afraid she knows how to use what she found—and has decided to get rid of her."

"Have you thought you might be in danger as well?"

"Yeah, but what's the fun of being safe all the time?"

"Living to an old age.

"And sleeping in flannel?"

Mildred gave him a playful slap on the arm. "I like flannel. It keeps these old bones warm. And it keeps Aubrey in check. He talked his doctor into giving him some of that Viagra. I'm not as young as I used to be, but Aubrey's as bad as he was in his twenties. He could probably keep up with you." She laughed heartily at her own joke. "Now stop prying into my sex life and help me get this child out of these wet clothes."

Eric didn't look forward to this. It wouldn't be easy on him under any circumstances. But with Mildred watching . . . After having betrayed him so many times over the years, he hoped his body would be kind to him for once.

Mildred began to unbutton Claire's blouse. "I don't know where they find this material these days. You can see right through it."

He'd already noticed that. He'd also noticed that the material clung tightly to her breasts.

"Here, hold her up so I can get her blouse off," Mildred said.

Eric knelt down, slipped his arm under Claire's body, and raised her from the bed. Her body slumped against his chest.

"You never realize how limp a person can be until they're unconscious," Mildred said. "Or how heavy."

Or that they can still have a profound effect on a man's body.

"You're going to have to take her blouse off," Mildred said. "I can't do it with you holding her."

Eric allowed Claire to slump over his arm while he removed one arm from her blouse, more aware of her breasts pressed tightly against his arm and chest than of cold, soggy material. When he moved her so he could slip the blouse off her other arm, her body fell backward, her face turned up to his, her throat, shoulders, and the tops of her breasts exposed.

He'd already noticed she was attractive. Now he noticed her skin was flawless. Even unconscious, cold, and wet, it had a soft glow that made him want to run his hands over it, to explore it with his lips.

"Here, let me unhook her skirt before you lay her back down."

Mildred's voice yanked him back to reality. Claire had been hurt. She was in danger. Mildred Strickland stood at his elbow, ready to take a dim view of anything that could be interpreted as a sexual response.

Then there was his own conscience.

He didn't see why God should have saddled him with such a prickly conscience *and* an overactive libido. They weren't often in conflict these days—he guessed he'd worn his conscience down over time—but when they were, it was a doozie.

"She's got lovely skin and a nice figure," Mildred observed. "But I guess you've already noticed that."

"I noticed that *before* I fished her out of the water," Eric said.

"I expected you would."

"Give me a break. I'm holding a half-naked woman in my arms. I'm neither blind nor dead."

"I'm glad of that, but a little numb would make me happier."

Eric laughed.

"If you think I can't be trusted, you can spend the night here. I'll go sleep with Aubrey."

Mildred's hearty laugh filled the small room. "And what would you do when he grabs for you in the middle of the night?"

"Maybe I'll wear one of your flannel nightgowns."

Mildred chuckled. "Lay her down and lift her so I can pull her skirt off."

He ended up lifting her off the sofa while Mildred removed first her skirt and then her slip.

"She's wearing those dratted panty hose," Mildred complained. "Why can't women wear stockings like they used to?"

"Because men like to see them in tight, short skirts," Eric replied. "Stockings rolled above the knee would detract from the picture."

"I don't know what the world is coming to."

"Neither do I, but some things don't change. Young women who get in the way of criminals get hurt."

"Are you going to take her case?"

"You knew I would, didn't you?"

"I thought you were retired, that you'd given up on women."

"I never said that."

"Now you're talking about sex. I mean nice young women."

"I never gave up on *nice young women.* I just didn't seem to be running into any."

"Well you've got one here. I hope you mean to take good care of her."

"We'll see. She may not be too fond of me when she regains consciousness."

Aubrey returned with the nightgown. Mildred met him at the door, took the nightgown, and gave him instructions to fetch a long list of items from their bathroom. "Men never maintain a decent bathroom," she explained to Eric. "I hope yours is at least clean."

"It is."

"Good. Now go call your doctor while I get her out of her underclothes. I don't want to expose you to any more temptation than necessary."

By the time he'd finally located his doctor friend at a

social function and convinced him he needed him immediately, Eric found Claire modestly covered by a thick, flannel nightgown that came down to her ankles.

"I just kept inching it down little by little until I got it on her," Mildred said, obviously proud of herself. "Now you're safe."

But Mildred had misunderstood the situation. As long as Claire was in his life, he wouldn't be safe.

"That's a nasty blow, but I doubt she'll have a concussion," the doctor said. "I strongly recommend you take her to a hospital."

"I can't. I don't know who did this or when they might try again."

"That's a matter for the police."

"I've already called them."

"Good. But if she doesn't regain consciousness within the hour, take her to a hospital."

"I'll make sure he does," Mildred said. "She's a nice girl. What kind of man could do this to her?"

"I can't say, ma'am," the doctor replied. "Eric, could I see you outside?"

He'd been expecting this. He and Allan had been friends since college, but Allan had gone to medical school, served his internship and residency, gotten married to a nice young woman, settled into a quiet practice, and was in the process of raising two children with a third on the way.

"I've known you to get involved in a lot of bizarre situations," Allan said, "but this looks dangerous."

"It is. Someone tried to kill her. Stolen information and at least five hundred thousand dollars are involved."

"Don't you think this is something you ought to leave to the police? It's not exactly like digging up dirt for divorce court."

"I've quit doing that," Eric said, irritated he always seemed to be defending himself to Allan. "But I can't leave this to the police. They think she's guilty."

"What if she is?"

"She still doesn't deserve to be knocked over the head and pushed into the lake."

"That's for the police to worry about."

"What are they going to do? Send her home and tell her to call them the next time she sees some strange man with a blunt object in his hand sneaking up behind her. She'll be dead."

"You really think someone tried to kill her?"

"I saw it happen, Allan. If she hadn't turned, that blow would have cracked her skull."

"Then you're in danger keeping her here."

"I'm better prepared to protect myself than she is."

"Divorces are one thing. Organized crime—or whatever this is—is another. It's out of your league, Eric. Leave it to the police."

"If it were somebody you cared about, would you do that?"

"You don't know her. You said—"

"I didn't believe her. If I had—"

"Nothing would have been any different."

"I can't abandon her."

"I'm not asking you to. There's the hospital, where she ought to be right now. The police, who ought to be taking care of this crime."

"And what about her in the meantime?"

"She's bound to have family. I'm sure they'll want to take care of her."

"Maybe, but she can't tell me that until she wakes up."

"Which she'd better do very soon, or you've got to take her to the hospital. That was a nasty blow. I can stitch up the cut, but that might not be all."

"I promise." He heard footsteps at the other end of

the dock. He expected to see one of the old couples returning from bingo, but it was a policeman.

"I'd better go," Allan said. "Call me. I want to know what happens."

Good old Allan. He disapproved of Eric's lifestyle, but he wouldn't refuse to help him.

Allan and the policeman passed each other.

"You the party calling about an assault?" he said when he reached Eric's boat.

"Yes."

"You look pretty healthy to me."

"I didn't get assaulted. A young lady did."

The policeman was a rookie, practically a cub scout—downy cheeks, blond hair, blue eyes, the works. He probably hadn't been on the force more than a couple of months. Headquarters clearly didn't attach much importance to the attack on Claire.

"Where is she?"

"Inside. She hasn't regained consciousness."

"Then how do you know she was assaulted?"

"I saw it."

"You'd better tell me about it."

The young policeman faithfully made notes of everything Eric told him. "I need to talk to the girl," he said when he was finished.

"I don't imagine she'll be too clearheaded when she wakes up. Why don't you come back tomorrow?"

"We're supposed to talk to the victim right away."

"Then you'll have to wait until she wakes up."

"I don't know if I can do that."

"Then I guess you'd better come back tomorrow. And you will contact the Charlotte police? I'm sure this has something to do with that theft."

"I'll have to talk to the sheriff. I can't do nothing like that on my own."

Just Claire's luck to have the theft take place in North

Carolina and the assault in South Carolina. The two police forces would be working on this from two different angles. They might not even consider the incidents connected.

"She's waking up," Mildred said. "She wants to go home."

"She can't," Eric said, turning away from the policeman. "Have you told her what happened?"

"She's not too coherent," Mildred said. "And she's mad at you."

Great. He was doing his best to help her, and she would probably accuse him of having something to do with her assault.

He found Claire sitting up when he entered his tiny bedroom. He wasn't a medical expert, but she didn't seem to be suffering from a concussion.

"I want to go home," she said.

"You can't just yet," Eric said. "Somebody gave you a nasty blow on the head and pushed you into the lake. Right now you couldn't even stand up, much less drive your car. Besides, the doctor has given me orders to keep you under close observation for the next hour. If you start acting even a little bit funny, he wants me to take you straight to the hospital."

"I don't want to go to the hospital."

"I don't want you to go, either. But if you don't stay here, I won't have any choice but to take you."

"Don't worry, dearie," Mildred said. "Eric is a nice man. And I'll pop in from time to time to make sure he stays that way."

Claire didn't look as if she meant to give in without further argument, but the sight of the policeman distracted her. "What's he doing here?"

"I had to call the police," Eric said. "Someone tried to kill you."

"Are you sure?" she asked. "I could have hit my head

when I fell in. If you hadn't called out to me, I wouldn't have lost my balance."

"You didn't lose your balance because you turned when I called," Eric said. "And you didn't hit your head when you fell in the water. A man came out from between the boats, followed you, hit you on the head just as you turned, and pushed you into the water."

"I don't remember seeing any man."

"Are you certain?" the policeman asked.

"Of course she's not," Eric said. "She's in shock. She can't remember anything."

"I'm not in shock," Claire said. "And I didn't see any man. Maybe you pushed me in."

"He couldn't have, dearie," Mildred said. "I was standing next to him when he yelled at you. I didn't see the man who hit you, but I did hear someone running along the dock."

"Mrs. Strickland tells me I have you to thank for pulling me out of the lake," Claire said to Eric. She seemed reluctant to relinquish the chance to blame Eric for what had happened to her.

"Don't sound so surprised," Eric said.

"Let's get back to this supposed assault," the policeman said. "You say you didn't see or hear anybody, Miss—" He stopped to consult his notes. "—Miss Dalton."

"No, I didn't."

"And you didn't see anyone?" he asked Mildred.

"No, but I heard someone running away."

"But that could have been anybody, couldn't it?"

"No, it couldn't," Eric said. "I saw the man. I saw him hit Claire . . . Miss Dalton. I saw him run away."

"Then how come she didn't see him?" the policeman asked. "She was closer than you."

"Because she had her back turned."

The policeman didn't look convinced. Eric decided at that point he couldn't expect any help from the police department. Nor did he expect them to contact the Charlotte police. The case would slide through bureaucratic cracks and be lost forever.

The policeman stopped writing for a moment. "I have to report she didn't see or hear anyone."

"Of course you do, young man," Mildred said. "But you also have to report that she fell in the water. And something did split her head open."

"There's stumps in this lake," the policeman said. "It was farmland before they flooded it."

"There are no stumps in the marina," Eric said. "They were cleared out to protect the houseboats."

"They could have missed one."

"You make sure you report everything I said," Eric told him. "And I expect to see an investigator out here tomorrow. Miss Dalton will be more herself then, and she might remember what happened."

"I know what happened. I—"

"Don't worry about it tonight," Mildred said to Claire. "You can think about it tomorrow. My husband was on the boat with me when this happened," she said to the policeman. "He might have seen more than I did."

"Where is he?" the policeman asked.

"On our boat," Mildred replied. "Come with me, young man, and leave Claire to Eric. She's seen too many people already. Considering what's happened to her, she ought to be prostrate."

Eric chuckled to himself. Mildred's generation might have responded to something like this by being prostrate with shock or whatever, but Claire Dalton was more likely to go out and start looking for clues herself. If she believed anything had actually happened to her, which seemed doubtful at the moment.

"You lie back and let Eric take good care of you," Mildred said to Claire as she pushed the policeman out of the room before her. "The doctor will be back to see you in the morning."

Eric wasn't sure it was a good idea for him to be left alone with Claire. She appeared angry and distrustful. He was tempted to offer to take the policeman to Aubrey and let Mildred stay with Claire, but he had to talk to her, explain what had happened, make her understand her life was in danger.

Claire almost reached out to grab Mildred's hand as she moved past the bed, to beg her to stay with her a while longer. She would have gotten up and followed if she hadn't been so weak she couldn't even sit up without having several pillows behind her back. Whatever had happened had left her feeling nauseated with a throbbing pain in her head.

She felt frightened, shocked, uncertain about being left alone with Eric Sterling. She felt a childlike desire to run away and hide. But even as a child she'd had no one to depend on but herself.

"Don't put your hand to your head," Eric cautioned when she started to reach up and find what was hurting so.

"Why not?"

"The doctor had to put several stitches in your scalp. I'm afraid he had to shave a part of your head."

A horrible vision of herself—bald with a bloody bandage over half her head—flashed into Claire's mind. She wasn't any more vain than the next person, but a shaved head was enough to give her nightmares.

"Where's a mirror" she asked. "I've got to see what you did to me."

"Wait until tomorrow. You'll feel better and—"

"I want to see it now."

Eric picked up a small shaving mirror. "The assailant did that to you. I had nothing to do with it."

Maybe not, but she remembered he hadn't believed her, wouldn't take her case, had advised her to throw herself on the mercy of the court. A man who would do that would do anything.

"I really didn't see a man," she said. When she'd heard him call her name, she'd turned, hoping he had changed his mind, had decided she was innocent and would take her case after all. She didn't remember anything after that.

"I called because I saw the man heading toward you. If you hadn't turned, your injury would have been worse."

"That would mean somebody was trying to kill me." She supposed she ought to believe him, but it was hard to believe anyone would want to kill her. She was good with numbers, something concrete, with rational thought. She didn't know how to handle this nightmare.

"Do you honestly not know what you . . . what was stolen?"

"I have absolutely no idea. I never even heard about the theft until the police came to arrest me. I told you they wouldn't explain anything."

"Well, apparently this involves more than just information sold to the competition. When you mentioned half-a-million dollars, I knew it was more important than you were letting on."

"But you thought I'd stolen the information and just wouldn't tell you what it was."

"Unless you were paid by someone to steal it for them and you sold it to someone else for an ever greater amount of money."

"If you believe that, I'm surprised you didn't leave me in the lake and save everybody a lot of trouble."

"You're the kind of woman who can't help being a lot

of trouble. Once you get an idea in your head, you won't stop no matter what. You're stubborn, blinded by a rigid sense of right and wrong, and you'll sacrifice yourself for a principle."

"What's wrong with that?"

"It may be great for national heroes and martyrs, but it's wasted in a situation like this. All you'll get for your granite sense of honor is a long jail term."

"I didn't think it was possible for you to think less of me than when you turned me down, but it seems I was wrong."

"That had nothing to do with my turning you down," Eric said. "I was retired. I'm not retired any longer. I'll take your case."

Claire didn't know whether to jump for joy or whether the knock on the head was causing her to hear things. "Why did you change your mind?"

"Two things. I felt guilty about what I said, letting you go away so preoccupied you didn't see that man."

"And the second?"

"I don't like it when things like this happen under my nose. Since the police aren't going to do anything, it's up to me to try. Now you'd better take a look in that mirror so I can tuck you into bed. You need all the rest you can get. Tomorrow is going to be a busy day."

Her heart beating fast with happiness that Eric Sterling was going to take her case, Claire raised the mirror. The reflection she saw staring back at her caused her to shriek.

FOUR

Claire had always tried to look as attractive as possible. It made good business sense. An attractive woman got more attention, more promotions, but Claire had never yielded to vanity. She didn't have the looks for that. But never, in her worst moments, had she looked as awful as she looked now.

Approximately four-fifths of her hair, uncombed since being pushed into the lake, had dried in a tangled mass. The other fifth had been removed, exposing her bare scalp as well as a bandage that covered the wound the doctor had stitched up. She looked like a wartime casualty.

"I was afraid you were going to be upset," Eric said.

"Why did you let him shave half my head?" she cried. "I look like something out of a grade-B war movie.

"He said it would be okay to wash your hair in three days."

Three days! She could have burgeoning colonies of lice living in her head in three days. She would die of embarrassment in three days. She would have to live with her head in a paper bag. She couldn't leave this boat to go to her car, not even in the dead of night. She'd have to stay here, locked away in this miserably small boat until her hair grew out.

Locked in with Eric!

Her gaze flew to his face. What could he think of a

woman who looked like a mangled scarecrow? She'd be safe from any improper advances, that was for sure. He was used to beautiful women. The lawyers had had quite a lot to say about Eric Sterling and his reputation with women. If only half of it were true, he would have to be a remarkable man.

Yet the thought of being forced to spend the next few days in close proximity to Eric excited her. No woman could think of being in the same room with that man—especially the same *bedroom*—and not have heart palpitations. He might be rude, stubborn, high-handed, generally a terrible example of the male sex, but he looked positively wonderful. She guessed it was his compensation for being such a terrible human being. Hers had been brains. More than once she had wondered if looks might not have served her better.

She was letting herself think like an idiot, letting her hormones take over. She was too old for that, had resisted too often to give in now. Besides, looks didn't last forever. Brains did. But neither was going to put hair back on her head.

"Where did you put it?" she asked.

"Where did I put what?"

"My hair."

Before he could answer, they heard a rapid knocking on the door.

"Is anything wrong?" Mildred called out. "I heard a scream."

"Did she see me?" Claire asked.

"Of course," Eric said as he moved to open the door. "Who do you think undressed you?"

Claire had been so preoccupied with her injury, the pain, Eric, her case, the whole situation, she hadn't realized someone had removed all her clothes and put her in a nightgown. She felt heat flood her body. She prayed it really had been Mildred who'd undressed her. Knowing

Eric had seen her naked—had touched her—would be too much on top of everything else. She'd have to leave no matter what she looked like.

"Mildred insisted on seeing for herself that I haven't assaulted you," Eric said, returning with his neighbor.

"He wouldn't do such a thing," Mildred said. "I tried to tell him you're upset and frightened—what woman wouldn't be who's been knocked on the head, nearly drowned, and come to in a strange man's bed. Men never understand. They have no feelings."

"She survived all that pretty well," Eric said. "It was losing her hair that sent her over the edge."

"I didn't go over the edge," Claire protested. "I was shocked."

"Do you always scream when you're shocked?"

"What's wrong with screaming?" Mildred asked.

"She wants to know what we did with her hair."

"You don't want it back, dearie. It'll just remind you of how much you lost."

"I don't really want it," Claire said. "I can't explain it, but it's like I feel violated, that if I have my hair back it won't be so terrible."

"That doesn't make any sense," Eric said.

"Of course it does," Mildred said. "If you were a woman, you'd understand perfectly."

"Well I'm not, and I don't."

"I know, but we forgive you." Mildred smiled, patted his cheek, then turned back to Claire. "I brought you a few things I thought you might need," she said, showing Claire a bag she then set down on a chair. "A man's bathroom has hardly any of the things a woman needs."

Claire felt a sudden urge to cry. This dear woman had been so kind, so thoughtful. "Thank you, but I'm going back to my apartment as soon as I can talk Eric into letting me out of here."

"You're not to even think about going anywhere,"

Mildred said. "If you need anything, Aubrey can drive me over to your apartment and I'll get it for you."

"Nobody's going near her apartment," Eric said.

"Why not?" Mildred asked.

"Somebody's got to," Claire said. "I need clothes, my toothbrush—"

"You need to stay alive," Eric said.

"But what has my apartment got to do with—"

"You do believe someone tried to kill you, don't you?" Eric asked.

Claire hesitated.

"Someone hit you over the head and pushed you into the lake. They wanted you dead."

"I'm afraid he's right," Mildred said.

"So why—"

"I hope they think you're dead," Eric said. "That man didn't stay around to see what happened. But you can be sure he'll know if your car is moved. I can guarantee the man who ordered you killed will know you've returned to your apartment before you've been home an hour."

"But what could have been stolen that's so important?" Claire asked.

"You're the only one who can answer that. But when a half-million dollars and a hired killer are involved, I'd say it was something very important. If they've tried once, they'll try again."

"But I can't stay here forever," Claire said.

"I know. We'll have to develop a plan," Eric said. "Since you're wide awake, we might as well start now."

"You don't need me for that," Mildred said. "Besides, planning gives me a headache. I gave all that up when Aubrey retired. Here," she said, retrieving a small bag from the chair and handing it to Claire. "This will get you through until tomorrow. By that time Eric will have figured out what to do next."

"Nobody can figure this out," Claire moaned.

"Eric can," Mildred assured her. "He's very clever."

"You seem to have a lot of confidence in him."

"He's a very nice man despite all his women."

Claire didn't think that was a very good recommendation. From her experience, men who entertained a lot of women were fickle, shallow, and completely uninterested in anything beyond a physical relationship. And not even that for very long. Variety seemed to be a necessity with them.

"I'll be over tomorrow to see how you're doing," Mildred said. "Make a list of the things you'll need for the next few days. Eric and I will figure out how to get them for you." She leaned over and surprised Claire with a kiss on the cheek. "Make sure you don't let anything happen to her," she said to Eric.

Eric followed Mildred out of the room and Claire let herself sink down into the pillows. She couldn't stay here for several days. She didn't know what she would do, but she definitely had to leave. Just the thought of sleeping in such close proximity to Eric caused the blood to pound in her head, making the wound hurt even more.

"We need to talk," Eric said the moment he returned to the room.

He seemed to fill up the small room with his energy, his fierce concentration, his body. She couldn't imagine how such a big man could feel comfortable in such a small space.

"My head's pounding," she said. "Can't we wait a little while?"

"No. The doctor gave you something to kill the pain *and* something to help you sleep. Within thirty minutes you're going to be unconscious."

Panic returned in full force. "I don't want to be unconscious."

"Okay, I exaggerated; but you will probably be too sleepy to think clearly."

"I can barely do that now."

"Still, we have to begin. First—"

"Oh," she said, sitting up straight, "I've got to call my answering service."

"Why?"

"To tell them where to route my calls."

"I thought you said you worked all the time."

"I do, but when I work late, I have my calls forwarded."

"Well, the first thing to understand is that you can't call anyone. The killers have got to think you're dead."

"They would hardly be asking my answering service if I'd called in lately, would they?"

"They might have tapped your phone."

"Don't be ridiculous. Why would anybody—"

"Anybody willing to have you killed wouldn't stop at tapping phones."

She didn't like it when he made sense, particularly not that kind of sense.

"Okay, I won't call the service, but I'll need to call the office."

"Why?"

"I'm supposed to explain one of my projects to my replacement."

"Forget it. They fired you; so let them figure it out themselves. Besides, whoever's trying to kill you is at that bank."

"Don't be ridiculous. It's an internationally respected institution, not some Mafia operation. Somebody else did this."

"If so, why did they give the police an anonymous tip? Why would they want anybody to know information has been stolen and sold?"

"I don't know, but—"

"Somebody in your company is the guilty party. You know something, and they've decided to get rid of you before you can tell anyone or attempt to blackmail them. It's probably your boss."

Claire couldn't help but laugh. "You wouldn't say that if you knew Mr. Deter. He's about the most ordinary man you've ever met. Besides, he's been my mentor almost from the first. I wouldn't be where I am now without him. I mean, where I *was.*"

"I'd stick with your first statement."

"That's impossible."

"Look, Claire, somebody tried to kill you. There's always an outside chance it could be somebody you've never seen or heard of; but most times people are murdered by relatives or close friends, people they've known for years. To be on the safe side, let's assume your boss wants you dead. What could you possibly know about him that could destroy him?"

"Nothing. Mr. Deter is devoted to his wife and children, has spent his whole career with the bank. He never misses work and is always cheerful. Well, he hasn't been too cheerful recently. There's some trouble at home, but he tries hard to keep it from affecting him in the office."

"What was bothering him?"

"I don't know. That's not the kind of thing you ask about."

"Think. What could you know about him? It could be something he said, something you found, something you saw when you went to his house."

"I don't know much about his personal life. I haven't found anything wrong in the office, and I haven't been to his house since before Christmas."

"It would have to be more recent. Didn't you say you'd just been assigned to work on a new project?"

"Yes." She'd been working toward that project for more than a year. She'd been certain if she could just get it, she'd have the chance to get a really big promotion. She could almost taste success, and then it had been snatched out of her grasp. "But there was nothing secret about that. I had been assigned to look into a new investment strategy. At least five others were being studied. We were to present our reports this summer, then make a decision about which one to develop."

"Are you sure there wasn't anything there?"

"All the information we use is available to anyone else. It was simply a matter of collecting it, analyzing it, and coming up with a strategy for using it to make the most money possible."

"Something must have happened. You've just got to try to remember what it was."

"I don't even know what was stolen. How can I figure out what I might have seen or heard?"

"I don't know, but if you're telling me the truth, you—"

"Do you still think I'm lying?"

"No."

It sounded like a reluctant admission.

"But there's something peculiar about this whole situation. I think you stumbled into something so big your boss had to get rid of you."

"It can't be Mr. Deter."

"He's the most logical candidate. Anyway, this thing you discovered—"

"Which, even though it's big enough to involve millions and my murder, I didn't think was important enough to remember."

"Hey, don't blame me if you don't pay attention to what you're doing."

God, he was an arrogant man. "Believe me, I know precisely what I'm doing all the time." She didn't know how he persuaded a steady stream of women to keep coming back. If she were his girlfriend, she'd walk out on him so fast his head would spin.

It startled her to realize that just thinking about being

intimate with Eric Sterling had the power to cause her body to heat up, her muscles to tense, her heart rate and breathing to increase. It made her angry. She wasn't about to let herself get excited over this man. She wasn't very good at judging character, especially male character, but she'd already been told this man was a minefield. She'd have to be an idiot to let him get to her.

Besides, he showed every sign of being nearly as much of a chauvinist as her father. No, it was impossible for anybody to be that bad without being born in the eighteenth century, but he would certainly expect the "little woman" to be at his beck and call.

"Okay, I'll admit that something may have slipped my attention," she conceded, "but it has nothing to do with my job. I don't know what it is, but it's not that."

"Let's go over everything you did the last week before you were fired."

"What do you mean *go over everything*?"

"I mean start with the moment you woke up and don't leave anything out until you put your head on the pillow and went to sleep that night."

"I can't remember everything I did."

"People can remember a great deal more than they have any idea they know. It just takes a while. Begin with the Monday of the week before you were fired. What had you done that weekend?"

"Worked."

"Do you always work on the weekend?"

"Usually."

"Did you see any clients that weekend?"

"No. I was trying to tie up all the loose ends so I could start on the new project."

"Okay, start with Monday morning."

"Nothing much happened at the office. I—"

"I mean start from the beginning. What time did you get up? What did you have for breakfast? How long did

you shower? When did you get to work, earlier or later
than usual? How much earlier or later?"

"I can't possibly remember all that."

"Okay, we'll start with what you can remember. But
don't leave anything out—no matter how small."

Eric stopped writing. Claire had fallen asleep in the
middle of a sentence. She had to be exhausted. She probably hadn't gotten a good night's sleep, maybe no sleep
at all, since her arrest. He had come to the conclusion
that regardless of how foolish her story sounded, she was
innocent. A guilty person would have provided herself
with some kind of defense. She had none, admitted she
didn't know what had been stolen, couldn't believe anyone in her company had done it, and couldn't remember
half the things she'd done for the last ten days.

Most likely she'd done exactly what she said—worked
nonstop, nights and weekends. He couldn't imagine why
an attractive young woman in the prime of her life would
be so consumed by her work. Every social event she attended had been work related. She couldn't remember
anything that sounded useful to Eric. That might change
tomorrow when she was more rested and could remember more. They'd only gotten through six of the nine
workdays before she was arrested. Her speech had become too slurred by exhaustion for him to be certain of
what she said. The one clear thing was that she was a
workaholic.

But lying there, her hair an unholy mess, the bandage
making her look like the victim of a car bombing, she
didn't look like a young woman more comfortable in
power suits than flannel and consumed by a rabid desire
to excel in a career dominated by men.

She looked lovely, fragile, and very vulnerable.

She'd probably hate that description. Most women who

felt powerless did. Though Claire might not have felt powerless before, she did now. He couldn't forget the picture of her standing on the dock after he'd refused to take her case. She must have felt too helpless and defeated to do something as simple as walk back to her car. She probably wouldn't have remembered seeing the man who attacked her if he'd been standing in front of her.

Now she sat propped up on the pillows and a cushion from the couch. She had slumped to one side, her body limp, her face in repose, her bandaged head facing him. He felt the old familiar surge of anger when he found a woman mistreated by men. He would never forget his father's treatment of his mother. Though the women he'd helped in his career didn't always come from situations like his mother's, they somehow connected with her in his mind. That's why he'd been drawn into handling women's divorces, to give them choices, a way out when they thought there wasn't one.

That was why he had quit when he found himself helping women whose main objective was money. He had become disgusted with them and himself. But Claire's situation rekindled his pure rage, his determination to help a woman who found herself in a position where she had no way out.

He had only one problem.

He'd never had to share living space with one of his clients before. He willingly admitted he was hopelessly addicted to women. He loved to help them, and he loved to make love to them. But he didn't want to *love* any one of them. He'd bought this boat as an escape from his house and the women who employed him. The stream of women had been a defense against falling for any one of them.

He tended to fall in love with his clients. He could already feel it happening with Claire. She looked so sweet, so much in need of someone to lean on, someone to comfort her . . .

He had to stop thinking like this. This is how it always started. He ought to put her to bed properly, take his pillows, and get out of the bedroom.

He laid his pen and notepad aside. He got up, walked over to the bed, and leaned over to sit her up so he could take the pillows from behind her back. But putting his arm behind her back, pulling her forward, reaching around to pull the pillows from behind her, brought his face inches from the side of her neck. The barely recognizable fragrance of her perfume reached his nostrils, and he felt himself beginning to slip. He couldn't think of anything but the remarkably lovely skin of her neck, the softness of her body in his arms, her nearness, her warmth, the nearly overpowering desire to kiss her, to taste her with his lips.

He cursed his weakness.

He jerked the pillows from behind her and tossed all but one aside. Putting his other arm under her legs, he lifted her to slide her down into the bed. Her head fell over on his shoulder. He stood there a moment, unable to move. Gathering his willpower, he forced himself to lay her down on the bed. He adjusted the pillow under her head and pulled the bed covers up over her, leaned over, and kissed her lightly on the lips. Then he grabbed up the extra pillows and left the room.

Once on the other side of the door he leaned against it as if he'd barely managed to get through the doorway before some pursuing monster caught him. It would have been funny if it hadn't been so serious. He couldn't let himself become infatuated with this woman. If he did, she would get hurt. She'd feel grateful to him for helping her. If he managed to get her freed from the charges, to find out who had framed her, she'd be so grateful she'd be convinced she would love him forever.

He lost interest in his clients the minute the case was over. If Claire were the kind of woman he thought—weak, needy, clinging—she'd be devastated, and he'd feel like the scum bucket he was. That was why he had to get away from private investigation, from handling divorces, from handling cases involving women. He ought to go into something like corporate law. It was so male dominated he'd be perfectly safe.

He might even be able to establish a normal relationship with a woman, to see if he could truly fall in love. The fear he might not be able to love anyone deeply and truly terrified him when he lay in bed at night, alone, thinking of his future. As much as he loved many women, their loveliness, their willingness to share themselves with him and demand little in return, he knew he wanted to be loved deeply and truly. He'd been able to push the fear that he might not be able to love in return out of his mind by escaping to his boat.

Now Claire Dalton would be here for the next several days. He would have to see her, think about her, talk to her, be near her, want her.

But this time he wouldn't give in. He'd concentrate on her case, solve it, and get her out of his houseboat as soon as possible.

He fixed himself a scotch and water, picked up his notepad, and started to go over Claire's activities. He had to memorize her days, become so familiar with every detail he could crawl into her head. Maybe then he'd find the illusive clue, the piece of information she didn't know she knew, that would help him solve this puzzle.

He took his pad outside. People were returning from bingo, all ignorant of the fact his life had changed completely in the few hours they'd been gone.

FIVE

A painful throbbing in her head woke Claire. Instinctively she put her hand to her head. When she felt the bandage, the events of the last evening came crashing down on her. She looked around the unfamiliar room. She was sleeping in Eric Sterling's bed, in his bedroom, on his houseboat. Someone had tried to kill her. She'd ended up with part of her head shaved and stitches in her scalp.

Could she still be sleeping, dreaming all of this?

She felt the bandage again. No, that was real. So was the bald spot. So was the throbbing pain. She tried to sit up, but the pain got worse. She eased back down in the bed. She didn't want to be here. She especially didn't want to stay here. She felt an almost desperate need for the familiar surroundings of her own apartment, her own things—her own bed. Too much had happened to her in the last three days. Without warning, her entire life—years of planning, years of unremitting hard work—had been shattered.

She'd lost everything she'd ever wanted and didn't know why.

But Eric Sterling would find out what had happened, why she'd been framed, fired, and forgotten. She suddenly remembered a dream she'd had last night and blushed. She seldom dreamed about men, certainly never in that way. It had been a foolish dream.

She'd been a wealthy, successful, executive in some transnational company, but her offices seemed to be unlimited expanses of fur rugs, enormous sofas covered with white Italian leather, walnut paneling, walls of glass. Her clothes changed from one exotic costume to another, all seemingly out of the Arabian Nights. Eric was a movie star, achingly handsome. Women from all over the world pursued him—great beauties, great heiresses, queens draped in jewels and ermine—but he wanted no one but Claire.

He pursued her from one luxurious office to another—she wondered why they were always in an office but concluded since she worked all the time, her imagination couldn't think of any other location—from one country to another, offering to give up his career, his money, his freedom if she would only let him love her.

But she had refused!

He'd made love to her on couches, on fur rugs, on a desk that seemed to stretch to the horizons. Though he'd turned her body to liquid flame, she'd insisted that nothing mattered but her career. Then he'd dissolved, disappeared, and she'd been left with nothing but her gilded cage of glass, fur, and leather.

She would never forget the expression on his face as he grew smaller, fainter, then disappeared like an ice cube melting on a hot stove. Never had she seen an expression of such pain, of pure emotional heartbreak. It was as though, through her rejection, she had willed his death. Yet even in those last moments, he still loved her, regretted not the loss of his life but the loss of a chance to adore her.

She had been left with a feeling of loss that lingered still, giving her dream a touch of reality that made her uneasy. She didn't want to feel that way about love. It was an unreliable emotion, one that could derail a career. But more important, she didn't want to fall in love with Eric Sterling. The list of reasons was so long the thought should never have occurred to her, not even after she discovered he was handsome enough to be a movie star.

She couldn't lie down any longer. It made her feel incapable of doing anything about her life, of even thinking about it sensibly. She pushed herself up, folded the pillow behind her, and leaned back until the throbbing in her head faded enough to be bearable. She remembered Eric had said the doctor had given her a shot for the pain. If he hadn't left pills, she might have to ask for some. She couldn't think sensibly. Which was probably why she found herself thinking about something as absurd as falling in love with Eric Sterling.

Not an affair. Love.

Which would be the height of folly. She didn't have time for love. Her career took up every moment of her day, all her energy.

Her career! She didn't have a career anymore. Even if she managed to prove her innocence, no one would hire her for any position above low-level administration. She'd been around long enough to know that rumor, innuendo, even a baseless accusation could stick to a person as tenaciously as the truth. Her career as a brilliant, high-level executive in an international bank was history.

Which was all the more reason she couldn't fall in love with anybody. She wasn't going to depend on a man to support her. She'd seen firsthand what that did to a woman, and she didn't intend to give anyone the power to control her life. She would build another career—somewhere, somehow. It wouldn't be the same as before, but it would be a career. She was good. She'd proved that. If she had to, she'd start her own company.

Why hadn't she thought of that before? The same skills

necessary in banking were applicable to lots of other areas. All she had to do was get this theft business behind her.

Which brought her back to Eric.

Everything depended on him. But what could he do? The police said they had solid evidence connecting her to the money, proof she had access to the stolen material. It infuriated her that no one would tell her what had been stolen. She felt like a blindfolded child told to find her way out of a maze. There had to be a way, but she couldn't see it.

Eric believed the key lay in something she'd done in the last ten days to two weeks, but she'd just worked. Day and night. She hadn't done anything, seen anything, heard anything unusual. The sense of frustration threatened to overwhelm her. He had to be on the wrong track. But she didn't know what to tell him to do. Until she did, it only made sense to follow his advice. She would, but she would come up with something else soon. She had to.

He wanted to know everything she'd done. She'd started last night, but she didn't remember much of what she'd said. She was so sleepy. If he thought it was important, she'd humor him. She couldn't afford to drive him away, even if she thought he was doing it all wrong. She needed a notepad. Her mind couldn't hold thoughts very long now. She looked around but didn't see anything to write on. The tiny room didn't have space for tables and chairs spilling over with all the things one rarely uses but wants close at hand when the need does arise.

A knock on the door interrupted her search.

"Are you awake?"

Eric knocked and spoke softly.

"I'm awake," she said. "Come in."

He entered with a tray in his hands. "I didn't know

what you ate for breakfast," he said as he pushed the door farther open with his foot, "so I fixed everything."

He'd come close. Coffee, juice, milk, cereal, eggs and bacon, toast with grape jelly.

"That's more than I eat in a week," she said.

He set the tray down on the side of the bed. She noticed that there was an extra plate, an extra bowl, extra silverware. "I'm going to eat what you don't," he said.

"Since you fixed it, you choose first. It's not fair for you to have to eat something you don't like."

He smiled. Her stomach flipped and her head started to pound.

"I eat everything. No matter what you leave, it'll be one of my favorite foods."

Right now her favorite food would be a pain pill. She'd had no idea how strongly his presence could affect her.

"Do you prefer juice, milk, or coffee with your medicine?" he asked.

"What medicine?"

"The doctor left a prescription. I got it filled after you went to sleep last night. You were supposed to have one during the night, but you were sleeping so peacefully I didn't want to wake you."

It gave her the oddest feeling to know he'd been in the bedroom while she slept, watching her.

"A pill and some juice," she said.

He handed her the glass of juice and a single tiny white pill. "You can have one of these every six hours if you need it. I'll be back in a minute."

He disappeared. She had barely swallowed the pill and the orange juice when he returned with a TV tray. She hadn't seen one of those in years. He sat down on the bed. She felt it move under his weight.

"Now tell me what you don't want."

She had never cared much about food. She could get

through an entire reception without approaching the buffet, but now she wanted everything in sight.

"Why don't we divide everything?" she asked.

"Is your head hurting too much to think?"

She was sure he wasn't the kind of man to go overboard worrying about someone else, but she could sense his genuine concern. "No. It's just easier to have some of everything."

He grinned, and she decided she needed a pill to make her immune to his attractiveness. She could see why so many women were drawn to him. But she was also aware his relationships were begun with the end already in sight. She didn't want a relationship, but she especially didn't want one like that. Yet it seemed her heart—or some other part of her mental or emotional systems that wasn't showing much sense—had decided an affair with Eric was exactly what she wanted.

It would be easy to give in. She felt hurt, vulnerable, at a loss, unable for the first time to control the course of her life. It would be wonderful to hand him all her worries and lose herself in a glorious orgy of delight. She could just imagine—

She refused to allow herself to think about that. He was exactly the kind of man she'd sworn to avoid.

"Do you mean we share everything, the drinks as well?"

"Yes." She hadn't, but it seemed reasonable.

"I need more glasses." He disappeared.

"Did you have them outside the door, just in case?" she asked when he returned almost immediately.

"Everything is close at hand when you live on a boat."

"Do you live here all the time?"

"No." He divided the juice and coffee. "Cream and sugar?"

"I like it black."

"I like lots of cream. By the way, it's decaf."

That surprised her. She would have guessed he drank

high octane everything. She watched as he divided the granola cereal between two bowls. She usually had shredded wheat without sugar. He poured milk over the cereal and handed it to her. She put a spoonful into her mouth and chewed.

"I never had anything like this before," she told him when she finished swallowing her first mouthful.

"Do you like it?"

"The hard lumps feel strange, but I love the taste of honey and nuts." She decided shredded wheat was definitely lacking.

"You can find a dozen cereals like it in any grocery store."

She didn't remember having seen it, but then she usually dashed in and out as quickly as possible. Most of the time she skipped eating altogether if she couldn't eat out.

"Do you like to shop for your own food?"

She didn't know why she asked that question. She'd never known any man who did.

"I do my own cooking, so I have to do my own shopping."

"You cook?"

"You sound surprised."

She was. She had thought men only cooked as a hobby, or to show off. That they considered the preparation of regular meals beneath them.

"The men I know are mostly married. They're so involved in their careers they don't have time to cook."

She finished her cereal. He took the bowl.

"The scrambled eggs have cheese in them," he said. "I hope you like cheese."

"Doesn't everybody?"

"I don't know. I haven't cooked breakfast for everybody."

It was on her tongue to ask him whom he'd cooked for, but just in time she remembered the stream of women Mildred had said paraded in and out of his bed. She didn't care about those women, but she didn't want to know he'd shared the same breakfast with dozens of them. This morning was special to her, and she wanted it to remain that way.

She couldn't remember when she'd last eaten eggs, but they tasted very good. She knew she hadn't eaten bacon since high school. She avoided pork and all kinds of fatty meat. But how many times did a woman get hit over the head and pushed into a lake? She hoped never again, but that ought to give her the right to eat bacon this once.

"I don't think I've ever had a breakfast like this," she told Eric. "Nearly everything on this plate is supposed to be bad for you."

"Nutritionists have changed their minds about eggs, nuts, butter, and even the amount of fat you can have," Eric said. "I figure they'll soon decide all the things our grandparents used to eat—you know, the people who are still hale and hearty into their nineties—are good for us, and all this fat-free stuff that's so full of additives is turning us into a chemical reaction that isn't so good after all."

Claire laughed. She had a mental picture of herself as a beaker in a chemical laboratory, bubbling over while emitting strangely colored gases that caused plants to wilt, paint to peel off the walls, and the air to fill with a dense fog.

"Are you one of these back-to-nature people?"

"All the animals of the world, man included, ate natural foods for millions of years. We not only survived, we thrived. How can that be bad for you?"

She shrugged and took a bite out of her piece of toast. It tasted wonderful. He'd melted butter on it before covering it with a generous helping of grape jelly. She'd never thought of breakfast as a feast for the senses, but this morning it had turned into just that.

She wondered how much Eric's presence, his having cooked and served the breakfast, contributed to that feeling. She had to admit she liked being pampered. She hadn't known men did such things, not even for the women who warmed their beds. She had driven Eric from his bed, and he'd still treated her like a queen.

"Do you want anything else?" Eric asked when she had finished her toast.

"Yes, but I'm too full to eat another bite. I'll probably fall asleep in a few minutes—like wild animals do after gorging—and will only wake up in time to eat again."

He took the tray from her lap and carried it into the kitchen. "How does your head feel?" he called back.

"Like it's about twice its natural size, but it doesn't hurt so much anymore."

He returned with the notepad from last night. "You fell asleep last night before you could finish."

"I'm sorry."

"I expected it. Allan said you would."

"Allan?"

"The doctor. He's a friend of mine. He made me promise to take you to the hospital if you didn't feel better. You do feel better, don't you?"

"Yes."

"Good. I'd rather the killers think they succeeded. If your apartment remains empty and your car stays where it is, we may be safe."

"But won't they be expecting someone to fish my body out of the lake?"

"Ultimately, but not right now. They'd probably be glad if it never showed up. Then no one would have to answer any questions."

"Whom would they ask?"

"Your boss, people you work with, your family."

"My family wouldn't care. I'm already dead to them."

She hadn't meant to let that slip out. She couldn't keep the anger from her voice when she talked about her family. That always made people curious. They got irritated when she refused to answer their questions.

Eric didn't ask.

"Would you like some more coffee?"

"Yes."

It was amazing that, despite being accused of grand larceny and nearly killed, the little things of life never changed. She still got hungry, got tired, had to sleep, still needed several cups of coffee to get going. She guessed it was good. At least there was something of the familiar amidst all the insanity that had consumed her life.

Then there was her attraction to Eric. She didn't know how a woman in her situation could spare the mental or emotional energy to be attracted to a man, particularly a man who would be nothing but trouble. Seeing him dressed in shorts and a T-shirt did nothing to affect the magnetism. In fact, it raised her temperature a couple of degrees.

A fine cover of dark brown hair covered his arms and legs. A few chest hairs peeked over the neck of his T-shirt. But the hair looked soft and warm rather than coarse and heavy. His long legs and strong arms still showed some of last summer's tan. Eric Sterling didn't spend all of his time sitting in cars. She wondered what he liked to do. She'd never learned to swim. Hard work was the only physical activity her father had thought suitable for a woman.

"There's more coffee if you want it," Eric said when he reentered the room. He set her cup down on the table next to the bed, set his on the TV dinner tray, and settled in his chair with his notepad. "We stopped with you moving into your boss's office to work. Tell me about that."

"There's nothing to tell."

"Then tell me what there isn't to tell."

He seemed willing to wait until he got what he wanted. She supposed he had to be patient. It was probably a requirement for getting accurate and complete information from women who were upset and angry, even hysterical. She was impatient, wanted everything done immediately. Since she worked mostly with computers, she could indulge her impatience most of the time.

It had to be quite different when you worked with people, especially people who were unwilling to tell you the little secrets, the dark, shameful feelings, to confess their resentments and hatreds. She didn't know how he had the patience. She found most people annoying. They didn't do what she wanted or they didn't do it fast enough or well enough or they asked questions, half of which were a foolish waste of time.

She felt that impatience rising now. She'd already told him her boss had nothing to do with this. She'd also told him going into his office didn't mean anything. She forced herself not to ask the question that trembled on her lips.

Why wasn't he up and out trying to find out who'd done this to her?

"I was working late," she began.

"Just as you'd done every night that week."

"Yes."

"Does your boss work late?"

"Yes, but he has a computer at home that is linked to the office so he can work from there."

"Wasn't your computer linked, too?"

"Yes."

"Then why didn't you work at home?"

"I told you I preferred staying in the office."

"Okay. You were working late. Tell me what happened hour by hour, minute by minute."

Claire clenched her hands under the covers, took a

deep breath, reined in her temper. "My computer went down."

"What time?"

"About ten-thirty. I can't remember exactly."

"You weren't working on anything new?"

"No. I told you I was trying to tie up loose ends before I started the new project."

"Okay. What did you do then?"

"I grabbed everything and headed into Mr. Deter's office."

"Anybody there?"

"No."

"Any signs anybody had been there recently?"

"No. The computer was on, but he never cuts it off."

"Okay, tell me exactly what you did."

"I sat down at his desk and started to work."

"What was his desk like?"

"Why do you want to know that?"

"I want to know everything."

Again Claire had to get a grip on her impatience. "I don't see how all this can help."

"You never know where you'll find a clue," Eric said.

Claire took another deep breath. "Mr. Deter's desk is always cluttered. He's not one to put everything away the minute he's finished. He prefers to have things within reach."

"What did you do with his stuff? Did you push it aside or put it somewhere else?"

"No. I would never move things around on his desk. I put my stuff down on top of his. I always do that. He told me to."

"Okay, you've spread your stuff over his stuff. What next?"

"I put my disk into his computer and started to work."

"Was there anything on the screen when you went in?"

"No. The screen saver was up."

"But something could have been on the screen."

"No."

"Okay, what did you do?"

"I put my disk in and started to work."

"You said the whole system went down."

"I'd hardly gotten started."

"Do you know why?"

"An overload somewhere, I suppose."

"You didn't try to find out what had happened?"

"Why? I couldn't fix it."

"So what did you do?"

"I waited a few minutes to see if the system would come back up."

"How long?"

"I don't know."

"Guess."

"Less than five minutes. I'm impatient."

She looked to see how he responded to that, but his expression didn't change.

"Then what?"

"I grabbed everything, cut off the lights, and left."

"And you finished your work at home?"

"Yes."

"Any problems with your computer?"

"No."

He made her tell him everything she'd done on the project. She was certain he didn't understand half of it, but she explained it anyway. It gave her a perverse kind of pleasure to see him struggling with the information. If he insisted upon putting her through this unnecessary torture, it was only fair that he suffer as well.

"When did you get to the office next morning?" he asked.

"My usual time, seven-thirty."

"Is there anybody else there that early?"

"No."

"What did you do?"

"Printed out all the reports and left them for my secretary to make copies."

"Okay, take me through your day minute by minute."

SIX

It frustrated Eric that Claire couldn't remember anything she hadn't already told him. He didn't know whether she truly didn't remember, if she kept skipping something because she thought it too unimportant to mention, or whether she was hiding something to protect herself or someone else.

He was certain of one thing. The clue to this whole mystery was buried somewhere in the events of the last two weeks. Before then, things had been going so well Claire's boss had given her an important promotion. Whatever had occurred to cause the trouble had happened after that.

But he couldn't convince Claire. She was certain her boss and everyone else in the investment department were innocent. That frustrated him, too. It was obvious only a person at the bank could have had the means to frame her. Or a reason. As far as she was concerned, there was nothing in her life but her job and everybody connected with it had to be blameless.

Eric thought that was almost as great a tragedy as being framed for a crime she hadn't committed. He didn't know much about Claire Dalton, but he did know she was a smart, attractive, energetic, appealing woman of strong principles. Not many people these days would refuse the easy way out of a situation like this; yet Claire had made up her mind to go to jail rather than admit to a crime she hadn't committed. It was a foolish thing to do, but it was admirable. That alone made him want to protect her, to find out who'd done this to her.

Eric had never met a woman quite like Claire. His first clients had been abused women who lacked the energy to fight for themselves. They felt trapped, helpless, without options, and they had given up. At times he'd almost had to force them to accept his help.

Claire was just as helpless, caught in a net wrapped tightly around her, but she was a fighter.

Was she protecting anyone? And if so, whom? Why?

Why was he so worried about whom she might be protecting? *Worried* wasn't exactly the right word. Irritated. Angry. But that made no sense. Women always lied to him, tried to protect themselves. Even the helpless ones lied, usually to protect the worthless man who was abusing them. Lying was expected. He would have been surprised if she hadn't tried to protect someone.

So why was he so agitated?

Jealousy?

The emotion seemed too ridiculous to consider, but he couldn't dismiss it. He knew himself, knew he became protective, then involved, finally infatuated. This was his cycle, one reason he was giving up this line of work, one reason he had stopped dealing directly with his clients. He let his sympathy for their situation become confused with warmer emotions. Only this time he couldn't banish Claire to the other end of the telephone. She was in his boat, in his bed, in his *life* for the next several days, and there wasn't anything he could do about it.

The attack on her had convinced him of her innocence. But during the long night he had had to force himself to consider the possibility that the attempted murder could have been the result of a partnership gone wrong.

Even though a busted partnership fit the facts even better than her being an innocent pawn, Eric couldn't bring himself to believe she was a crook, especially one clever and determined enough to hire a private investigator to prove her innocence. If she had been in on the plot, she ought to be asking him to help her arrange some kind of blackmail, some kind of exchange for money, protection, safety.

No, she had to be innocent. She didn't show any sign of understanding what the whole thing was about. She believed everyone was as good as they said they were. She was exactly what she seemed, a young woman obsessed with her career, so blinded by her ambition, her desire to get ahead, her willingness to devote her life and all her energy to her job, she hadn't noticed when she stumbled into some kind of criminal activity. She probably held the clue in her mind, had seen it, worked with it, put her hands on it, and didn't know because she'd been too preoccupied with her work to pay attention to anything else.

He wondered what had happened in her life to cause her to drive herself so relentlessly. She didn't seem like the kind of woman to sacrifice herself on the altar of worldly success. That kind of woman played the odds, would have taken the plea bargain, gotten out of the tangle with as little damage as possible, kept right on after her goal. Claire hadn't even considered the odds. She'd set her course and meant to follow it regardless of the cost.

A strange combination of idealism and ambition. He'd never seen anything quite like it before. But he intended to keep his distance. If he didn't, the next thing he knew he'd be making love to her.

"That's enough for this morning," he said, getting up to take the breakfast dishes and trays to the kitchen. "We'll go over it again later."

"Why? There's nothing more to tell."

He lifted her tray from her lap. "There has to be more. I don't know what it is or what it will take to uncover it, but there'd better be more. If not, there's nothing I can do to keep the police from putting you in jail for a long time."

"You don't believe it's somebody outside the bank, do you?"

"No. It doesn't make sense."

"But Mr. Deter's not a crook. He wouldn't know how. And if he did, he wouldn't do this to me. He's been too kind, too helpful. He promoted me when other people were against it."

Eric didn't want to upset her. She couldn't leave the boat for a couple of days. He would try again later to get his information. In the meantime, he'd see if his friend in the police department could get a copy of the charges against her, or at least get a look at them. He'd already asked marina security to keep an eye on her car. And if he called in another favor, he could have someone watch her apartment. That would help, but it wouldn't be enough. She would have to help him with his investigation. This was one case he couldn't solve alone.

"I'm sure you're right," he said, as he turned to take the trays to the kitchen. "After all, you know him a lot better than I do. Don't worry about it. You need to get some more rest."

"I'm not sleepy and I'm not tired. I want to go home."

"You're not strong enough to go home, and you know it," he called as he scraped the dishes and put them into hot water. "Besides, we can't take the chance they'll be looking for you."

"I can't believe anybody's trying to kill me. Last night must have been an accident."

"Claire, I saw that man stalk you, hit you on the head,

and push you into the water. Do you really believe it was an accident?"

She didn't answer.

"Stop trying to convince yourself you're not in danger. It could get you killed."

"But why would anybody want to kill me?"

"That's what we have to find out."

"But they've already framed me for a crime that will send me to jail."

"Maybe they don't think that's enough. Maybe they expected you to give up, not hire a private detective."

She was getting agitated, exactly what he didn't want.

"It doesn't make sense."

"It'll make perfect sense once we know who's behind this and what he's trying to hide. You can't do anything about that now, so just settle back and relax."

"How can I relax when my whole world is turned upside down? I can't even sleep, knowing this is your bed, wondering how many women have been here before me."

Much to his surprise he felt a flush of embarrassment. "Then don't think about it."

"That's like asking me to ignore the stitches in my head."

"Those stitches represent a threat to your life. What I have done in that bed has nothing to do with it. As far as you're concerned, I'm a stranger who's stepped into your life. In a few days I'll step out again. You'll soon forget you ever saw me."

But he hoped that wasn't true. How foolish, but it would be pointless to pretend he wanted Claire to forget him. Even more alarming, he didn't want to step out of her life. He'd better get this case solved quickly. At the rate he was going, he'd be hopelessly infatuated by dinnertime.

"If you can prove my innocence, I'll remember you for the rest of my life."

"No need to do that. Paying my fee will be enough."

"But you will have given me my life back. No amount of money would be sufficient reward for that."

"Then you can name your first son after me."

He didn't know why he said that. Maybe he was trying to be funny. If so, he failed miserably. She looked shocked. He suddenly realized that he would like very much to have a son. Even more disturbing, he'd like to have that son with Claire.

Or at least some innocent, idealistic woman like her.

Don't kid yourself, Sterling, you meant Claire Dalton herself. No substitutes accepted.

He was falling into the old trap faster than usual. He'd better do something about it or he could find himself romantically involved with a woman headed for jail.

A knock on the door and a cheerful *yoo-hoo* interrupted his troubled thoughts.

"Come in," he called to Mildred. "We've just finished breakfast. You're just in time to wash the dishes."

Mildred gave him a brilliant smile. "I left Aubrey doing ours. You can't think I'd come over to wash yours."

"No, but I could hope. Claire has absolutely refused."

"I should hope so. She has to stay in bed for several days."

"I didn't refuse to wash the dishes," Claire protested, blushing charmingly. "He didn't ask. I really should have offered to help. I'm not helpless."

She started to get out of the bed, but Mildred put a stop to that immediately.

"I'm not letting you do more than sit up until this afternoon. And then only if I think you're strong enough."

"But I can't let Eric—Mr. Sterling—do everything."

"Of course you can. It'll do him good. And call him *Eric*. Mr. Sterling makes him sound respectable, and I assure you he's not."

Mildred didn't try to hide her wink. Claire blushed. Eric had never been around a strong woman who blushed so often. He was certain a very different woman lived behind the facade of a dedicated career woman. He wondered what could have happened to cause Claire to work so hard to hide her true self.

"I still don't feel right taking advantage of him," Claire said.

"You've hired him, haven't you?"

"Yes."

"Then consider it part of his job."

"I doubt he had this in mind when he set his fee," Claire said.

"We haven't discussed a fee," Eric said.

"And you won't until she feels better. He'll take advantage of your weakness," Mildred warned. "It's very expensive to support his kind of lifestyle."

"I thought you were my friend," Eric said, grinning.

"I am," Mildred said, "but women have to stick together. That's why I've come."

"And I thought you were just being nosy," Eric teased, "coming to make certain I hadn't seduced her." He had to be more careful what he said. Claire's blushing cells were going to wear out from overuse.

"Don't be ridiculous. I know you wouldn't take advantage of a young woman in her condition. You're susceptible, Eric, but you're not a lecher."

"Enough with the compliments. You'll give me a swelled head. What did you come over for if not to spy?"

"This poor child is bound to be feeling dreadfully out of place. She'd be a lot happier and more comfortable if she could have her own things. She can make a list of what she wants from her apartment, and Aubrey and I can get them for her."

"I couldn't ask you to go to so much trouble," Claire said.

"It's no trouble," Mildred replied. "Aubrey and I have nothing to do this morning."

"Nobody is going near that apartment," Eric said. "Not today or any day soon."

"But why?" Claire asked. "I can't live in Mildred's nightgown forever."

"You still think her apartment's being watched?" Mildred asked.

"I'll soon know," Eric replied. "I'm going to ask a friend to watch it for me."

"They think I'm dead," Claire said. "Why should they watch my apartment?"

"They can't be certain you're dead until your body is discovered," Eric said. "And there's always the chance that that police officer did relay the report of the attack on you to the Charlotte police."

"So?"

"So, they could have a contact in the police station. Any group that can afford to spend a half-a-million dollars to get rid of you is no small operation."

"I still need clothes."

He reached for a notepad and pen and handed both to her. "Make a list of what you feel you absolutely have to have right away. I'll go into town and get it for you."

"Don't be ridiculous," Mildred said. "If they're watching Claire's car and apartment, they're probably watching you, too."

"They don't know I pulled her out of the water."

"They know she came to see you. If you start buying a lot of female clothing, that'll make them mighty suspicious."

"What do you propose I do?"

"Let Aubrey and me buy everything. We have enough grandchildren to account for just about anything we want to buy."

"I don't have money to pay you," Claire said. "Eric won't let me go to the bank. Not even an ATM."

"I should hope not," Mildred said. "You're far too weak to leave the bed. Now get busy with that list. Aubrey wants to get back in time to watch a golf tournament on television. I don't know how he can stand it. It's boring enough when you're there."

"I've got a few things I'd like for you to pick up if you don't mind," Eric said.

"Sure. But there's no reason why you can't shop for your own things."

"It's not for me," Eric said. "We need to buy a wig for Claire when she's ready to go out."

Claire's hand went instinctively to the bandage on her head. "I'd forgotten about that. I'll probably need two or three before my hair grows back."

"One will do for the time being," Eric said. He handed Mildred a list. "Do you think you can buy all these?"

She looked at the list. Her eyes grew wide, and she cast Eric a questioning glance. "Are you sure about this?"

He nodded. "Do you think you can manage it?"

A slow smile spread over Mildred's face. "I don't know, but I'll have fun trying. Are you paying?"

"I'll pay for it," Claire said without raising her gaze from her list. "But I can't right now."

"Use your credit cards and I'll write you a check," Eric said. "That way it'll be easier to return anything we don't use."

"I need more sizes," Mildred said to Claire. "What size shoe do you wear?"

Eric figured that having to concentrate on her own list prevented Claire from becoming overly curious about Mildred's questions. Finally, each woman seemed satisfied her list was complete.

"I'd better get going," Mildred said. "Now you make sure you stay in bed," she said to Claire. "Don't let this man make you do anything. And don't let him aggravate you. Make him let you watch what you want on television. If he doesn't like it, he can use our television."

"I want her to take a nap," Eric said.

"I think that's a good idea," Mildred said. "And don't eat too much lunch. Eric is a great cook. Save room for dinner."

"What can he cook besides scrambled eggs?" Claire asked.

"Dearie, you're in for a big surprise," Mildred said. She bent over to give Claire a kiss on the cheek. "I'm sorry you got hit on the head, but I'm glad I've had the chance to get to know you. You take good care of her," she said to Eric.

"Does she always mother people?" Claire asked Eric after Mildred left.

"Always. But she can be right fierce when people don't do what she says. So you're to stay in bed. I'll close the bedroom door so I won't keep you awake."

"I don't think I can sleep. I just woke up."

"Try. If you don't, I'll grill you on your activities again. I still haven't found a clue."

"I'll go to sleep. I don't think I can go over everything I've done one more time. You've actually got me wondering if my mind isn't playing tricks on me."

"Go to sleep. Doze. It's in your subconscious. Maybe it will come out if you don't try so hard."

Eric closed the door and breathed a huge sigh of relief. He didn't know what it was, but he couldn't relax around Claire. A tension existed between them that was unlike anything he'd ever experienced. He realized Claire was different, not helpless or manipulative, but a strong woman of firm moral principles who needed help. That didn't fit into his pigeonholes. It disturbed his ideas about women, and he didn't like it. He liked his women to give him pleasure, relief from tension, not to tie him up emotionally.

On the other hand, maybe, with Claire, he'd finally gotten over his tendency to fall in love with his clients. It was about time. He'd worked on it long enough.

But as he washed the dishes, dried them, and put them away, he wasn't encouraged to believe he'd accomplished his goal just yet. He might not be infatuated with Claire, but he was rapidly becoming obsessed with her. As far as he was concerned, that was even worse.

Claire woke with a start. She'd been dreaming about people chasing her, trying to kill her. She didn't know who they were, why they were chasing her, even where she was, but she had been filled with stark terror. She had no one to help her, no one she could depend on. Everyone had turned their backs on her. Even kindly Mildred had laughed before turning away.

Worse still, the faces of the people pursuing her were people she knew—her boss, one of her friends, someone she thought she remembered from a party, a man who looked disturbingly like Eric. It was a frightening dream. She was relieved to be awake.

She wasn't alone anymore. Eric was going to help her. Mildred and her husband had gone shopping for clothes.

She looked around the room, hoping to see a telephone, but didn't. She doubted a boat this small had more than one. She didn't remember seeing one in the bedroom, but she was sure Eric would have removed it if it had been there. He had been adamant that she not contact anyone at all.

That wouldn't be a problem. She had no real friends at work, and no one in her family wanted to hear from her. Nor, to be honest, did she really want to hear from them. Not if it meant they would start criticizing, interfering, putting pressure on her to do what they thought was right, what they wanted. She'd tried to explain that she was different, why she needed to leave their community, but no one had understood. They couldn't fathom why she should want something they themselves had never wanted, something they thought was wrong, even evil.

So she'd cut herself off from her family, become even more involved with her work. Now what did she have left?

She wouldn't think about that. She was capable. She was energetic. As soon as Eric proved her innocence, she'd be right back out there, making people stand up and take notice. She would prove that a woman could do anything a man could do.

But would anybody care?

That was a useless question. She didn't care what people thought. She was doing this for herself.

But somehow that explanation didn't satisfy her. What had happened to make things different?

For the first time in years, she had nothing to do but think. Not about her job, not about how to make it to the next level, get that next promotion, or complete her work so brilliantly it would impress men who were determined not to be impressed.

Now she had time to reassess her life, figure out where she was, what she'd accomplished, what to do next. What stunned and horrified her was the realization that after all her work, despite her great success, she suddenly had nothing—no job, no prospects, not even a record she could use to get another job. She was about to become an indicted criminal, a fact that would virtually insure she was unemployable. Everything she'd studied and worked for over the past fifteen years had suddenly been wiped out, her work and effort made worthless.

She had been stripped down to herself, to Claire Dalton. Nothing more, nothing less.

So, what did she have? She was a little frightened to realize she didn't know who Claire Dalton was, what she wanted, what she thought and felt about practically anything. For years she'd defined herself by her ambition. After college, she had defined herself by the job she held, the job she wanted next. Claire was the director of this, the vice president of that, the brightest star in her bank's assortment of young executives. Outside of work, Claire Dalton had no definition, no personality.

Outside of work, she didn't exist.

It was a terrifying thought, but one she couldn't ignore. She got out of bed, went into the bathroom, turned on the light, and looked in the mirror. She was relieved to see her face staring back at her. For one crazy moment, she had been frightened the mirror would show no reflection at all.

But the likeness she saw there might as well have been that of a stranger. Her face looked drawn, her skin pallid. Any makeup had come off in the water or been scrubbed off by Eric or Mildred. Her lips seemed pale and thin, her brows and lashes lighter than she remembered. She didn't even want to think about her hair. She had always worn it short, but it would be months before she would look like herself again.

But what *was* herself?

A black, gray, or navy blue severely tailored business suit, medium heels, makeup carefully applied so as to be effective without being obvious, hair short, businesslike. That had been her image of herself. What she looked like at home, or the few times she took what passed for a vacation, didn't count. That young business executive in severely tailored gray was the only Claire Dalton who existed.

Claire shivered, turned away from the mirror. She was too agitated to get back in bed. She opened the curtain. All she could see was the side of another houseboat, its curtains drawn. It seemed a simile for her life, closed away in a cubicle, eyes turned inward, shutting everything out but the tiny world inside.

She hadn't minded her career taking up her time, but she'd never intended for it to consume her personality as well. She did have a personality, didn't she? Claire Dalton had to exist outside of the job. She used to.

Or had she? Had she ever existed beyond this all-consuming passion to get ahead, to succeed, to make a place for herself in a world her family had forbidden her to want?

She had no husband, no friends, no hobbies, no passions, no possession she cared about. Not even a pet. She had an apartment she slept in, furniture that served its function, a car that got her to and from work. Other than that, she had nothing.

Surely somewhere along the line she'd had other ambitions, things she wanted, *needed,* to be happy. What were they? When had she forgotten about them? Why had she cast them aside?

She had no answers, but she knew she must find some. If not, she might as well go to jail.

She had already entombed herself.

A knock sounded at the door.

"Time to wake up," Eric called. "Lunch will be ready in ten minutes."

SEVEN

"Stay in bed," Eric said. "I'll bring lunch to you."

"I need to get out of this bedroom," Claire said. "I'm beginning to feel like I'm shut up in a cell."

"I know it's not very big, but no woman ever compared my bedroom to a prison cell before."

Claire felt herself flush. She figured Eric was trying to raise her spirits, but the image of some voluptuous creature lounging on his bed, beckoning Eric to join her, her body covered only by sheer material, was too strong to be ignored. She started to ask Eric if she could borrow his bathrobe, but the thickness of Mildred's flannel nightgown made additional clothing unnecessary.

"I feel locked away with nothing but my thoughts," she said. "They're not very good company these days."

"The living room isn't much bigger," Eric said.

"At least I can look out the window."

The combined kitchen, dining, and living area would have been crowded for a party, even a small one, but it was rather roomy for two people. Eric probably hadn't bought a bigger boat because he'd never planned to have more than one guest at a time. The image of the voluptuous female on his bed flashed through her mind once more. She didn't blush, but she could feel her temperature rise. She'd always felt equal or superior to any other woman when it came to her job. When it came to feeling feminine, seductive, desirable, she felt like a throwaway, a nonfeminine female.

Odd. That had never bothered her before, but now everything had changed. Could it be her vulnerability, the danger, her feeling of helplessness, or was it something more fundamental?

Could this change be solely because of Eric Sterling? That seemed a silly reason. He would have no interest in her if she hadn't been attacked right before his eyes and he hadn't been forced to let her stay on his houseboat. She would be very foolish to attribute his change of attitude, any show of interest, any small kindness, to anything other than the conduct of a gentlemanly host.

He certainly couldn't have any interest in the woman she'd seen in the mirror.

She banished the image of the voluptuous blond. She hadn't been able to compete with a woman like that before she'd been pushed into the water. Now she didn't even appear to belong to the same species.

"You have to sit down," Eric said. "If Mildred or Allan find me letting you wander all over, I'll catch hell."

Claire almost asked *Who's Allan?* before she remembered he was the doctor. Strange that a man she didn't know would be concerned about her. But he was a doctor. It was his job to care.

What about Mildred? Why did she care? She'd never seen Claire before last night. She had no reason to be interested in her well-being. She certainly had no reason to volunteer to do her shopping. But she had.

Claire walked slowly and deliberately out of the bedroom and over to the sliding glass door that separated the living area from the open deck. The view was of the decks of other houseboats, some occupied, some empty, all looking very much the same.

"You can sit over here," Eric said, pulling out a chair

from its place against the wall. He waited until she seated herself. "I don't have a proper dinner table."

"It doesn't matter. I rarely eat at a table unless I'm on a business lunch."

He set up the card table and set it over her lap. "I do have a tablecloth."

She was surprised he'd even thought of that. Her family never used a tablecloth. Her mother said it was easier to clean a wood surface than wash a tablecloth.

"I feel guilty letting you cook and do all the cleaning up," she said.

"Don't. Besides, there's not enough room in my kitchen for two."

"It hardly looks big enough for one."

Her mother's kitchen was huge. All the girls had helped prepare the meals. And everyone sat down at a table large enough to seat a dozen people, half again that many when necessary.

Claire sometimes felt lonely for the company, but she never missed the constant disapproval, the censorious looks when she expressed an opinion that ran counter to her father's beliefs. Going away to college in the face of strenuous opposition had been a liberation, getting a job and setting up her own apartment an empowerment.

But there was something about Eric's tiny kitchen, his small living-dining room with its intimate atmosphere that brought back a kinder feeling for that huge kitchen, a nostalgia for something she hadn't recognized then, couldn't identify now.

"I don't do a lot of cooking here," he said.

She hadn't expected he would. He was too busy making love to an endless stream of women.

"I guess it would be too crowded for a party."

"Not really. People can spill over on the deck and walkway if necessary."

"Do you have many parties here?"

"No. I bought a small boat because I like to keep to myself."

And the beauties he invited to join him. She had to get her mind off the women in Eric's life. They had nothing to do with her. He had nothing to do with her except to help prove her innocence. After that, she'd never see him again.

But she couldn't possibly forget the man who had saved her life, who had protected and cared for her while she recovered. No, he would be the one to forget her. After all those voluptuous beauties, why should he remember a scarecrow?

"I hope you like tuna fish," Eric said. He set a plate down in front of her with a large mound of tuna fish salad in the center surrounded by crackers. "I ought to give you milk or hot tea, but we drank all the milk at breakfast and I don't have anything else except Coke and beer." He set down a glass of Coke. She stared at the tuna fish. She'd never seen any quite like it.

"What's wrong?" he asked.

"Nothing."

"Then why are you staring at your plate as if there's a worm crawling out of the lettuce?"

"I was wondering how you fix your tuna fish salad. It doesn't look like what I'm used to."

"Taste it. If you hate it, I'll fix something else."

She picked up her fork, took a small amount, and put it in her mouth. It was delicious. "What do you put in it?"

"Eggs, pickles, mayonnaise, and a dash of mustard. And before you ask, I don't have an onion on the boat. I hate the things with a passion."

She couldn't help it. She laughed. She'd never heard of anybody hating onions. Her entire family wanted them on everything.

"That must make it very difficult to eat out."

"Now you understand why I learned to cook."

He brought his own plate to the table, drew up a chair, and sat down. Suddenly the room felt much smaller, the meal more intimate. She tried to tell herself not to be a fool, that not even voluptuous blonds got romantic over tuna fish salad, but she couldn't deny the charged atmosphere.

Okay, it wasn't charged with romance. That was too foolish even for her bruised brain to believe, but the tension was unmistakable. It didn't, however, seem to be bothering Eric.

"Tell me about yourself," he said.

"There's nothing to tell."

"You're twenty-seven years old. You've got family, friends, been to college, gotten a job, been arrested for theft, been pushed into a lake. There's always something to tell." He spread some tuna fish on a cracker, popped the whole thing into his mouth, and washed it down with Coke. He fixed another cracker, ate that, and settled back in his chair. "I'm not trying to be nosy," he said when she remained silent. "I need to know everything I can in order to protect you."

"Where do you want me to begin?" she asked. She had never told anybody about herself, not even in college. She wasn't sure she could do it now. The past carried too much pain, too much bitterness.

"Anywhere you like."

He popped another cracker. She decided to use eating as a delaying tactic. She spread tuna fish on a cracker. "You'll have to tell me about yourself," she said, then bit into the tuna fish. It really did taste good. She'd have to ask him for the proportions. She could fix this on a weekend and have it for meals all week.

"Sure, if you don't mind being bored."

She swallowed her mouthful. "I don't mind." She put the second part of the cracker into her mouth. She sat there watching him eat, wondering what he thought of her, what he would think after he knew something of her life. She'd learned long ago that people distrusted anyone who was very different from them. She was certain there wasn't one single thing in common between Eric Sterling's life and her own.

"I wouldn't ask if it weren't necessary," Eric said.

He sounded so understanding, as if he knew how hard it was to break the shell that protected her. Oh well, she might as well get it over. He was a private detective she'd hired to gather information. It didn't matter what he thought as long as he did his job. She took a deep breath.

"I guess you could say I grew up in a very religious community. At one time I thought everybody lived the way we did. I probably still don't appreciate the extent of the differences between my family and the rest of the world."

"You make it sound as if you were reared in another country." She could see no hint of surprise, disgust, or condemnation in his expression. He ate another cracker covered with tuna fish, took a swallow of Coke.

"It might as well have been. From childhood we were expected to work in the fields, at home, in the family business, whatever that might be. We were educated in some of the ways of the world, but only enough to enable us to survive. We were expected to marry and stay in the community."

"Why didn't you stay?"

"For as long as I can remember, I knew I wanted something different. I didn't mind the work, but I loved school, learning. The more I knew, the more I wanted to know. We were supposed to keep to our own kind, but I made friends with a girl from the outside. She brought me magazines, books, told me about things she'd seen on television. She fired my imagination for a world I could only glimpse in isolated moments."

"What did your parents think about that?"

"They ordered me to drop the friendship, even stopped me from going to school when I wouldn't. When they let me go back to school, I picked up my old friendship and threatened my sisters with bodily harm if they said a word. It was through this friend that I learned of a scholarship that would allow me to have the kind of education everybody outside of our community took for granted."

"Did your parents let you go?"

Nobody would ever know the pressure brought to bear on her to keep her from accepting the scholarship. She had been given extra chores, treated to weeks when no one was allowed to speak to her, was even beaten, all in an effort to get her to change her mind. They were determined to break her spirit, to force her to stay where they thought she belonged.

"My parents never tried to understand why I should want to leave the community to go to school. I heard them talking about locking me in my room until it was too late to accept the scholarship. In the end I had to run away."

She wondered what he thought of that. She looked closely, expecting disapproval, surprise, worst of all, pity. Incredibly, he smiled.

"That took guts," he said, "especially for a girl. You must be one tough cookie." He ate another cracker, drank some more Coke, and waited for her to continue.

Claire didn't know what to say. She knew all about approval in her professional life, how to go after it, how to handle it when she got it, and how to put up a good front when she didn't. She didn't know how to handle approval of herself. She couldn't remember when she'd gotten any.

"There's nothing much to tell after that. I went to a private boarding school for the daughters of rich men. I didn't have any friends—it wasn't surprising. I had nothing in common with those girls—but I got the education I wanted. I did well enough to earn a scholarship to college."

She'd known from the moment she ran away she'd have to win a scholarship if she wanted to go to college. Every assignment, quiz, test, or paper became a threat to her future. She *had* to get the top grade in the class. She didn't miss the friendships, the gossip sessions, or just hanging out with other girls. She was too busy studying.

"It doesn't sound as if you had much fun."

"I wasn't looking for fun," she said. "I was looking for success. After college, I had to get into graduate school. After that, I had to find a job. I didn't have anyone to help me. I couldn't afford to slip, not even once."

She'd planned very carefully. She completed undergraduate school in three years, graduate school in one. But she'd almost slipped once. She'd let herself get interested in a fellow student facing pretty much the same struggles she faced. Only his family demanded academic perfection. She started helping him with his work. That came to a screeching halt when one of their professors threw out their term papers because they'd turned in the same one. The young man had accused her of copying his paper.

She had been so shocked, so hurt, she'd almost been unable to react. Fortunately anger had restored her backbone and her common sense. She had insisted they both be required to defend the paper orally without recourse to their notes. The teacher had wanted to refuse her, to dismiss her from school—the young man came from a prominent family, one that couldn't be thought guilty of cheating—but she took the issue to the student honor council, which backed her position.

In the examination that followed, it quickly became clear she had prepared her own work. The other student didn't bother to appear, a tacit acceptance of defeat. He was put on probation, and she was reinstated with a clean slate.

"I assume you graduated first in your class." Eric said it like a statement of fact, nothing more.

"No, but I was second. I got a job with the investment arm of the bank and worked there for six years until they fired me last week."

She leaned back in her chair. She felt drained. She never let herself think about those long, bleak years. She'd told herself it was worth being miserable to have the future she envisioned. Now she sat on a houseboat, wearing a flannel nightgown, eating tuna fish, and being stared at like some sort of science exhibit by the man who held her future in his hands. What did she have to show for all those years of suffering, self-denial, the unending hours of grinding hard work?

Nothing.

"What about you?" she asked. Let him bare his soul. She didn't want to be the only one feeling vulnerable.

"Nothing nearly so interesting," he replied.

He'd finished his tuna fish and was eyeing hers hungrily. She pushed the plate toward him.

"You're not hungry?" he asked.

"It's very good, but I've had enough."

"You'll be hungry in an hour or two."

"I ate enough breakfast to last a whole day."

"If you're sure—"

"Go ahead. Eat it."

He didn't need any more encouragement. He spread tuna fish on two crackers and popped them into his mouth in quick succession.

"I can't make this very often," he said after he'd swallowed. "I like it too much. I'd be so fat I'd sink my boat."

She couldn't imagine him fat. He looked remarkably fit to her. She wondered if he worked out at a gym. For years she'd told herself she ought to join an exercise program, to help work off the tension if for no other reason, but something else always seemed to take precedence.

"Come on," she said when it became clear he'd rather eat than talk. "It's your turn."

"I have nothing much to tell." He washed down the last of the tuna fish with Coke, settled back, and grinned at her. "My parents were disgustingly rich. I didn't have to struggle. Everything was pretty much done for me."

Now that she thought about it, he had the look and feel of old money, the subtle differences about a man who had money, social position, and acceptance from birth. He would never think to question his own worth. Who else would have so many clients he could afford to talk with them only by phone or dress with complete disregard for current fashion?

He combed his light brown hair straight back, but it kept falling in his eyes. He must have run his fingers through it to push it back into place at least once every fifteen minutes. The gesture had become part of his personality. Despite having an outstanding physique, he wore baggy shorts, a worn T-shirt, and sandals. Everything about him looked untidy. But she could tell that when he did straighten himself up, dress to impress, he would cause more than one woman to gasp for breath. He had patrician good looks. Nothing spectacular. He'd never make a model for a perfume ad, but he could step right into *Town and Country* anytime he wanted.

He had nothing in common with her.

"How did you end up as a private investigator?" He was the kind of person who *hired* investigators, not became one.

"A case of being soft in the head. I finished law school with the laudable intention of helping women who were too abused or downtrodden to get out of bad marriages. I intended to see that these women were set up so they had a chance to make something of themselves, to take pride in what they had become."

"That sounds wonderful, but what does it have to do with investigating?"

"You have to have evidence in divorce cases. The more money involved, the more evidence you need and the harder it is to get. I soon found I was better at getting the evidence than the men I hired. One morning I woke up to find that we'd switched roles."

His face wasn't expressionless now. She had no difficulty seeing he didn't like what he did, that he didn't like himself for doing it.

"But what you do now is just as important as what the lawyer does," she said. "He couldn't help any of those women without you."

"Our backgrounds are different, but we do have one thing in common. We've both become so consumed by what we've been doing that we've lost our sense of direction. One day I found myself pursuing an honorable man whose only desire was to get out of the miserable marriage and into a life with a woman who adored him. His wife, the woman who had hired me, wanted money and vengeance. She didn't care what she had to do or whom she hurt to get it."

"What happened?"

"I quit the case and burned all the evidence I'd gathered. Then I retired."

"What are you going to do?"

That wasn't any of her business. Besides, if he were rich, he might not have to do anything.

"Go back to law," he said. "I'm thinking about setting myself up as a small-town family lawyer, sort of like a doctor who becomes a general practitioner."

She hadn't expected that. She'd have guessed corporate law or private law for wealthy clients. Something about Eric's handling traffic tickets and boundary disputes didn't fit.

"Have you picked out your small town?"

"No. I'm still mulling it over. I don't want to get things wrong this time."

She'd be doing a lot of mulling over herself in the near future. Only she wouldn't be worried about getting things right. She'd be trying to get any sort of job at all. She'd sacrificed her youth and her family. She didn't intend to let being framed for a crime rob her of her success.

But becoming a top executive in one of the world's largest banks didn't have the appeal it once did. She didn't feel a need so strong it was like acid burning in her gut, a need that drove her on when her body screamed for rest, a need that was so voracious it devoured any desire for friends, family, time to herself. She still wanted it, but she could feel an as yet unnamed yearning for something else. She couldn't imagine why she should feel differently after all these years, but the feeling wouldn't leave her. Something inside her had changed. She just didn't know what.

Eric got to his feet. "Now that we've spilled our guts to each other, what are you going to do with your afternoon?"

"What are you offering?"

"I was thinking about taking the boat out for a spin."

"I'd love to go," she said before she remembered her head looked like it had been hit by a land mine, that she didn't have anything to wear but Mildred's flannel nightgown. "You go on. I'll find something to read or watch a little television."

"You probably don't even know how to turn the TV on, much less what shows to watch. I'm certain you haven't read a book since college that wasn't either a corporate report or a study on some aspect of banking."

"I'm not ignorant."

"Yes, you are. You haven't had time to pay attention to the outside world. The closest you've come was probably buying clothes, and even then you had your job in mind."

"Fine, have it your way, but I still can't go. My head looks like I spent the last hour banging it against the wall. And I refuse to be seen anywhere in a flannel night-gown."

"You can wear some of my clothes."

"You're about six inches taller and fifty to sixty pounds heavier. Your clothes would swallow me. They look like they're about to fall off you."

He glanced down at his shorts. "I don't like tight clothes."

"Tight is one thing," she shot back. "A proper fit is another."

"I dress to suit myself. Do you want me to find you something to wear or not?"

He irritated her so much she wanted to throw his offer in his face, but she couldn't stand the idea of staying cooped up in this houseboat knowing he was riding around the lake. Besides, she might as well admit she liked being with him. Maybe it was his strength, his absolute self-confidence, the fact he didn't seem to care what anybody thought about what he did. Her whole life had been ruled by what others thought of her and what she did. The freedom he represented seemed like Nirvana.

"I thought you wanted me to concentrate on remembering everything I've done for the last week."

"I do, but you're too tired and upset right now. It'll be better if you relax and take it easy for the rest of the day. Besides, a change of scenery might jog your memory."

"If I can't go to my car or my apartment, why is it safe to go for a boat ride?"

"They think you're dead. If they are watching, they'll take you for one of my women. You won't look a thing like yourself swallowed up in my clothes."

She was willing to be convinced. "Let's see what you can find. I can't go out looking too ridiculous."

"You look ridiculous now. Anything else would be an improvement."

So much for enjoying his company. A little more and she'd absolutely adore watching television, even if it were one of those horrible talk shows she'd heard about. She just might be in the mood to watch people throw chairs at each other.

"I know I'm not pretty, but that's no—"

"I didn't say a word about your looks," Eric said, interrupting her. "You might look ridiculous in a night-gown with an unsightly bandage stuck to the side of your head like a piece of misplaced plaster, but you're a pretty woman. If you wore something to set off your spectacular figure, you'd have half the men on the lake asking for your telephone number."

She couldn't think of a word to say. She'd always thought she looked rather nice when she dressed for work, but nobody had ever said she was pretty. As for having a spectacular figure, the thought had never entered her head.

"You don't have to try to make me feel better," she said. "I'm quite used to the way I look."

Eric showed signs of losing patience. He picked up the plates and took them over to the sink. "I don't flatter women. Outside of the fact it's a bore to say things you don't mean, once you start, you can't stop. Each lie has to be a little bigger than the last."

This man was full of all kinds of surprises. "I didn't mean that."

"I doubt you have any idea how men see you. You've been dressing for success for so long, and avoiding the pinch on the butt, you haven't given any man a chance to tell you what he thinks of you. I'll bet you haven't had a date in three years."

"I've had several," she said, firing up.

"A date that had nothing to do with your job. I bet you haven't even let a man take you to a bar for a drink."

"I have."

"Did you talk business?"

She always talked business. "Probably."

"Don't lie, not even in little things. Remember, I'm on your side."

"Whether I talked about bank mergers or stock figures has nothing to do with proving I didn't sell that information."

"It may. You never know. Now let's see if I can find you something to wear."

He left the dishes in the sink and disappeared into his bedroom.

"I don't have any bright colors," he called back. "Everything seems to be brown, blue, khaki, or dull white."

"I don't care." She probably wouldn't wear it, so it didn't matter.

"I've got lots of T-shirts. Let's hope your bra is dry."

EIGHT

She wasn't used to a man talking about this sort of thing. It probably was an everyday occurrence with him—she hadn't forgotten his string of women—but it wasn't with her. Her parents never mentioned an item of intimate female apparel. As for sex, well, she wondered how her parents had managed to figure out how to have babies, though they obviously had. There were nine children in her family. Some families in the community had more.

"I'm sure all my clothes are dry." She couldn't bring herself to explain that a bra made of synthetic fabric dried quickly. Just the thought to talking to a man about her underwear caused her stomach to knot.

"You couldn't wear your clothes even if they were cleaned and pressed," he said. "You'd look ridiculous sitting on the end of a pier dressed in a business suit, dangling your high heels in the water." He emerged from the bedroom with two pieces of clothing and a belt in his hands. "Here, see how these fit."

For a moment she hesitated to take the clothes from him. She'd never worn a man's clothes. Wearing his seemed too intimate. She told herself not to be ridiculous. After sleeping in his bed and wearing only a nightgown in his presence—not to mention his helping undress her—she shouldn't feel the slightest twinge of embarrassment at wearing his clothes.

"If you don't like them, you can choose something else. Just dig through my drawers until you find something you like."

"I'm sure these are fine," she said. She would wear what he'd chosen or she would stay on the boat. Getting to her feet, she felt a little wobbly and reached out to steady herself against the table. He took her hand.

"Are you okay?"

"Yes. I just stood up too quickly."

"Maybe you shouldn't go out just yet. That knock on your head was pretty severe."

"I don't want to be trapped inside."

"I don't know how it's any different from being closed up in an office all day."

She wasn't going to argue with him. He obviously thought the life she had led was insane. Maybe it was, but it was her life and he had no right to keep criticizing it.

"I had something to do there. I have nothing to do here except think about my aching head and my looming jail sentence. I'll get dressed. I may not get to enjoy the sunshine again for a long time."

She didn't know why she kept acting like the police were about to lock her up, but she did know talking to Eric Sterling had a way of making her forget her problems, at least for the moment.

"I can't stay out long. I sunburn easily."

"I'm glad you reminded me. I've got some suntan lotion around here somewhere. I'll be glad to help you put it on."

She retreated to his bedroom. She didn't want him touching her body. Compared to the women he was used to, she probably rated a two. Or a one. For all she knew, she might not even make his scale.

She tossed the clothes on the bed. She didn't know why she was getting so agitated over a boat ride. She didn't want him to think of her as a woman, only as a client. That's how she thought of him, as a man she employed to do work. The fact that she'd been forced to stay on his houseboat was a mere coincidence. It was his job to keep her safe until he could get the evidence to prove her innocence.

No, it wasn't. He was supposed to gather evidence for her. There was nothing in his job description that said he had to house, care for, protect, and pamper her until she could remember some illusive detail. Actually, she probably shouldn't even consider herself a client yet. She hadn't paid him a retainer. But he hadn't asked for one. She wondered why.

She began to unbutton the nightgown. There was no point in torturing herself with these endless questions. Or worrying about his reaction to her. She ought to treat this just like any other business experience. She knew how to do that. She'd dealt with many powerful men over the years. Compared to the sharks she'd been swimming with for the last six years, Eric Sterling was a goldfish.

She slipped the nightgown over her shoulders and let it drop to the floor. She reached for her bra, but instead walked over to the mirror on the back of the door. She looked at her body, tall and slim. Eric said she had a spectacular figure. Was he just trying to make her feel better or did he really think her figure was something special? She'd never given it any thought. It had made buying clothes easier. She could wear almost anything regardless of how severely tailored. She didn't have big breasts or hips. She wasn't model thin, but she wasn't voluptuous, either. She would have thought Eric would like a woman with more curves, more flesh, bigger—

She turned away from the mirror with a grunt of disgust. What was she doing, standing naked before a mirror, examining her body, wondering which parts of it could be attractive to a man like Eric Sterling? That knock on the head must have done more than break the skin. Maybe it had knocked all her common sense into the water, leaving her a brainless, quivering mass of female insecurities.

Okay, things weren't going too well for her right now. She wasn't in control of her life. She didn't know if she'd ever be in control of it again. But she did know she could survive without Eric Sterling's approval.

She picked up her bra and put it on. It made her feel kind of funny to know Eric had handled it, but she put that out of her mind. All kinds of hands had touched that bra before she bought it and the thought hadn't bothered her a bit. It was silly to start thinking about it now just because she knew the man.

She picked up the T-shirt and pulled it over her head. She hardly needed pants. It came to her knees. She wondered why Eric insisted upon wearing clothes that were at least three sizes too big. The men she worked with dressed just as carefully for informal occasions as they did for work. Shirts, shorts, pants, hats, shoes, everything looked new or freshly laundered, and everything fit perfectly. Not even those executives with protruding stomachs tried to hide them with ill-fitting clothes.

His shorts would swallow her. She stepped into them, bunched the extra fabric in her hand, and left the bedroom.

Eric's laugh greeted her. She felt herself turn red.

"I hadn't expected everything to be that big on you."

"You did notice we're nowhere near the same size, didn't you?"

"Okay, what do you need?" he asked, ignoring her snipe.

"Something to hold these shorts up," she said. "Your belt didn't have enough holes in it."

"I've got just the thing." He disappeared into his bedroom and came out moments later with an adjustable belt.

"Try this."

"The material will bunch at the waist."

"Your T-shirt will hide it."

"And the rest of me."

"You need shoes," he said, ignoring her once again. He turned and went outside. She slipped the belt through the loops on the shorts and pulled it tight. She spread the bunched material around her body until she looked pleated all over.

Eric returned a moment later with a pair of tennis shoes. "Try these. They belong to Mildred. They look about your size." He handed her a pair of socks.

"Did you steal these, too?"

"Mildred keeps all kinds of stuff around in case her children visit."

Claire told herself to stop trying to be disagreeable and get dressed. She wanted some fresh air. She had known she didn't have anything to wear. She had known she'd look awful in anything Eric could find on his boat. If she didn't like it, she should shut up and stay inside.

She sat down and put on the shoes. They fit surprisingly well.

"See. I told you they'd fit."

Actually he hadn't said any such thing, but she didn't bother pointing that out.

"I need a hat," she said.

"I've already thought of that," Eric said. He reached into a bin next to one of the kitchen cabinets and pulled out a hat. "Here, put this on."

He had handed her a pith helmet!

"I'll look like I'm going on an African safari and have lost my way."

"It's the only thing I've got other than baseball caps. Besides, you need to shade your face."

"Maybe Mildred has a straw hat," she said, willing to wear anything rather than this helmet.

"Mildred doesn't wear hats. She says she likes to let the sun bleach her hair. It keeps her from having to do it so often."

Claire almost gave up the idea of going out, but the thought of staying in and doing nothing for the rest of the afternoon was too oppressive. She'd never been unoccupied for such a length of time. She'd probably go nuts.

"Okay," she said, "but if you ever tell anybody what I looked like today, I'll never forgive you."

"I doubt we'll ever see each other again after a week or so," Eric said. "Whom can I tell?"

Odd that statement should hit her so hard. She'd known the man for less than twenty-four hours—much less than that when she considered how much of it she spent asleep—and already she couldn't imagine never seeing him again. How did a person do that to you? She could imagine leaving the bank for another job, leaving Mr. Deter and all the people she'd known and worked with for years. Yet a man she'd known for a few hours seemed like a permanent part of her life.

"Nobody I work with would believe I'd wear anything like this," she said to cover her confusion.

"Nobody would who had anything else to wear. Now stop obsessing about your looks and come on."

"Sunglasses," she said.

"They're on the boat."

"Where's the suntan lotion?"

He picked up a bottle from a table. "Here, I'll put it on you."

"I can put it on myself," she said, holding out her hand for the bottle.

"You can't put in on your back."

"The shirt will cover my back."

"You sure I can't help?"

"Positive." She didn't dare let him touch her. She doubted anything would happen if she did, but she couldn't afford to take the chance. She poured lotion out into her hand and rubbed it over her arms. Eric watched. "Don't you have something to do?" she asked.

"No."

"You can't stand here watching me."

"Why not?"

She couldn't think of a good reason. She capped the bottle. "I can finish on the boat."

"After you," Eric said, holding the door for her.

She had no choice but to leave the safety of the house-boat and step outside on his deck. Several couples were sitting on their decks, watching television, talking, moving from one boat to another. Most took no notice of them as Eric locked the boat and slipped his feet into a pair of worn deck shoes.

"I keep the boat at another dock," he said.

They had to pass the spot where Claire had been pushed into the water. Much to her surprise, she felt herself shy away from the edge as they walked by.

"You don't have to worry about that happening again," Eric said. "If he comes back, he'll do something different."

"Thanks. That's the kind of cheerful news I really needed."

"No point in not facing facts. It only causes trouble."

Those words could have come out of her own mouth. She used to be a stickler for the truth, facts, doing things now, heading off trouble before it got worse. Now she felt like hiding until everything went away. She couldn't understand how she could have changed so much. *Don't be a fool. How many people get framed, almost killed? Of course you're going to feel differently about things.*

Maybe that would account for the desire to stay close to Eric. She was feeling out of her depth. She needed someone to lean on until things got back to normal. Once that happened, she wouldn't need him or anyone else anymore.

"Tell me what your boat's like," she said. They were approaching the pathway that led to the parking lot. She couldn't help but glance in that direction. She wondered if her car were still there, if anybody were actually watching it to see if she returned. She wanted to ask Eric to look, but she knew he wouldn't.

"It's a regular boat," Eric said. "I can't really describe it. It's better if you wait to see it."

Claire had been on boats before. Several executives of the bank had huge homes on nearby Lake Norman. A couple with a home at Myrtle Beach had hosted parties on their yacht. It had been very much like a house sitting on the water. The rooms were huge, the view wonderful, and the yacht had never left the dock. She didn't much like water because she'd never learned to swim. After the experience of last night, she liked it even less.

Eric led her to a walkway that led out into a forest of boats.

"Is yours a sailboat?" she asked. A lot of them were. She had no desire to ride on a sailboat. She knew nothing about them except that they could get caught in a stiff wind and capsize.

"No. Inboard motor. I come out here to relax. A sailboat is too much work."

She breathed a sigh of relief.

"There it is." The boat he stopped before seemed much too large for one person, but it made her feel better. Maybe it was harder to capsize in a big boat.

"Let me help you on board," Eric said. "The boat will rock under your weight. It's easy to lose your balance if you're not prepared."

He held her hand steady while she stepped up onto a ledge then over the side of the boat onto one of the seats. She didn't tell him that his holding her hand was more likely to cause her to lose her balance than the rocking boat. She sat down, relieved to be safely off her feet.

Eric cast off the ropes that moored the boat to the dock before he climbed aboard.

"Once we're underway, come on up front with me," he said. "You won't be able to see nearly as well back here. Besides, you'll get windburned."

If she'd known it was so hazardous, she'd have stayed at the houseboat.

"Where are the sunglasses?" she asked. "I need a life jacket, too."

"The jacket is under the seat. The sunglasses are up front."

She stood up and immediately lost her balance. Eric grabbed her. She sat down in the seat behind her and held onto the arms.

"Looks like it'll take awhile before you get your sea legs."

"We're on a lake and we haven't even left the dock. How much worse does it get?"

"Not much unless we hit a big wake."

She had no idea what he was talking about. The only wake she knew about was celebrated after a funeral.

"You'll have to take care of yourself for a bit. It takes all my concentration to get the boat out of the dock."

She didn't see why. All he had to do was back up, turn left, and head out. It must be like driving a car.

She quickly learned her error. Water didn't remain in place like concrete. It moved. Up and down. And sideways. They started drifting toward the boat on the other side. Some big rubber things hanging on the sides of the boat that looked like spools with all the thread gone kept them from bumping.

The motor started with a dull cough, caught, and purred reassuringly under the floor of the boat. Slowly, gradually, Eric backed out into the narrow channel between the lines of boats. He turned and inched forward out of the marina.

"Why don't you go faster?" she asked. Now that she was on the boat, she was impatient to get out into the middle of the lake.

"There's a speed limit inside the marina," Eric said. "If you go too fast, you create a wake that starts the other boats banging into each other."

At least she now knew what a wake was. She could understand why people didn't want their boats banging about. One could easily spend a hundred-thousand dollars on a rather modest boat. She'd rather invest toward her retirement.

"Are there a lot of boats on this lake?" she asked.

"Too many. Everybody who lives out here wants a boat. You ought to see this place on a holiday weekend."

Claire decided she liked it just as it was. Theirs was the only boat leaving the marina.

"Come on up here," Eric said. "I can't keep talking over my shoulder."

Claire preferred to stay where she was, but she grabbed hold of the side of the boat, stood, and held on tightly as she made her way to the front.

"Sunglasses are in the drawer," Eric said. "Coke is in the refrigerator. If you want something to eat, we'll have to stop."

"We just had lunch. I'm not hungry."

"Good. I hate having to dock this thing any more than I have to."

She chose a pair of green sunglasses, put them on as

they left the marina and moved out toward the open water. Eric increased their speed. The nose of the boat rose, and the wind began to whip at her clothes, threatening to blow her disgusting hat off her head.

"Face into the wind," Eric said. "It's the only way."

That didn't work. The wind kept catching under the hat, lifting it off her head.

"Here, put on a baseball cap," Eric said as he opened a drawer filled with half a dozen caps.

"It'll blow off, too."

"Not if you put it on with the bill backwards."

Claire had never in her life worn a baseball cap. She considered them childish and looked down on grown men who wore them. But she saved her greatest scorn for anyone who wore it with the bill backwards. She looked up to see Eric had turned his cap around. She didn't understand how he could still look so handsome. It had to be the money. People who had everything from the beginning couldn't look ugly no matter what they did.

"Come on. Choose a hat. I can't open her up until you do."

Claire resisted the idea, but she decided nothing could make her look any worse than she did already. She looked at the collection of hats. She chose a white one, but it was several sizes too large.

"Adjust the strap at the back," Eric said. "Come on. We're almost in the channel."

Claire cast the hated pith helmet aside, adjusted the strap until the cap fit her head, then put it on backwards. "There."

"Hang on," Eric shouted. "I'm going to open her up." He pushed down on the throttle. The nose of the boat rose at least two feet; the motor's purr changed to a mild roar.

Claire felt as if she were being hurled along at a breakneck pace even though the speedometer registered only twenty. She glanced back at the retreating shoreline. The houseboats looked very small, the trees and houses like part of a toy village. She'd read about Lake Wylie many times, even attended social functions at some of the homes along its shore, but she'd never realized the lake had so much water in it. It looked huge. She didn't understand how it could ever be crowded.

"Stand up and face into the wind," Eric shouted to her. "There's nothing like it."

She didn't know if she could. The boat's sudden acceleration had thrown her against the back of the seat. She felt pinned to the cushion.

"Take hold of the bar," Eric said, pointing to a bar along the front of the boat. "Plant your feet firmly, and stand up."

She did as he said, surprised at how easy it was. Until her head rose above the protection of the windshield and the wind hit her full in the face. She felt as if someone had put his hand on her face and pushed.

"Face into the wind," Eric said.

"How can you breathe?"

"You get used to it."

She didn't know how. But she remembered seeing some old newsreels of women dancing and doing acrobatics on the wings of airplanes. If they could breathe going that fast, she could, too.

She was pleased to find that after her first few fearful moments it was easy to breathe. In fact, she became so enthralled with the exhilarating sensation of speed she forgot all about breathing. She'd never owned a convertible, would never have considered getting into one because of what it would do to her hair and clothes, but she didn't have to worry about either today. She could forget her appearance and just enjoy the wind in her face, the wonderful freedom of *not caring*.

It seemed that for as long as she could remember, she'd been worried about what someone would say, agitated about how a boss, teacher, or dean would see her action, how it would affect a promotion, grade, scholarship. It was all out the window now. Nothing she did mattered. Nobody cared. While it was frightening, it was also liberating.

"This is fun," she called out to Eric over the roar of the motor. "I'm glad you talked me into coming."

"It's a great way to unwind," he said. "Even on the hottest days, it's cool on the lake."

"Can you go faster?"

He laughed and turned to her. "I thought you were afraid of speed."

"I thought so, too, but I've never been on a boat before. I like the feel of the wind in my face."

"They have speed limits on the lake, too, but I think we can squeeze in a few more miles per hour."

He pushed down on the throttle and the boat responded like a thoroughbred getting its second wind. The nose of the boat rose another foot; the sound of the motor changed to a roar, and the wind hit her in the face with such force she was certain she couldn't breathe.

She loved it.

She couldn't explain the change that had come over her, but she felt like an entirely different person. For the first time she could remember, the pressure inside her that had driven her since childhood was gone. The harder the wind hit her in the face, the more it liberated her from herself. She had no past, no future, just the present. Nothing but the wide expanse of blue sky, the rippling waters of the lake, and the wind in her face.

And Eric.

She wasn't able to put him into a neatly defined category, either. On the surface he was a private detective who'd reluctantly taken her case and then been forced to take her in when she was attacked practically at his front door. The same thing could have happened had she tried to employ another detective.

But she didn't feel that way. It frustrated her that she couldn't find the words to express what she was feeling. Maybe that came from spending her whole life dealing with figures. There was no doubt with figures. They were concrete, real, easy to perceive. You simply stated the results of your calculations and moved on to the next problem, also to be solved by a formula and expressed in a set of numbers.

But her relationship with Eric—if you could call a less than twenty-four-hour acquaintance a relationship—couldn't be reduced to a set of numbers. It involved feelings, and Claire had spent years ignoring her feelings, telling herself they weren't important, that feelings only got in the way of success. She'd gotten so good at it, she didn't feel much of anything anymore. She'd even denied the feeling of panic that set in when she was arrested. She kept telling herself it was a mistake, that all she had to do was find a lawyer and a detective who could produce the necessary evidence and everything would get straightened out. Follow the steps, the logical path, and it would all work out.

But nothing about Eric followed a logical path. He was born into wealth but lived like a vagabond. He'd been trained as a lawyer yet ended up a private detective. He wanted nothing to do with her or her case; yet he'd taken excellent care of her after the attack, even prepared her meals. Now he had given up his afternoon to help her relax and try to forget, at least for a short while, the trap threatening to close around her.

She could learn to love a man like that.

The thought frightened her so much, she sat down with a plop. "Where did you say those Cokes were? I need something to drink."

NINE

Eric didn't know when he'd enjoyed an afternoon more. He had expected to be bored. Claire had kept herself so tied to her job, he'd doubted she'd know anything about boats. Nor did she have any social skills he could see. He'd taken her out in the boat because he felt sorry for her. And to keep from being closed up in the same room with her all afternoon.

He'd been right. She didn't know anything about boats. Or the lake. Or how to entertain a man. He supposed if he'd been an account executive in a dark suit, she'd have known exactly what to do. Still, he enjoyed her simple pleasure in the ride. After ten minutes, everything about the world seemed to retreat. The wind slapped them about the face as if it had form and substance. The roar of the engine cut them off from the rest of the world. The smell of the water, the panorama of the enormous blue sky, and the taste of the spray transported them to a different world, brought their senses into full play.

No matter what was going on in his life, a boat ride always had the power to cleanse his soul and calm his spirit. It appeared to have the same effect on Claire. She smiled, even laughed. For a few moments she let herself be the little girl he suspected she'd never been. He wondered what kind of person she'd be if she were freed from the ambition that held her in its grasp.

He hadn't liked her when she'd hunted him down at his boat. He'd seen too many women like her, driven, ambitious, unable to understand that a good life had to be made up of relationships with people, not financial, social, or career goals. But he couldn't hold that mistake against her. He'd let himself get on the wrong track and stay there for far too long.

"Does your skin feel tight or dry?" he asked as they cruised into the marina. It didn't look that way. It looked soft and supple and warmed by the sun. She'd put lotion on her face three times, but the bridge of her nose was pink.

She put her hands to her cheeks. "No, but I feel awfully warm."

"That's from the wind. You'll feel more normal in a few minutes."

He wasn't sure he wanted her to return to normal. He liked her better this way, thrown off stride, not trying to achieve anything or be anybody. She was a good companion, but he doubted she knew this. She probably hadn't given herself a chance to discover it.

"I hope Mildred has come back with some of the clothes she promised," she said, looking down at herself.

"What's wrong with what you're wearing?"

"I feel like I'm wrapped in layers of material."

He glanced over at her. "You don't look bad to me."

"Yeah, right. I probably make you feel like you're out with one of the fellas."

"You don't look like a guy. As a matter of fact, you look more feminine than you did in that power suit you were wearing last night."

"But that's one of my most successful outfits. My boss asked me to wear it once when we were courting some very difficult accounts."

"You looked like a female barracuda. Today you look like a cute bunny rabbit."

"I never met a man who thought a rabbit was cute!"

"Did you ever ask?"

"No. They'd think I was crazy."

He laughed. Maybe he was crazy. He didn't know, didn't care. "Ask sometime. Most guys are pretty human behind those suits."

"Why can't a woman be human behind a suit?"

"I guess she can. It's just that I'd want to shake her hand rather than kiss her, and that's no way to find out."

Claire flushed and looked away. He hadn't meant to say that. It had just popped out. He wondered why he'd said it. He hadn't even thought of kissing Claire.

That wasn't true. He'd spent hours last evening and during the night thinking of just that. But he hadn't counted that. He always wanted to kiss a female when there was one close at hand, especially when she was in his bed. And for that very reason he'd discounted his feelings. They were merely the results of a habit—a bad habit at that—and would vanish as soon as Claire passed beyond his orbit.

He concentrated on bringing the boat into the marina without a wake.

But that wasn't the way he felt now. He didn't feel the compelling physical urge which usually grabbed him. This felt different. There was a little bit of sympathy, a little bit of pity, a little bit of commiseration. And a little bit of physical interest. Things weren't *that* different.

But that wasn't all. He admired her courage in refusing to plea bargain, but he admired her even more for all she'd overcome. Unfortunately, her success hadn't made her happy. He wanted to do something about it. It was a rather foolish wish. She had no reason to have anything to do with him after her case was over, especially if he couldn't come up with the evidence to prove her innocence. Still, he would be unhappy if she disappeared.

"Do you take your boat out every afternoon?" Claire asked.

"I do when I'm here. Occasionally I take it out at night."

"Is that how you romance your women?"

Mildred. Nobody else could have been telling her about his women.

"Sometimes, but most of the time I go out by myself. It's peaceful. The moonlight on the water is beautiful."

"I'd like to see that."

"It's just as pretty from the deck of the houseboat. And not nearly as dangerous."

"Dangerous?"

"There's always some idiot who thinks he can navigate the lake in the dark at supersonic speed."

"Probably some of the men who work at the bank. Several of them live here."

Fortunately, a couple of friends were on the dock when he came in. They helped him moor his boat. He was certain Claire would have tried, but she didn't know enough to be able to help. He'd teach her later.

There he went again, acting as if their relationship had a future.

"Thanks for taking me with you," she said as he helped her out of the boat. "I'm sure it's a bore to bother with someone who knows nothing about boats, but I really enjoyed it."

"It's always fun to make a convert," he said. "I just don't want to make so many there won't be room for me anymore."

"I can't imagine the lake ever filling up."

"Wait until you see it on the Fourth of July weekend."

Damn! He couldn't stop. He needed to halter his tongue before he said something to put that haunted expression on her face again.

"Then you'd better get to work and find out what really

happened about the stolen information. If you don't, I'll be sitting in jail on the Fourth of July."

She readjusted the sunglasses and pulled the bill of her cap to the front and lower over her eyes. She was looking around to see if there was anybody who might recognize her. He couldn't tell whether she was more afraid it might be the man who'd attacked her or someone from her office.

"We'll get back to that tomorrow," Eric said. "There are still several hours of the afternoon left, time to have a drink, settle back, and soak up some of the spring warmth."

She didn't look like that agenda appealed to her. She probably hadn't settled back and relaxed in her whole life. He doubted she knew how.

"I don't drink," she said.

"That must be a hindrance in your line of work."

"I just have the bartender keep filling my glass with soda water."

"Soda water is for mixing with scotch, not drinking straight."

"I've never drunk scotch."

"Do I have a treat for you."

She kept a wary lookout as they left the marina and skirted the parking lot. She craned her neck to see into the parking lot.

"Are you still worried about your car?"

"I left my briefcase in it," she said.

"Why did you bring it? You don't work at the bank anymore."

"I always carry it with me."

Habit. Maybe a denial that the firing was permanent.

"Is there anything in the car you absolutely can't do without?"

"No, but—"

"Then we'll leave it for another day or two. We'll decide what to do about it after that."

She tensed when they passed the spot on the boardwalk where she had been pushed into the water. But her attention was distracted when Mildred called loudly from the deck of her boat.

"Did you have a nice ride?"

"It was wonderful," Claire said as they came closer. "Eric says I'll have a sunburn, but I don't care."

"You will tomorrow," Mildred said. "Let me see."

"He said it's my nose," Claire said. "Do you think it's going to peel?"

"Yes, but not badly. I'm glad to see you had the good sense to put on plenty of lotion. You're much too pale. You don't look like you've been in the sun more than five minutes in the last ten years."

But her skin looked wonderful. It seemed strange that such an unhealthy habit could have such wonderful results.

"Did you behave yourself?" Mildred asked Eric.

"I tried, but she kept asking me to go faster. Don't ever let her behind the wheel. She'd have the shore patrol out after you in less than a minute. The woman is speed crazy."

Claire blushed slightly. "That was my first time on a boat, and I loved it."

"I like going fast, too," Mildred said. She turned to Eric, gave him a questioning look. "I got most of the stuff you asked for. I'll get the rest tomorrow."

"I don't want you to go to all that trouble," Claire said.

"Don't worry. I've never had so much fun shopping."

"What was so exciting?" Claire asked.

"Wait until you see what I bought."

The first bag contained all the things Claire had asked Mildred to purchase. Eric would never understand why women had to have so much stuff. He liked the results, but he was certain it could be accomplished with less than a wheelbarrow load of bottles, jars, cans, tubes, and little pots of cream.

Mildred took a wig out of the bag. It was a modest wig, short hair with a cluster of curls about the head. Eric didn't think red was exactly the right color for Claire, but maybe it would make her less self-conscious about the bald spot.

"Try this on to see if it fits," Mildred said. "You'll need a mirror. There's one in Eric's bedroom."

Claire looked at the wig a little doubtfully.

"I can take it back and get another," Mildred said

"It's not that," Claire said. "I've never worn a wig. Somehow it seems sinful."

"It's probably something your parents told you," Eric said, remembering the oppressive home she had described.

Claire took the wig, but she didn't seem convinced.

"You just put it on like a hat," Mildred explained. "Go on. Try it on. If you need help, give a holler."

"Can I holler now?" Claire asked with an apologetic smile.

"Sure. Just give me a minute. I've got to talk to Eric about something."

Sensing Mildred wanted privacy, Claire went inside.

"I got the stuff you asked for," Mildred said in a whisper. "Are you sure this is what you wanted?"

"Yes."

"If Claire is nervous over that wig, you'll never get her into this outfit."

"I expect it will make her a little uncomfortable."

"Uncomfortable!" Mildred said with a squeak. "She'll balk."

"She won't when I explain why she has to wear it."

"Why does she have to wear it?"

"She can't stay on this boat forever. When she leaves, she can't look like herself."

"I understand that, but I'm still not sure it's the best way to go. But if you need help convincing her, let me know."

"I'll make sure you're standing between us."

"I'd better go see how she's coming with that wig."

But it wasn't necessary. Claire emerged from the houseboat with the wig on her head and a smile on her face.

"I don't look a thing like myself," she announced. "I feel like a totally different person."

Eric thought that was probably a good thing. The old Claire Dalton must have been a very unhappy woman.

Claire settled back with a glass of wine, her stomach pleasantly full. This had been one of the very best days of her life. A week ago she wouldn't have believed it was possible. She wondered why she hadn't seen long ago that something was very wrong with her life. The harder she worked and the more successful she became, the harder she made herself work so she could become even more successful. Success had become an obsession, an addiction she couldn't break. She demanded more of herself every year. She'd had to lose it all, to find herself fired and without a job, injured and in hiding, before she could stop working long enough to realize she didn't want to do that anymore.

She had to admit the most enjoyable part of the day had been Eric. He was nothing like the ill-tempered, irascible, rude man she'd met yesterday. He'd worked very hard to help her put her troubles aside and enjoy herself.

He had grilled a steak for her dinner, served it with a baked potato, a salad drenched in Roquefort dressing, and an expensive red wine. While the steaks cooked, he'd kept up a running conversation about everything from the rapid growth of downtown Charlotte to what the states were going to do with their money from the tobacco settlement to the problems of gambling on the Indian lands in South Carolina. Claire could barely follow him. She rarely got beyond the business section of *The Charlotte Observer.*

But she didn't really care. Eric had fixed her a drink made with scotch. He said it was called a Highland Cooler and that it had a kick. It was delicious. She didn't know what he put in it besides scotch; but she was certain if people knew about this drink, everybody in Charlotte would be drinking Highland Coolers. She had trouble remembering to drink it slowly, to take sips instead of swallows.

About five minutes before the steaks were done, she was glad she'd been careful. She didn't get a kick, but she got a definite nudge that pushed her over into a very pleasant state of not caring a whole lot about the bank, her job, or the evidence the police were holding over her head.

"Are you sure you like it medium well?" Eric asked.

"Yes."

"A good steak ought to be served rare."

"If I see one drop of blood, I lose my appetite."

Eric sighed. "It kills me to do this."

She started to get up. "I'll finish it."

"Keep your seat." He pushed his steak over to the side to keep it warm. "How is your drink?"

"Lovely. I would like another, please."

He laughed. "Only one of those per evening. Two, and I'll have to put you to bed."

She heard herself giggle. She couldn't figure out how it happened, but she was certain it was her own voice. "I'll tell Mildred."

"You won't have to. She's been peeping around the

corner all evening. I think she's afraid I have designs on your virtue."

"She ought to know I'm safe. I'm not beautiful like your other women."

She knew her references to his women were beginning to make him uncomfortable. She didn't mean to do it, but in a way she was glad. Though she'd only hired him as a private detective, she was glad to know he wasn't a womanizer.

"I've told you at least a dozen times you're very attractive. Now that you've got some clothes that fit you and a wig to cover your bandages, you look very pretty."

"Thank you."

She didn't believe him, but it was nice of him to compliment her. She was wearing a long-sleeved blouse, slacks, and a pair of gold sandals. It was warm enough to wear shorts, but her very strict upbringing had never allowed her to be comfortable exposing her limbs. She could still hear her father's thunderings against females who exposed their bodies for men to stare at. He had said no matter how men acted toward these women, what they said to seduce them, they felt nothing but scorn for them. Claire didn't think what he said was true, but she couldn't forget it. She'd been to dozens of parties and receptions around pools over the years, but she'd never once put on a bathing suit. She didn't even own one.

Dinner had passed very pleasantly. Her steak was cooked to perfection. She put all the butter she wanted on her potato, and she didn't pause to think of the calories in the Roquefort dressing.

By the time she finished eating, she was so full of good food and wine she didn't feel that she could move. All the tension that had kept her going for years, that had earned her a reputation for being a bundle of nerves, an endless source of energy, had deserted her.

She felt deflated. She was a balloon that had sprung a

leak, exhausted itself in one frantic flight, and had now sunk to the floor incapable of stirring to life. Only she didn't want to stir to life. She wanted to stay right where she was.

She'd been relieved when Mildred and Aubrey came to visit. She didn't have to move, didn't have to do more to participate in the conversation than nod or murmur agreement. She was disappointed when they decided to leave so soon.

"I guess it's time we toddled off to bed," Mildred said, getting to her feet. "I'm getting to the age where if I don't get my ten hours sleep, I can't keep my eyes open the next day."

"And if she can't keep her eyes open, she can't fix my breakfast," Aubrey said.

"I told you to learn to cook," Mildred said. "Look at Eric. He's a great cook."

"He's a traitor; that's what he is," Aubrey grumbled.

"Watch it. I'll steal your Viagra," Eric threatened.

"I'll show you where he keeps it," Mildred offered.

"Touch it and die," Aubrey said. "That's the only good part about getting old." He winked at Mildred. "We get to stay in bed longer."

"That's your side of the story," Mildred replied.

But Claire noticed Mildred's smile when she said it. She obviously didn't mind Aubrey's attention as much as she pretended.

The thought of what would happen between them later both embarrassed and intrigued Claire. The physical relationship between men had women had been a taboo topic in Claire's home, except for making it clear that girls should stay away from boys and keep their bodies and limbs covered at all times, that unmarried women should occupy quarters well separated from those of unmarried men, even those in the same family. Nothing was said about the adult relationship between men and women.

The message had come through loud and clear. Any physical relationships between a man and a woman before marriage was evil. Claire wasn't sure she believed that, but she had been too busy studying and working to give it any real thought. Being stuck on the houseboat with Eric had changed that. She'd thought about it last night. She'd thought about it during the boat ride.

She was thinking about it now.

She didn't believe a physical relationship between a man and woman who cared for each other was sinful, even if it took place outside of marriage. It might be inadvisable but not evil. If she could believe some of the talk she'd heard, it might be fun. Maybe even for the woman. Everybody knew men liked it.

"Don't get up," Mildred said when Claire started to get up to say good-bye. "You look far too comfortable."

"I am."

"I told you Eric would take good care of you."

"He has, but I can't keep imposing on his hospitality."

"Keep right on until the man who pushed you into the lake is behind bars," Aubrey said. "We don't like having his kind running loose."

"I'm not too fond of him either," she replied, "especially since I can't swim."

"Eric can teach you, but you'll have to go to a pool. The lake isn't very clean."

She glanced at Eric, but he smiled in the good-humored way she'd come to expect when Mildred was around. She wondered if he would teach her to swim. She doubted he wanted her to stay that long. He might say it wasn't safe for her to leave, but he'd probably be very glad to get his bed back.

"I think I'd better wait until my stitches heal," Claire said.

"Nah," Aubrey replied. "The chlorine would probably be good for them."

"Come on," Mildred said to Aubrey, "before you say something else ridiculous. He needs his sleep," she said to Claire, "or he turns into a silly old man."

"Not so silly I can't keep up with you," Aubrey replied following his wife as she left Eric's houseboat and started toward their own.

"You're so senile you just think you're keeping up," his wife said.

They went back and forth until they disappeared inside their own boat and Claire could no longer hear their voices.

"Are they always like that?" she asked Eric.

"It's their way of showing they adore each other."

It seemed to her an unusual way to show affection, but she supposed it didn't matter how you did it as long as you did it.

"Are you tired?" Eric asked.

"A little."

"You've had a long day, on top of being injured."

The Highland Cooler had kept her from having to think too much about her injury. The wig wasn't her favorite style or color, but it made her feel racy. She'd always considered redheads a little fast. She'd always worn her hair short and straight. That vision of herself in the mirror, her face surrounded by abundant red curls, had given her an entirely different picture of herself. With no job and no career, her mind had been free to wander. And it had wandered right over to Eric Sterling.

Claire had been aware of men all her life. But they were disapproving fathers and brothers, students competing for grades and scholarships, men competing for jobs and promotions. Eric didn't fit into any of these categories. He was the man who'd saved her from drowning, who was going to save her from going to jail. He was her champion. He was already a saint. She'd had time to observe him very closely during the course of the day, and she'd come to the conclusion Eric Sterling was just about the most handsome man she'd ever met.

She wished his clothes weren't so baggy, but she liked looking at his tanned, slender legs. She supposed they were ordinary legs. They weren't especially powerful; his calves didn't bulge with muscles, and the light covering of brown hair didn't make her think of hulking cavemen. She liked his feet, too. She almost giggled thinking of that. She couldn't remember noticing a man's feet before, but Eric kicked off his shoes as soon as they got back to the houseboat. She didn't understand why Eric's feet should hold such an attraction. She supposed they were quite ordinary, long and slim with even toes. Nothing special.

There was nothing special about his arms and hands either; but she'd watched, fascinated, while he cooked, served, and ate his food. He had long, slender forearms, ordinary hands with long slim fingers. Let's face it. All of him was long and slim.

"We'd better go in," Eric said. "The night chill can be penetrating."

"I don't think I can move."

"I'll help you up."

He reached out, took both her hands in his grasp, and a jolt went through Claire that practically lifted her from the chair. She wanted this man, and she wanted him in the physical sense. That was unmistakable.

TEN

Claire resisted the impulse to snatch her hands away. She couldn't let her feelings or his nearness cause her to panic. Nor the winning smile that curved his lips. She had to remember he was being nice to a woman who'd been injured. Though he continued to say nice things about her looks, especially her figure, she had not forgotten what she looked like last night when she'd first seen herself in the mirror. She was certain he hadn't, either.

"I can get up by myself." She hadn't meant to sound abrupt or ungrateful, but it sounded both.

"Then why haven't you?"

"Because you filled me too full of food and wine. I don't know when I've enjoyed a meal so much." She hoped that would take the edge off her rude reply, but she really meant it. It was amazing to find a man who cooked and cleaned up after himself, especially a lawyer who could find any information required. What a recommendation for a husband!

She didn't know where that thought had come from, but she put it out of her head immediately. She'd done some foolish things in her life, but to let that notion take root in her thoughts, to seriously consider anything permanent existing between her and Eric, was foolish to the extreme. Just because she was feeling a very strong attraction to him didn't mean he was feeling one toward her. She had to keep reminding herself of his parade of beautiful women. A man used to filet mignon wasn't likely to settle for corned beef hash.

She got to her feet. "See. I can get up by myself."

"Good. Why don't we go for a short walk before we turn in? It'll help settle your dinner."

Her first impulse was to agree. The words had almost left her mouth when she remembered last night's attack. Her relaxed calm fled to be replaced by nervous dread. Despite the lights that came from inside the many houseboats, she couldn't help but notice the dark shadows between the boats. In fact, the light made the shadows deeper and harder to penetrate.

"I think I'd rather stay here," she said.

"Is it because of last night?" he asked.

"Yes." She didn't see any point in denying the obvious.

"I'm sure there's nobody here tonight."

"Maybe, but I'd rather stay here."

"You went out in the boat."

"That was out in the open. There are a lot of tall bushes at the back of the parking lot. And what about the trees that come right down to the lake?"

"I'll stay between you and the land."

"How can you be so sure I'll be safe?"

"You were this afternoon."

"But it was daylight. We could see for miles around."

"I got involved in investigation in the first place to help women who were frightened, who felt helpless, who were too afraid to do anything to change their situation."

"I'm not like that."

"Once you start being afraid of one thing, you'll soon be afraid of something else. Before you know it, you'll be afraid of life itself."

"So you think I ought to stick my head out there and

let someone shoot at it. Is that your prescription for living a long and full life?"

"It's a start."

"I'd rather live a long one that's not so full."

"If you give up now, you won't be living, just existing."

Oh, well, if the police did have an open-and-shut case, what did it matter if she got shot? It might be better than going to jail.

"Okay," she said. "But if anybody jumps out at me, you've got to be my shield."

"Scouts' honor. And I was really a scout."

"I should have known. That's probably why you're so intent upon saving damsels in distress."

"No. I'm doing it for my mother."

She hadn't meant to intrude on his personal life, but now he'd gotten her curiosity aroused. "I'll walk, and you tell me about your mother."

He didn't seem eager to comply with her request.

"It'll help me forget about the gunman hiding in the bushes."

"There's nobody hiding in the bushes."

"Then talk."

"Start walking."

Everyone they passed spoke to Eric. He was the youngest of the houseboat owners—everybody else looked old enough to be retired—but they clearly considered him part of their community. That surprised Claire. She wouldn't have thought a temperamental private detective would have had the time or the inclination to make friends with a lot of retired people.

"Are you on a first-name basis with all of them?" Claire asked.

"Just about. They treat me like a son, somebody to look out for and give advice to."

"Do you take any of it?"

"I listen a lot. These people have lived twice as long

as I have. Their cumulative knowledge is greater than any I'll ever have. I consider myself fortunate to be able to listen to them."

That was something else that surprised her. She wouldn't have thought he'd listen to anybody. He seemed far too used to the habit of command.

Claire breathed a little easier after they passed all the deep shadows without anyone jumping out at her. The walk up to the marina office was well-lighted. She could relax for a short while at least.

"Now tell me why you fell into the habit of rescuing helpless women," Claire said.

"It's not a happy story."

"It can't be worse than mine."

"Yes, it can."

"Then it'll make me feel better by comparison."

"My mother was a very nervous and excitable woman. She would probably have benefitted from psychiatric help, but her parents refused to admit anything was wrong. The doctors said she would never have children. She suffered through every operation and treatment available. My birth was considered a miracle, but her nerves were so fragile she couldn't care for me. I was brought up by nurses and nannies."

"Did she love you?"

"She adored me and did her best to spoil me. My father was equally determined that I would always be aware of how fortunate I was to be the only son of a wealthy, socially prominent couple."

"How awful."

"It wasn't nearly as bad as his treatment of my mother. As the only grandchild of the founder of the family business, she was an heiress. Unfortunately, she was also very ugly. Along came a handsome young man, a brilliant executive, clearly the successor to her father's position as head of the company. What could be more natural than for him to marry the boss's daughter to make sure he made it all the way to the top?"

Claire had wondered about his relationship with his parents. She hadn't heard him mention them or any other member of his family.

"Rather than put a good public face on his marriage, my father constantly berated her for her nervous condition, for being unable to entertain his business acquaintances. He told her she was lucky anybody would marry her, that she was useless as a wife and mother. He belittled her at home, ignored her in public, and was unfaithful to her at every opportunity. When she complained to her family, they told her to ignore it, that she was lucky to have such a handsome, brilliant, successful husband, fortunate her son looked like his father instead of his mother. She wanted to divorce him, but they were afraid he would leave the company and go to their competition. When she tried to divorce him anyway, they threatened to have her committed."

"What a horrible thing to do. What happened?"

"She committed suicide."

Claire hadn't expected that. It shocked her badly. "How old were you?"

"Fifteen. I was away at boarding school at the time. I wasn't even told until after the funeral. They were afraid I would create a disturbance."

"You loved her?"

"I adored her. I knew she wasn't a particularly good mother, but her love for me was uncritical and unqualified. With my father, I always had to measure up."

"Does your father know what you do?"

He laughed, but it wasn't a laugh of amusement. "Oh, yes. He knows very well."

"You're going to have to explain that remark."

"My first client was my father's second wife. I couldn't help my mother, but I could help this woman."

"And that's when you started doing your own investigating."

"Who better to get the goods on my father? I knew all his habits, his tricks. When I got through with him, he had lost half his personal wealth."

"Where's he now?"

"Still running the company. He really is a brilliant executive."

"Do you still see him?"

"Only if I go to a stockholders' meeting."

She looked up.

"My mother left me all her stock," Eric said. "I own controlling interest. He knows I can throw him out anytime I want."

"Would you?"

"No. I don't want anything to do with the company."

They walked in silence for several minutes while Claire tried to absorb what she'd learned. She couldn't understand why, if he preferred a houseboat, he had such a modest one. And why did he want to become a lawyer in a small town? With his connections, he could join just about any firm he wanted.

She also got the feeling Eric hadn't been able to forget his father any more than she had been able to forget hers. His expression told her that despite the still-simmering anger, other equally strong emotional conflicts remained. She doubted Eric could ever be happy until he faced them. She wondered if that didn't apply to her as well.

She came out of her absorption to discover they'd walked much farther than she'd intended along a path that skirted the edge of the lake. She thought she could make out picnic tables in the shadows under the trees. It was dark enough to hide a hundred killers.

"Let's turn back," she said.

"Nothing's happened."

"Something could have. I was so busy listening to you, I forgot to watch."

"And you enjoyed your walk a lot more, didn't you?"

"Yes, but—"

"No buts. I told you I'd take care of you."

She stopped. "You think I'm like your mother, don't you?"

"No. I think you've been caught in a net not of your making and you don't know what to do about it. You're a strong-minded, straightforward, honest, hard-working woman; but you have no idea how evil people can be. I do."

"You still think I'm helpless." She *was* helpless, but she didn't want to admit it. It made her seem small and foolish.

"Only for the moment. Now let's head back."

He turned and she was next to the darkness of the park. She changed sides. "You promised to stand between me and any bullets, remember?"

He laughed. "Yes, I remember." He reached out and took her hand. "There, does that make you feel better?"

"Yes." She lied. It made her feel safer, but it caused her body to go into an orgy of odd tremors and flutters. Her stomach did enough swoops, dives, and dipsy-doodles to qualify as a roller coaster.

But she didn't take her hand out of his.

She knew he couldn't save her without evidence. She knew it wasn't going to be easy to find, but everything felt better with Eric close by. She'd never felt this way about a man before.

"It's a beautiful night," Eric said. "I often go for a walk before bed if the sky is clear. The only places you can see more stars than here are in the desert or on a mountain. Or at sea."

She'd never been at sea, never seen the desert, never climbed a mountain. She felt that she'd never done anything, never been anywhere. She'd promised herself all those things *after* she'd become a great success. Only now did she realize that she'd never defined what *great success* meant to her. Up until now, it had always meant somewhere up ahead.

"I never realized so many people lived alongside the lake," she said. "The lights wreath the edge of the lake like a shimmering necklace."

"That's a pretty way to say it. Did they teach you that in business school?"

"It was the first thought that came into my mind."

"If they're all that nice, you ought to give in to more first thoughts."

He wouldn't say that if he knew one of the *first thoughts* whirling around in her head was to wonder what it would be like if he kissed her. She was certain the thought shocked her more than it would shock him. He probably expected her to want to be kissed. After all, he apparently kissed all the beautiful women he brought to the houseboat. But visiting houseboats and kissing their owners wasn't something she'd ever done. She didn't have any game plan, any expectations, so why was she wondering what it would be like to be kissed by him?

Because she *wanted* him to kiss her.

That was the craziest thought she'd had all weekend. She'd never been kissed before. Not even in friendship. She was a virgin, pure, unspotted, not even warmed up.

"Never advise a person to go with their first impulse," she said. "It's an axiom of business."

"But some of the greatest success stories are a result of gut feeling."

"The odds are against it."

"You're one to go with the odds?"

"That's the best way to ensure success."

"Don't you ever fly by the seat of your pants, act on instinct, go with the feeling of the moment?"

"No one can succeed all the time; but if you have a good reason why your plan failed, you'll be given a second chance. Without one, your career is down the tubes."

"Do you always think in terms of logical, well-thought-out business decisions?"

She didn't do it consciously. It just seemed natural. "No, not always."

"When did you last go against your best judgment?"

"When I left home."

He stopped, turned her to face him. "I disagree. I think you knew you'd die if you didn't get away, that you had the intelligence and the drive to succeed in anything you wanted to do. I think that was a decision based very much on facts."

She shrugged. "In that case, I've never done anything impulsive."

"Not when you sat down in my living room and refused to leave until I took your case?"

"I was desperate."

"What better reason to go with your instincts?"

"I knew you were the best."

"You'd been told that, but you didn't know. You still don't know. I haven't come up with a single clue. I couldn't even keep you safe from attack."

"I didn't have anywhere else to go. Is that instinctive enough for you?"

"Better."

"And I came for a walk in the dark even though I'm certain somebody's watching me this very minute."

He squeezed her hand. "That's even better."

She wished he wouldn't do that. It started her thinking about things that could never happen. She'd been struggling to keep any such ideas at bay. Every time he did something thoughtful, it made it all that much harder. She *knew* he was only doing it to be nice, but that didn't seem to make any difference. She couldn't understand why she had suddenly become such an emotional idiot. She never used to act like this. Maybe it was what came from being framed, fired, and nearly killed.

"Why are you so anxious for me to be impulsive?" she asked.

"I just want to see you do something because you want to, because it would be fun, not because it's sensible, safe, or useful to your career. I don't think you've had much fun in your life."

She resented that. It made her sound like some pathetic female without enough sense to take care of herself. "I had a lot of fun. It's just not the kind of fun most people want."

"Maybe, but for most people, career success comes under the heading of satisfaction. Fun is going skinny dipping at midnight, sneaking out to go to a rock concert with a guy your parents don't like. Painting your nails different colors and dying your hair green."

"That would be easier if I had any hair."

He stopped and turned to face her. "That's exactly what I mean. You're thinking in terms of what your hair used to look like. Think of something totally different, funky, something you wouldn't do in a million years."

"That wouldn't be fun. I'd be so self-conscious I couldn't leave my apartment. I wouldn't look like myself. I wouldn't even *feel* like myself."

He put his arm around her as they started back. "Good. Think of somebody you'd like to be, then start acting the way you think they'd act."

"That's a crazy idea."

"It could be fun."

"It could cause me to do something stupid I'd regret later."

He stopped, turned to face her again. "Maybe if you don't do it now, you'll regret it forever."

"Like what?"

"Like this."

He put his hand under her chin and lifted her head until she was looking right into his eyes. Then he kissed her.

Claire remembered a song with the words *and the world stood still*. She hadn't believed anything like that could happen, but this was obviously what the songwriter meant. For one moment, the world faded. Nothing else existed for her except Eric.

Kissing had always seemed like an overrated exercise to her, something kids did all the time because they couldn't keep their hormones under control. Adults, she thought, confined it to their more passionate moments in private. Kisses were not to be shared between friends unless something else was intended to follow.

But Eric was kissing her, brushing her lips lightly with his, moistening her lips with the tip of his tongue. They weren't friends. They hardly knew each other.

"Is this how you seduce those women you bring here all the time?" she asked.

She hated herself the moment the words were out of her mouth. She hated herself even more when she saw the expression on Eric's face. She might as well have slapped him.

"It's one way," he said, his voice constricted with a tautness she hadn't heard before. "But this wasn't about seduction. It was about a guy kissing a girl because she was in a tight spot and feeling a bit down. It was just my way of letting you know you're not alone. I guess it wasn't such a good idea."

He had let go of her hand. He turned and started back toward the houseboat. He stopped when she didn't follow. "I thought you wanted me to stay between you and the bushes."

She didn't think she could force her feet to move. She didn't know exactly what she was feeling—she was swamped by a flood tide of emotions—but she did know she was sorry and would have given anything to be able to unsay those words. "I wasn't sure you still wanted to walk with me."

"Don't be absurd. I'm not going to turn my back on you just because you can't tell the difference between seduction and friendship."

"I've never been kissed like that before," she said. "I didn't know there was a difference."

He looked for a moment as if he didn't believe her. Then suddenly the tightness left his expression. "No wonder you let yourself get framed and didn't have the slightest idea what was going on. You live in a world all by yourself. Don't you ever get lonely?"

She started to reply with an indignant negative. But then she remembered a weekend shortly after she'd come to work for the bank. She'd finished all her work and had had nothing to do. So she'd gone back to the office, come up with an idea for an independent project, and worked through the weekend. Over the years, she'd fallen into the habit of filling any free time with work, stifling any need for companionship with the need to get ahead on just one more project.

"Yes. I do feel lonely sometimes, but I was out two evenings last week, three the week before."

"That was business. Do you ever go out with friends, take in a movie, go scuba diving?"

"I can't swim."

"You know what I mean."

"There's nothing wrong with work."

"There is when it causes you to mistake an innocent kiss for a seduction."

"How is a woman supposed to know the difference?"

"Like this."

Eric grabbed her, put his arms around her, and crushed her body to his. His mouth captured her lips in a ragged, hungry kiss. His lips covered her whole mouth, devouring her like some starving animal. Then he opened his mouth and thrust his tongue between her teeth. Her gasp of startled surprise didn't slow him down. His tongue filled her mouth, searching, thrusting, probing until it engaged her own tongue in a dance that nearly paralleled that taking place between their two bodies.

He pressed her body so tightly against his she felt that her breasts were in danger of being permanently flattened. She could feel the power of his arms as they encircled her, the sinewy strength of his legs as he pressed them against her thighs. His hands roamed her back from shoulder to waist until they cupped her buttocks and pressed her against him so tightly she felt the bulge of his groin against her abdomen. Even as she struggled to break free, he thrust one hand between them to cup her breast in his palm.

Claire was certain she would faint.

Then just as suddenly as Eric grabbed her, he released her. "There," he said, sounding nearly as breathless as she felt. "Now you know the difference."

ELEVEN

Claire stared at Eric, her mouth open, her body rigid.

"We should get back," he said, sounding almost normal again. "It's getting chilly."

She was in such a deep state of shock she doubted she would notice. She offered no resistance when Eric took her hand and they started back to the boat. She couldn't decide whether she was angry with him for the way he'd handled her or disturbed to discover what a man considered seductive.

"Is that really the way you kiss the women you seduce?" She couldn't believe she was asking such a question. She could feel her face turn warm with the flush of embarrassment.

"I don't seduce women," he said. "The women who come to my boat do so because they enjoy what we share."

"But is that how you kiss them?"

"Sometimes." He sounded a bit aggravated, as if he'd rather not answer. "It's not the same with every woman."

She was not only so naive she didn't know how men kissed women they intended to sleep with, she didn't even realize that they acted differently with different women.

"I'm sorry. I shouldn't have asked that."

"Why not?"

"Because it's rude. It makes it sound as if I think you're some kind of sex fiend, and I don't."

Eric laughed, and the last of the tension seemed to leave him. "Mildred is the one who makes it sound as if I'm addicted to sex. You make it sound like something nice people wouldn't do." He turned to look at her. "Do you think I'm nice?"

She hesitated, unsure how to answer his question, unsure even of her opinion of him. He seemed so full of contradictions she had no idea which represented the real Eric Sterling.

"I think it's very nice of you to put up with this strange woman who forced you to take her case, then got herself attacked on your doorstep."

"I preferred it when you thought I was a sex fiend. Come on. It's time we get you in bed."

She felt dismissed, that he'd briefly given her some thought, then decided to move on.

"I'm sorry if I said anything wrong," she said. She didn't want him to be angry with her, but even that was preferable to being dismissed.

"You didn't say anything wrong. You just reminded me of how different we are."

"Now you're laughing at me."

"Believe it or not, I'm laughing at myself."

"Why?"

"I don't think I'd better explain."

She stopped abruptly, even though the shadows cast by the shrubs boarding the walk nearly swallowed Eric's face. "That's not fair. You got angry because I didn't know anything about seducing females. You grabbed me, kissed and handled me all over; then you laughed at me as if I were an innocent fool. Well I am innocent. I can't help that, but I'm not a fool. I can learn."

"I'm sure you can."

"And I don't like to be laughed at."

"I told you, I wasn't laughing at you."

"I don't believe you." She stopped, surprised at herself. "I shouldn't have said that, but you made me angry. There, I acted on impulse. That ought to make you a little bit happy."

"It does." He tugged at her hand, but she didn't move.

"I want to know what you were laughing at."

"No, you don't."

"Yes, I do."

"Do you promise not to get angry? No kicking, scratching, or slapping?"

"I've already acted on impulse once this evening. You can't expect twice. I'm still a novice." She sounded snippy, but she didn't care.

"Okay, but remember you asked for it. I was weighing the possibility of our sleeping together for the rest of the time you're on the boat."

She'd anticipated many things, but never that. She stood as stiff as her father's starched collars, unable to move or think.

"I knew you'd be mad."

"I'm not mad."

"Then say something."

"What am I supposed to say? This is the first time this has ever happened to me."

"That's exactly why I was laughing at myself. It would be like taking candy from a child. Sorry, that wasn't a very apt comparison."

"Why is it like taking candy from a child?"

"Because you're so innocent you wouldn't know we were doing it just for mutual pleasure. You'd get your feelings involved and get hurt."

"I may be naive and inexperienced and rather ignorant when it comes to sex, but I do know people engage in it for all kinds of reasons. Including fun."

She started toward the houseboat, leaving him to follow a step or two behind her.

"Okay, so I underestimated you. I'm sorry."

But it hadn't felt like an underestimation. She felt that she'd been measured and found unworthy. She'd experienced that often enough to remember what it felt like.

"You don't have to apologize. I'm sure I should be flattered you even considered sleeping with me. You probably thought it would be a kindness if you tried to wise up this little girl from nowhere, let her know what the real world was like."

"Claire, don't—"

"I know what it was. You found yourself saddled with this dreadfully plain female in a wig. You couldn't very well invite anyone else over for the weekend, so you thought you'd make do with what you had. I overheard one of the other vice presidents at a Christmas party—he'd had a little too much to drink—say that all women were alike in the dark. Is that true? Would I be just as good as any other women if you couldn't see my face?"

Damn! She was crying. She never cried. She never even got mad. It was a waste of time and energy.

"You shouldn't have encouraged me to go with my instincts. Never tell a woman to be herself until you're sure what that self is like."

"There's nothing wrong with you."

"Nothing except being a frigid, frightened, inexperienced, ignorant virgin. That may not seem like much to you, but it seems like a hell of a lot to me. Now you've got me cussing. I never cuss."

Eric grabbed her by the arm and spun her around. "Get mad all you want. Cuss all you want, but don't ever run yourself down like that."

"Why? It's true."

"Maybe, but they're not bad things. We were all there at one point."

"Were you ever frigid?"

He half grinned. "No."

"Frightened of sex?"

"No, but—"

"You were never unattractive, unpopular, poor, or forced to study and work all the time to make top grades so you could win a scholarship so you could keep going to school. Boys hate girls who get better grades than they do. They have some very unpleasant names for females like me."

"I'm sorry for whatever they said."

"You don't have to be. I know I'm not attractive."

"You are."

"I'm not. My father told me that."

"Then your father is blind or an idiot."

"My father is an oracle. All truth and condemnation come straight through him from God. He is the source of all wisdom, all—"

"Stop it. You're pretty, you've got a spectacular figure, you're nice, and you're obviously practically a genius when it comes to finance. After his being so far wrong in so many areas, I don't think you have to worry about your father's being right about anything else."

"It's not just my father. It's other people, too. They—"

Without warning, Eric pulled her into his arms and kissed her. Equally without warning, she threw her arms around his neck and kissed him back.

"Why did you do that?" she asked when Eric finally broke their kiss.

"Because I wanted to."

"Was that the only reason?"

"It seemed like the only way to shut you up. You've been saying those things about yourself for so long you've started to believe them."

"So you're taking me on as a charity case."

"Claire, is it impossible to believe a man can like you,

find you attractive, can want to express those feelings with a kiss?"

Yes. Totally impossible. "No one ever has."

"Well, I do. I have."

"Why?"

"I don't know. I just do. Don't try to analyze everything."

They started toward the marina.

"You just like me," she said. "It was just a friendly kiss."

"Yes."

She wasn't sure she could handle that. She wanted Eric to like her a lot, not just as a friend. She knew she was lucky he even wanted to be her friend, but it didn't stop her from wanting more. She told herself not to be a fool. To take what she had and be thankful.

But it wasn't easy to be thankful for a drop when you wanted the whole cup.

"It's a nice night for a walk," a woman sitting on the grass verge next to the lake said as they passed.

"A beautiful night," Eric agreed.

The moonlight shone on the water like a pale yellow streak against a gray-black background. The lights that twinkled along the shore started to fade against the stronger light coming from the mercury vapor lights that illuminated the parking lot and lined the boardwalk out to the houseboats. It was a world that seemed foreign and at the same time wonderfully protective. It had no connection with her previous world. She could be somebody different.

She had to be different. Eric had kissed her.

"Did you have a nice walk?" Mildred asked when they reached the houseboat.

"Yes, it was very nice," Claire said.

"See. I told you nothing was wrong," Aubrey called from inside their houseboat. "Now come on to bed."

"He took his Viagra." Mildred made a face, then

grinned. "It's driving him crazy that I insisted on staying up until you got back."

"Well, we're perfectly safe. We got to talking and went farther than we intended," Eric said.

"See. Didn't I tell you?" Aubrey called. *"Now* will you come to bed?"

Eric chuckled.

"I'd better go before he bursts something," Mildred said. "At our age, it's not easy to find replacement parts."

Coming so soon after their earlier discussion, this rather frank reference to sex caused Claire to feel warm. She knew it had more to do with her than with Mildred. She was thinking about having sex with Eric. She didn't want to think about it. She knew it couldn't happen, that she wouldn't let it happen, but she couldn't control her thoughts . . . or her desires.

She followed Eric onto his boat. "Thanks for the walk," she said. "I enjoyed it."

"Good. Now get a good night's sleep. We have to go back to work tomorrow."

She turned to go inside, but he didn't follow. "You're not going to bed yet?"

"I've got to put the chairs up and clean out the grill."

"I can help."

"You need your rest. Besides, you don't know where everything goes. On a boat this small, that's crucial."

He was probably trying to be nice, but she felt rejected. And she was tired of feeling that way. Now that she stopped to think of it, she'd felt rejected all her life.

The only two people in the world who seemed to care about her were a hard-bitten private eye and a little old lady whose husband gobbled Viagra, both of whom she'd known a little more than twenty-four hours. She was twenty-seven years old, Phi Beta Kappa, *summa cum laude.* She had won dozens of academic scholarships and prestigious promotions, but she had no one who cared a rap what happened to her. That didn't say much for her life up until now.

She walked through the living room and bedroom to the bathroom. She stared at herself in the mirror. A strange woman stared back at her. She'd forgotten the wig. She'd never get used to this mass of bright red curls.

Maybe that wasn't all bad. The clothes she'd worn in the past, the hairstyle, the success hadn't generated any interest in her as a person. And she hadn't been happy. She kept telling herself that she was working toward her goal, that she would be wonderfully happy and fulfilled when she got there.

But she'd come close enough to begin to wonder what lay beyond the next promotion besides more money and another promotion. If she hadn't been knocked off the merry-go-round, she might never have known she wanted more.

She might never have known what that *more* was if she hadn't needed to hire Eric Sterling.

Eric muttered to himself as he folded up the chairs and put them away. He had warned himself over and over, but he was becoming romantically involved with his client. He was thirty-five years old. He wasn't a kid anymore. He had made this mistake before. He knew the results. It was stupid to do it again. But even if he could have sent her back to her apartment in the morning without fear someone might try to kill her, he wouldn't. All the signs were there for the usual infatuation, but there was something unmistakably different about Claire.

For one thing, he couldn't remember having worked with anyone who had so little knowledge of people, of her own self. She might have an IQ in the stratosphere, but she knew nothing of the world outside her job. She was powerless, defenseless, clueless.

All of which ought to have turned him off, disgusted him. At least, irritated him. Instead it intrigued him. It made him want to protect her. It made him determined to prove her innocence though he knew damned well he didn't have a thing to go on. Maybe he was just as bad as she was.

That started him wondering what she was really like. He wanted to know why she was driven to achieve worldly success at the expense of everything else. He knew lots of people who wanted money and position, but most of them had goals concerning love and family that were equally important.

Claire never mentioned love, had said nothing positive about her family. That had to be a very important factor in her decision to pursue success to the exclusion of all else, but he would like to know why. No one could simply turn their back on their past and go on as if it didn't exist. He ought to know. He'd tried; yet it still pursued him as relentlessly as his shadow.

Claire's mention of her father had reminded Eric he hadn't been very successful with his own. He had tried to believe he didn't care about his father, that their lives were forever separate; but he'd known for some time that it wasn't true. Even knowing his father had been cruel and heartless couldn't change that.

He'd chosen his career out of anger, had become a private investigator to get revenge. But he didn't want to be a private investigator. He wasn't even sure he wanted to be a lawyer. His interest in the family business had grown over the last few years until he could barely keep his hands off it. He supposed he inherited that from both his parents. He'd let anger drive him in the wrong direction once before. He had to come to terms with his father and his past, or he might do it again.

He had the distinct feeling Claire had let her desire to prove to her father that she could succeed get so far out of control it had overshadowed everything else in her life. One day she would wake up and realize she had a great deal of what wasn't very important and none of what was essential to her happiness. It was a dead certainty she wasn't happy now. She might not realize it, but her success hadn't given her the satisfaction she needed. Their third kiss had proved that.

Their third kiss!

Here he was trying to keep his distance, and he'd kissed her three times in less than fifteen minutes. He doubted she'd been kissed three times in her entire life. You'd think by now he'd have learned to keep his hands to himself, but that seemed impossible when it came to Claire. He couldn't explain that. It was just so.

No, he could explain it. Stupidity. That covered the situation pretty well. He muttered several curses. Why should this time seem different? He was sure it would turn out like all the others. He ought to pull in his antenna and keep a low profile until it was over. But he wouldn't. This time was different.

He had to find out why.

He emptied the ashes from the charcoal grill and carried them to the dumpster at the end of the boardwalk. He met Mildred on his way back.

"I thought you and Aubrey were tangoing tonight."

She laughed softly. "Viagra can increase his potency, but it can't do a thing for his stamina."

Eric assumed a mock defensive stance. "Don't cast your lewd gaze at me, you lusty old woman. I passed my peak a good while ago."

"I imagine you can still get the job done."

He stood up straight. "What an unromantic thing for an old romantic like you to say."

"I wasn't aware romance had anything to do with your tangos."

That was cutting too close to the bone. "Are you going to turn moralistic on me?"

"I was just wondering about your attitude toward that young woman inside."

"You can stop with the mother hen act. I'm not in the habit of seducing virgins."

"I didn't think you were. I was referring to your habit of falling in love with your clients. You might be able to fall in and out of love with a minimum of emotional damage, but I think something like that would devastate Claire."

"What makes you think I'm infatuated with Claire?"

"You said you used to fall in love with the really helpless ones. I can't imagine anyone more helpless right now than Claire. She's pretty, she's sweet, and you've broken your own rule by letting her stay here. If I didn't know about the attempt on her life, I'd say you were setting yourself up for falling in love."

Eric liked Mildred a lot. In some ways she was like the kindly aunt he'd never had, but this was one time he could have done without a nosy relative. "You forgot innocent, naive, unsophisticated, inexperienced . . ." There were so many things about Claire that made her completely unlike any of the women he usually saw. That made her all the more dangerous.

"I didn't forget any of those."

"Neither did I. And you're right. I am having trouble keeping my interest purely professional, but I can't send her away. Not while she's still hurt, frightened, and in danger."

"I don't want you to send her away. I hope you keep her here until everything is straightened out."

"Then why—"

"I'm hoping you will fall in love with her, *really* fall in love. She's a nice girl. It's time you settled down."

Eric felt some of the tension ease. "You old fraud. You just can't stand to see me living free and easy."

Mildred laughed quietly. "Don't waste any more of your life. Find a nice girl, settle down, then go after your demons."

The tension returned. "What demons?"

"You need to go home. You left a lot of things up in the air. Now I've been nosy enough for one night. Tell Claire good night for me, and tomorrow you get busy finding out exactly what did happen to that poor child."

"I'm hoping my friend will have been able to get a copy of the police report, at least be able to tell me what it says. I'll also know something more about her car and apartment."

"Do you have spies everywhere?"

"Just about. Now that she's had a day to relax, I'll take her back over the last two weeks. There has to be something she's forgotten she knows."

"What if you still don't get anything?"

"She mentioned a company party tomorrow night. I thought we'd disguise her as best we can, crash the party, and see if some of her co-workers know something."

"Do you think she'll wear any of that stuff?"

"I hope I can persuade her."

"Let me know when you're ready. A woman's touch is always a good thing in situations like this."

"I'll be sure to call you. I've never done anything like this before."

"I have a feeling it's just the beginning to a lot of things that you've never done before. Now I'm going to bed. But before I do, I'm going to hide Aubrey's pills. I need a day off."

Mildred went inside chuckling. Eric's answering

chuckle died as soon as she closed her door. How could she possibly know he'd been avoiding going home for more than ten years? How could she possibly know he could never rest easy until he did?

Claire thought if he asked her to go back over her last week one more time, she was going to throw something at him. "You've been battering me with questions all morning," she complained. "I've told you I can't remember anything else. Why don't you believe me?"

"I do believe you, but I'm convinced the clue to all of this is buried in your mind. You obviously did something, heard something, saw something, that meant a great deal more than you know."

"But I've told you I didn't see, do, or hear anything out of the ordinary for the last few weeks. I don't think I've ever done anything out of the ordinary."

"Except work a hundred hours a week."

"That's not unusual. Up-and-coming young executives are expected to put in long hours. That's how management decides whom to promote. You've got to be able to do the job, but you've also got to be willing to make it come before anything else in your life."

"As far as I can tell, it *was* your life."

"It wasn't the work. It was the promotions, the success I craved. I'd planned my whole life around that."

"And now?"

She didn't want to answer that question. She didn't want to admit she had begun to question her goals, begun to see the last fifteen years of her life as a frantic chase after a rainbow that existed only in her head.

"You don't have a career anymore," Eric said. "Nobody is going to hire you."

"They will after you find out what happened and who really did it."

"Okay, for the sake of argument let's say they offer you your job back, maybe even throw in a promotion so you won't sue them. You resume your rapid climb up the corporate ladder. What happens when you're fifty and you've climbed as high as you can? What then?"

"What do you mean?"

"What will you have to show for all those years of work?"

"My success."

"You mean money, a fancy apartment, and a huge expense account."

"Among other things."

"What other things?"

"I will have proved I can succeed."

"You already know that. So do your bosses. Why do you have to go on proving it over and over again?"

"That will be a greater success."

"When do you say, I've had enough success. Now it's time to get on with the rest of my life."

She couldn't answer that question. She hadn't even thought about it until yesterday. She still didn't know how she felt about it.

"I'll know."

"Okay. You'll know. What about the rest of your life? What do you want to do when you've had your fill of success?"

She didn't know the answer to that, either. She'd always assumed that once she had her success, she would somehow end up happily married with a family. But she'd never given any thought to how she'd get that husband and family. It had always been at the end of her thoughts, something to be considered later when all the job-related decisions had been made and she'd gotten that next promotion.

"I haven't worked out the answers to all those questions

yet," she said, trying not to feel like a foolish child. "I have to take everything one step at a time."

"The next few days will be a good time to do some working out," Eric said. "First, what happens if you get your old job back and promotions rain down on your head like confetti in a New York parade? Second, what happens if you're cleared but find your career as a high-level executive is down the tubes? Let's face it. Some of the mud from this accusation will stick, even if we're able to prove you innocent beyond a shadow of a doubt. And finally, what happens if you're convicted and have to spend time in jail?"

Claire had refused to think about that. She was innocent. She knew that somewhere out there was the proof. She'd concentrated all her energy on finding a good private detective. Her father had said that truth always prevailed. It might take it a while, but it would finally come to light. He'd never told her much that stood her in good stead, but she had put her faith in believing him this time.

"I'm innocent. I don't have to worry about jail."

It was impossible for her to consider life after jail. For her, there would be no life. The destruction her family had predicted would have overtaken her.

"In that case we'd better get started proving your innocence," Eric said.

"I can't go over my movements again. It'll drive me crazy."

"We're not going to do that. We're going to a party."

"What party? I can't go anywhere looking like this." She wasn't wearing her wig.

"We're going to your bank's annual party, the one you told me was taking place this afternoon."

"They won't let me in.

"I know. That's why I had Mildred buy you a completely new outfit."

He reached into a bag and pulled out a different wig. Claire recoiled in horror.

"I can't be seen in public wearing that. I'd rather go to jail."

TWELVE

"Are you sure that's a wig?" Claire asked. "It looks like a whole sheep to me."

"It's a Dolly Parton wig," Eric said. "Your normal haircut makes you look almost like a man. This is about as far away as you can get from that."

"But I can't wear that. I'd die of embarrassment."

"Look, what's more important, pride or going to jail?" Eric asked, his tone sharp. "I haven't been able to glean a single thing from what you've told me. If I'm going to prove you didn't steal that information, I'm going to have to have something to go on. Maybe some of the people you worked with will know something."

"How can they know what I don't know?"

"It's an avenue we've got to try."

"I can't do it. I simply can't be seen in this."

What must Eric think of her to believe she'd appear in a wig like that? She might as well announce she was looking to spend the night with a man and the highest bidder would get the nod.

Eric put the wig aside. "Then you might as well let me take you to the police station. You'll be safe from the killer there, and the sooner you start your jail sentence, the sooner you'll get out."

"I'm not going to jail. I'm innocent."

"That won't matter. The police say they have an open-

and-shut case. I say we don't have the first clue who did this, where to look, anything. You'd better start preparing your plea bargain."

"No.

Eric held up the wig. "Do you have a better idea?"

She had no idea at all. She had assumed that she'd hire a detective, turn the case over to him, then go home and wait until he delivered the evidence that would free her. She hadn't anticipated any of what followed.

"You haven't left this boat," she said. "You haven't even started to look. Maybe you could have found what you need already."

"I have a contact in the police department who's trying to get a look at the charges against you. The friend watching your apartment tells me it's staked out, so you can't go near the place. But you're right, I haven't done anything because I don't know where to start. You've given me nothing. I don't know what was stolen, when, how, or who bought it. How can I find something when I don't even know what I'm looking for?"

"I can't tell you what I don't know."

"That's why we've got to talk to some of the people you work with, see if we can learn anything from them."

"We'll have to tell them who I am. They won't talk to a stranger."

"I know that, but we have to get in first. I doubt we can do that if they recognize you. Also, we have to remember that the man who tried to kill you might still be out there. If so, we don't want him to know you're still alive."

She looked at the large shopping bag sitting on the table next to Eric. It appeared to have quite a few more items inside. She had a sinking feeling Eric intended to do more than give her a new wig.

"What else is in that bag?"

"An outfit almost guaranteed to keep you from being recognized."

"Where did you get it?"

"Mildred bought it for me when she bought the clothes you wanted."

"You mean you planned this yesterday?"

"I knew we'd need a disguise. I didn't know exactly what we'd use it for."

"Let me see what's in that bag."

"You're not going to like it."

"I didn't expect I would."

"But you've got to wear it."

She withheld her opinion for the length of time it took him to pull a black leather mini skirt from the bag. Before she could swear she'd rather die first, he pulled out a halter top of such a brilliant red she was certain she'd blind anybody who dared approach her.

"Are you crazy?" she exclaimed. "I couldn't possibly wear that. I'd turn as red as that top. Well, nearly. I don't think there is anything in the universe that red."

"All the more reason for you to wear it."

"No.

"Do you remember what I said about jail?"

"There has to be another way."

"I'm open to suggestions."

She didn't have any. She'd been counting on Eric to know what to do.

A knock at the door distracted her. Mildred let herself in.

"I thought I heard the sound of anguished screams," she said with a cheerful smile.

"You heard Claire saying she'd rather go to jail than wear these clothes," Eric said.

"Look what he wants me to wear," Claire said.

"I know. I was rather doubtful when I bought all that stuff, but now I've decided it's just the thing for you."

"Why?" Claire's voice sounded like an anguished wail. She'd been certain Mildred would be her side.

"You'd better show her the shoes," Mildred said. "The whole outfit will be useless unless she can walk in them."

By the time Eric produced a pair of platform heels of an equally brilliant red, Claire was beyond shock.

"Of course I can't walk in those," she said. "If I fell off them, I'd probably break a leg."

"I'll hold you upright," Eric volunteered.

"I hope you have a mask," she said. "You can't expect me to show my face."

"I'll take care of that," Mildred said and held up a makeup bag. "By the time I finish, even your best friend won't know you."

Claire couldn't understand why the two people who said they cared about her would want her to humiliate herself.

"It'll be just like playing dress up when you were a little girl," Mildred said.

"I never played dress up. My father said it was a sin."

"Well, now you'll get to see how much fun you missed."

"Have you ever dressed like this?"

"Not with my figure, dearie. But if I looked like you, I'd go dancing every night. I'm not sure about the shoes, though. I'm afraid of heights." Mildred paused, then laughed. "Don't look so frightened. I'm just teasing. I'd love to be able to go out in clothes like that and not send people into hysterics "

"That's what I'll do."

"You'll send the women into fits of jealousy and the men into . . . maybe you'd better ask Eric what you'll do to the men."

"Mesmerize them," Eric said. "They'll be so stunned they won't know what they're saying . . . which is exactly what we want."

"I can't—"

"Let me make you up," Mildred said. "Then we'll decide about the clothes."

Mildred reached inside that seemingly endless shopping bag, drew out several packages, and pushed Claire toward the bedroom.

"We're going to be in the bedroom for at least half an hour," she told Eric.

"What are you going to do?" Claire asked when Mildred sat her down on the side of the bed. "I can't see."

"I don't want you to see until I'm finished," Mildred said. "I can't work if you keep exclaiming at everything I do."

"You're scaring me to death."

"I'm just teasing."

"Maybe you shouldn't tease so much."

"Aubrey says that, too."

Claire doubted she and Aubrey were talking about the same thing.

"Are you going to tell me what you're doing?" Claire asked.

"No. You can talk about anything you want except the makeup. I'll let you see it when I'm finished."

"I don't know how I ended up in this situation," Claire said. "Up until last week nothing unusual ever happened to me. Now you're about to make me up to look like somebody from MTV."

"See. You do know something about the outside world. Now you won't be upset at what I do. I do watch MTV. I love to see how they dress. Tell me about your family."

"I think I'll tell you about work."

So she started with her first job interview and progressed through all the positions she'd held in the six years since she'd finished graduate school. She was able to ignore Mildred when she washed her face and applied the foundation and color. She didn't even get too upset when Mildred worked over her eyebrows. The eyeliner tickled. She'd used it herself, but she had a feeling Mildred was putting it on much heavier than she had.

Claire expected the lipstick, but she hadn't expected Mildred to experiment. She put it on and took it off until Claire's lips were tender.

The false eyelashes were definitely weird. Her eyelashes felt as if they weighed five or six times what they usually did.

"Don't touch them," Mildred warned when Claire's hand went toward her face.

"But they're driving me crazy. How does anybody wear these things?"

"I don't know, but they make you look fabulous. You're not going to believe yourself. Wait until Eric sees you."

Claire realized she was just as upset about what Eric might think as she was about what people who knew her would say.

"He's not going to laugh, is he?"

"He's going to be stunned."

Claire decided being stunned with shock and doubled over with laughter weren't all that far apart.

"How much longer before I can see?" she asked.

"Not long. Let's get you dressed. I think it'll be easier to put on the wig last."

Claire didn't need a mirror to know she was indecently clothed. The nearly black net hose covered more of her body than her skirt and top together. She tried to tell herself she was wearing more than if she had on a bathing suit, but that was small comfort. She didn't go to the beach. She didn't swim. She'd never worn a bathing suit.

"I forgot your nails," Mildred exclaimed. "You can't possibly go out dressed like this and not do something about your nails. Do you have anything I can use? No, of course you don't," Mildred said, answering herself. "And

I don't either. But Orida, four boats down, probably does. That woman has no taste at all."

That pronouncement didn't make Claire feel any better.

"Okay, put those shoes on and see if you can stand up."

It took Mildred's help, but she finally got to her feet.

"I can't move," Claire said.

Mildred laughed. "Maybe we'd better practice walking. I don't think Eric will want to carry you everywhere you go. People are liable to think you're a talking doll."

Claire had never given much thought to shoes. She bought navy, brown, and black pumps with medium heels. She never thought about them as long as they matched her clothes. Perched on these stilts she could hardly think of anything else.

"Suppose I fall down."

"Eric will be beside you."

"He'd better be."

"Okay, time for the wig."

Claire carefully settled herself back on the bed and allowed Mildred to adjust the wig until she was satisfied. She stepped back and broke into a brilliant smile. "Your own mother wouldn't recognize you."

"I hope not. The shock would kill her."

She had a fleeting thought of how far she'd come from what her parents wanted. She wondered if she'd gone too far at last.

"Can I see myself now?"

"I want Eric to see you first."

"You promised."

"He might have some suggestions. He knows more about women than I do."

She couldn't stand the idea of Eric seeing her, reacting, making comments without her knowing how she looked.

"I'm not leaving this room until I know what I look like," she said.

"Okay, but be careful of that wig when you go into the bathroom. It's a real tiny room and that's a real big wig."

Claire was more afraid of falling off her platform heels than knocking the wig off her head. But neither of those emotions could compare to what she felt when she caught sight of herself in the mirror.

She screamed. It wasn't a loud scream, just intense and deeply felt.

Everything about Claire Dalton had been erased, covered up, or overshadowed by the hair, makeup, and the clothes. She looked like a rapper's girlfriend.

The bedroom door burst open. "What happened? What's wrong?" Eric demanded.

"Claire just saw herself in the mirror, and she's squealing with delight," Mildred said.

"That's a lie," Claire said as she slammed the bathroom door shut. "I'm in a state of shock."

"Let me see," Eric said.

"No," she shouted through the door. "I look like . . . I don't know what I look like, but I hate it."

"She looks wonderful," she heard Mildred telling Eric. "I wasn't too sure when I bought all those clothes, but you were exactly right. That wig adds just the right touch of impossibility."

Impossible hardly covered the situation. Insane came closer. Demented wasn't far off the mark, but nightmarish came closest to encompassing all the aspects of the situation.

"Come on out," Eric said.

"No."

"Stop sulking."

"I'm not sulking. I'm just trying to spare you a heart attack."

"I've got a strong heart."

"You look lovely," Mildred added.

"I thought you liked me," Claire said to Mildred.

"I do."

"You wouldn't tell such lies if you did."

"But you do look lovely. It's not the kind of look you're used to. If you were in Hollywood, you'd be the center of attention."

As a freak. She looked at herself once more. The bold, sassy stranger was still there. Claire Dalton was nowhere in sight.

"You might as well come on out," Eric said. "You can't stay in there forever. Besides, the party will be starting soon."

"I'm not going looking like this."

"Of course you are."

"You haven't seen me."

"Whose fault is that?"

"You wouldn't want to be seen with the creature Mildred created."

"If Mildred says you're lovely, then you are. I trust her opinion."

Great. It didn't matter if she felt she looked like something that had escaped from a drugged-out rock concert. Mildred was welcome to turn her into any kind of bizarre female she wanted.

"Mildred is a frustrated makeup artist. I bet she flunked finger painting in school."

"I never took art," Mildred said. "I don't have an aptitude for it."

"So why did you break a lifelong vow on me?"

"It was fun," Mildred said. "Besides, you do look lovely. In an unusual sort of way."

"Like a freak, a curiosity, an oddball."

"I can understand your reluctance, but it's silly not to come out," Eric said.

It infuriated her that he would dare say she was acting

silly. She knew the gravity of her situation, but women would look at him and think how handsome he was. Then they'd wonder why he'd hooked up with a female who looked like a Halloween joke.

"Come on, Claire. You've got to be adult about this."

No, she didn't.

"You're not changing anything, are you?" Mildred asked.

"No," she said, resigned, "I haven't changed anything."

She took another look in the mirror. The reflection was as horrifying as she remembered. There was nothing to do except keep reminding herself she was doing this to save her life. She would keep saying that to herself all afternoon. There were no other circumstances under which she'd ever go out in public looking like this.

She took a big breath and opened the door.

Eric's eyes widened a little, but he withstood the shock remarkably well. She didn't want an impassive mask. She wanted to know he was just as appalled as she had been. She wanted to hear him ask Mildred to take every bit of that makeup off and do it again.

"We forgot her fingernails," Eric said to Mildred.

"I know. I'm off to find Orida now. I'm sure she'll have something I can use."

"You mean you *like* me the way I look?" Claire asked Eric.

"It's fabulous," he said as a smile broke the solemnity of his expression. "It's even better than I had hoped."

She stamped her foot and nearly fell over sideways. "If you mean you've never seen such a bizarrely dressed female in your whole life, I'd like to remind you that you're the one responsible for this. You bought these clothes and forced me to put them on. I wanted nothing to do with it."

He took her hand, drew her forward, turned her slowly

around. "I don't like that wig. It makes you look a bit foolish. The shoes are over the top, but they're a necessary part of the impression we're trying to create. Okay, the makeup is exaggerated, but the concept is good, and the rest of you looks fabulous. You're going to need an entirely new wardrobe. You show up at work looking like this, and promotions would come so fast you wouldn't be able to keep up with them."

"What you mean is propositions would come so fast I wouldn't be able to outrun them. Don't you know what men think of women who look like this?"

"Yeah," he said, sounding a bit hoarse. "I'm thinking the same thing right now."

If she'd thought she could have moved both feet without falling into an ignominious heap on the floor, she'd have slapped him.

"You've got a fabulous body. No wonder your father wanted you to wear all those long, ugly clothes. You'd have had every male in your community in a fever."

"You think I'm *attractive!*" She couldn't believe he was telling the truth. He had to be trying to make her feel better about going out looking like a tasteless drag queen.

"You'll be the hit of the party. There won't be a man there who'll be able to take his eyes off you."

She'd momentarily forgotten about the party. "I don't want men staring at me."

"Sure you do. Every woman wants that."

"Not me."

She wouldn't mind Eric staring at her when she was dressed more sensibly, but she was definitely uncomfortable with the idea of having every man in a room looking at her and thinking thoughts that . . . well, she didn't want to think about what they'd be thinking.

"I wonder what kind of nail polish Mildred will find. I can't believe I forgot to put it on the list."

She was standing here, marooned on these platforms,

and all he could think of was adding to her embarrassment.

"Let's move into the other room," Eric said. "It's a little crowded in here for three people."

He looked surprised when she didn't move.

"Is something wrong?" he asked.

"Everything. I can't move."

"What do you mean?"

"I mean I can't walk in these shoes without falling over."

He grinned. "Hold my hand."

She teetered into the living room. "You really can't expect me to go anywhere wobbling on these shoes like a newborn giraffe."

"You can use the time until Mildred gets back practicing. You'll get the hang of it in a couple of minutes."

"Have you ever worn platforms?"

He looked amused. "No."

"Then you have no idea how long it takes to get the hang of walking in them. It took me months to learn to stand upright in two-inch heels. I must be six inches off the ground."

"Not that much. Come on. Start walking. You can lean on me if you need to."

Too bad Eric didn't have to go in disguise. He'd undoubtedly look better than she did, but at least he'd have some sympathy for her. Now he just grinned and tried to look like the patient, understanding male to her hysterical, mindless female.

She forced herself to stumble around the room. She supposed a person could learn to walk in these things, but it would take weeks. They had barely an hour. Still, she was getting the hang of these shoes a lot quicker than she'd expected. Maybe there was an acrobat somewhere in her family. Maybe a clown or two.

Just the thought made her smile.

"I knew you could do it," Eric said.

He backed away and left her on her own. She wobbled a bit, but she made up her mind she wouldn't fall off these shoes. She had also accepted the necessity of going to this party looking like an escapee from a Jerry Springer show. After all, she was trying to save her own neck, and a woman ought to be excused for doing anything under those circumstances.

"I found the perfect nail polish," Mildred said, bursting in without warning.

Claire lost her balance and went careening into Eric's arms.

"None of that," Mildred teased. "You'll mess up her makeup."

Eric helped her back on her feet. "I can't let you completely overshadow me," he said with a provoking smile. "While Mildred does your nails, I'll see if I can unearth something that will be worthy of you." He disappeared into his bedroom before Claire could think of a suitable reply.

Mildred's choice of fingernail polish proved to be unlike anything Claire had ever imagined, much less seen. She had expected the brilliant red, but she hadn't anticipated its luminous quality or the tiny flecks of silver in it. It was almost as if she had minuscule lights in each fingernail.

"It glows in the dark," Mildred said, delighted with her find. "The moment Orida told me it was her favorite, I knew it would be perfect."

Perfect to complete the outfit of the most outrageous tramp ever to attend a bank party. Claire had been to the six previous parties. Never had anyone shown up dressed in anything remotely like her costume.

Eric emerged from his bedroom looking like John Travolta in *Saturday Night Fever*. His hair was slicked back and greased until it shone. He was at least a dozen years too old for the outfit, but just looking at him in those tight pants caused Claire's temperature to escalate.

"Where did you find such an outrageous getup?" Mildred asked once she stopped laughing.

"I bought it for a job several years back. I'm surprised I can still get in it."

"You almost didn't," Mildred said.

Eric grinned. "I think it makes me look like a perfect partner for Claire."

Claire was sorry to say she agreed. They both looked as if they'd gotten caught in a time warp. She prayed even harder that no one would recognize her.

"We ought to get going," Eric said. "If we arrive too late, they could be too drunk to make sense."

"Nobody gets that bad," Claire said. "The only time anyone did, he was transferred to one of the branches within a month."

"I still prefer to catch them before their wits are too dull," Eric said. He pulled back the sliding door. "Ready?"

No, but waiting would only make it worse.

"Watch the wig," Mildred warned. "Maybe I shouldn't have gotten one quite so big."

"It's fine," Eric assured her.

Claire had been so worried about the party she'd completely forgotten she had to run the gauntlet of twenty houseboats. And that didn't take into consideration anybody who might be in the parking lot or at one of the other docks. Her getup would attract attention at a hundred yards.

"I need a coat," Claire said.

"You look just fine," Eric replied. "Now come on. Give me your hand."

He helped her navigate the deck of the boat as it bobbed slowly in the water. The short gangplank to the boardwalk was easier. She looked at the boardwalk and the hundreds of boards that had been used to construct it—and the cracks in between—and decided that if she made it to the end, she could walk anywhere.

A wolf whistle nearly caused her to stumble.

"Where did you get that filly, Sterling?" somebody called. "She looks much too lively for you. Bring her over here."

"And give you a heart attack?" Eric called back.

Claire blushed furiously, but she was certain no one could see it through all that makeup.

"Smile," Eric said. "Act like you're enjoying yourself."

"I'm not."

"Wiggle your hips a little bit. That ought to give Willie palpitations for sure."

"If I wiggle anything," she said between clenched teeth, "I'll pitch headlong into the water."

"I've got you. Now smile and look sassy."

She didn't know how to look sassy. She'd spent her whole life trying not to draw attention to herself, trying to be *one of the boys*.

The men grinned at her as she passed. One or two of the women smiled, but most either refused to look at her or gave her a look that said she was trash and they knew it if she didn't.

"They all think I've slept with you," she hissed to Eric.

"Don't worry. You didn't."

"I know that, but they don't."

"It doesn't matter. Give them your biggest smile. Let them know you know you're gorgeous, and what they think doesn't matter."

She'd been telling herself that about her parents for years, but it wasn't any easier now than it had been then.

Somehow they made it to the car, managed to fit her and her wig inside, and started to the party.

"Now let's go over what you're going to do when we get there."

"I thought I was supposed to ask questions."

"You are, but you've also got to flirt, be the kind of woman men come on to. I want those men panting so hard they won't think too much about what they say."

"You aren't going to leave me, are you?"

"No, but you've got to be the kind of woman who collects boyfriends, not the kind who's controlled by them."

He spent the next thirty minutes describing a kind of woman she could never be. It was possible to make her outside look totally different by using makeup, indecent clothes, and this abominable wig, but nothing could change the woman inside.

"We're here," Eric said, as he pulled the car to a stop in the parking lot. "Time to put on an Academy Award performance."

Claire took a deep breath and prayed they'd gotten the date, time, and address wrong.

THIRTEEN

The first person she met was the only woman Claire thought she could consider a friend. The woman stared back at her with a look that said *I don't know who the hell you are or what you're doing here.*

"I'm Linda Parker," the woman said, introducing herself. "I'm acting as hostess today. Welcome to the party. I don't believe I've met you."

Eric had told Claire what to say. She had the words memorized, but they refused to leave her throat. Eric prodded her in the back to jostle them loose.

"I'm Susan Egan," Claire said. "I got hired two days ago."

"You must have worn something else when you came for your interview," Linda said. "I'm sure I would have remembered an outfit like that."

"I'd never wear this for an interview," Claire said with a giggle. "I wouldn't think a stuffy old personnel manager would like it."

"I'm sure you're right," Linda said. "But I'm surprised I don't remember that hair."

"Please don't mention it," Claire said, trying to act flustered rather than ready to faint from embarrassment. "It didn't feel clean, so I washed it twice." She made a face. "It frizzed."

"There sure is a lot of it."

"My boyfriend says it's my best point." Claire had out-stripped Eric's coaching several sentences ago, yet the words kept coming.

"I doubt that," Linda said with an expression perilously close to a sneer. "I see several men looking this way. I expect they'll be more than happy to tell you what they think are your best points." Her gaze raked Claire. "You've made them so easy to see."

"I don't like to get hot," Claire said. "I've been to a lot of dos like this, and it always gets hot."

"I bet it's hot wherever you go."

"I'm so glad you understand." Eric prodded her in the back. "Just talking about it makes me warm. I think I'll get something with ice in it to cool me down."

"Whatever you do, don't go near the ice sculpture. We want it to last for most of the evening."

"Keep smiling," Eric said as they moved away. "And make eye contact with all the men. You're supposed to enjoy parties like this."

"I'm trying," Claire said, hoping her face didn't crack from the falseness of her smiles.

"Who was that woman?" Eric asked.

"The woman I thought was my friend," Claire replied. "I can't believe she talked to me like that, like I was a . . ."

"I think *easy lay* is the phrase you're looking for."

"It is not!" But it was what she meant.

A middle-aged man from the overseas investment department came up to them. She cringed, grabbed Eric's hand, waited to be identified and thrown out. The man didn't like her and had tried several times to deny her promotions.

"Hi. Welcome to the party," he said. "I don't think we've met."

Her stomach turned a flip. "I just got hired," she said, hoping she managed to gush despite the feeling of nausea that threatened to overcome her. "I don't know anybody here."

"I'll be happy to introduce you around."

"We're heading to the bar," Eric said. "We're dry down to our toes."

"I'll tag along," the man said, eyeing Eric up and down, trying to decide just how much competition he might be. "My drink's about down to ice."

Actually his glass was half full, but Claire figured Eric wouldn't want her to mention that.

"Where do you work?" he asked.

"I'm a receptionist," Claire answered, "but they haven't decided where my talents can best be used."

"I'm sure they have," the man replied. "Just not who's going to get the benefit of them."

"Personnel seemed to think there wouldn't be any problem placing me. The nice man who interviewed me said I was highly qualified."

She was beginning to enjoy this. She'd never considered pretending to be someone so completely different from herself. But now that she was here and had no choice, she liked the fact that no one knew her. She could be outrageous, and it didn't matter.

Suddenly, the years of repression she'd endured to win favor with teachers and administrators, to gain promotions, the thousands of times she'd smiled and swallowed what she really wanted to say, all came welling up like a bad taste in her mouth. It was childish; it was probably petty, but she didn't care.

"Fix me a drink, honey," she said, turning to Eric. "You'd better make it real weak. I have no head for alcohol," she told the man. "Two drinks and I'm liable to do anything." She moved a little closer to him and whispered. "Last time, I got so hot I dived into the pool. My boyfriend was real mad. I got his car all wet."

The man's eyes grew a little wider. "I'm sure we could

find some towels. We can't have him getting mad at you again."

He frowned at Eric, and Claire giggled. "It wasn't him. That was another boyfriend."

"Do you have a lot?"

"No. I think seven is enough for one girl, don't you?"

"Maybe you could find room for one more?" He looked hopeful.

Claire giggled. "Maybe I'll push one in the pool." She took her drink from Eric and put the glass to her throat. The shock of the cold almost threw her out of her role. "Aaah, that feels so much better. I'll see you around." She took Eric by the arm and headed toward a larger group of men who'd been eyeing her ever since she arrived.

"You've been holding out on me," Eric said. "Where did you learn to act like this?"

"I'm trying to act like Marilyn Monroe in *Some Like It Hot*. How am I doing?"

"Better than I thought possible. There must be a little bit of hussy buried in you somewhere."

"My father's sure there's a whole lot, but actually it's revenge. Can you imagine what would happen to the man we just left if his wife knew how he was acting?"

"Yes, I can. Where are we going now?"

"Toward that group of men over there. If anybody here will know what's going on, one of them will."

Claire had to admit that the next hour was one of the most exciting of her entire life. She was the center of attention. Every executive seemed to feel he needed an extra person in his department. Claire felt certain there'd be at least a dozen requests on the personnel manager's desk next morning, all claiming the services of Susan Egan were essential to the smooth operation of such-and-such department.

She thoroughly enjoyed imagining the confusion when

they couldn't find any record of Susan Egan. The personnel manager hadn't always been cooperative. She didn't mind giving him this little headache.

"You've flirted enough," Eric said. "It's about time we start trying to ferret out some information."

He sounded irritated. Claire didn't know why. She'd done her best to do everything he wanted. He'd even complimented her several times. But that had been earlier. Now he seemed to spend most of his time steering her clear of the men following in her wake.

"Whom do you want to talk to?"

"A woman is probably the best bet."

"Maybe Linda has used up all her acid."

Not quite.

"There are no unattached men *here,*" she said when Claire approached her.

"I'm glad. A girl gets tired of talking to just men, doesn't she?"

"Some women do, but I never imagined you'd be one of them."

"I don't usually," Claire said, settling down next to Linda, who didn't look happy with her company, "but I'm a little depressed."

"I hope I never see you happy. The place couldn't contain you."

Claire tried to disguise her surprise at Linda's venom.

"A friend of mine is in terrible trouble, and it's been preying on my mind."

"I'm sure I'm sorry for your friend, but since I can't possibly know her, I don't see—"

"But you probably do," Claire said. "She worked here. Her name's Claire Dalton."

Linda looked as if she'd been stuck with a pin.

"I'm surprised you know Claire. She's not exactly your type."

"We have apartments in the same building."

Linda's expression indicated how she thought a woman like Susan Egan could come up with the rent for an expensive apartment. "If you want to keep your job here, you won't mention that name to anyone."

"Why? Claire is a sweet girl."

"I wouldn't call her sweet. A little ruthless, if you ask me; but she was honest and she worked hard. I didn't know her well, but I liked her."

"I do, too; but the poor thing is so depressed, she won't do anything but stay in that apartment and mope. And that's not like Claire."

"No, it isn't."

Linda wasn't going to offer any information without being asked directly. "She won't tell me, but she says the police are going to put her in jail."

"She's right."

"But they can't!" Claire said. Genuine indignation almost caused her to lose her breathy Marilyn Monroe voice. "She hasn't done anything. The police said she stole something off a computer. Why should she do that? Anybody can read what's on a computer."

"Not everything."

"Do you know what it is?"

"No. Nobody's talking. As far as I can tell, they don't even want to admit it happened."

"Who discovered it? The poor girl told me she went home a rising young executive one day, showered with praise by her boss, only to find herself out of a job and indicted for theft the next. She's devastated."

"I'm sure she is. Look, we've got to stop talking about this. I don't know what happened. I just know it's big, something that involves the suits. You only have to look at them to know half of them are tied in knots. Tell Claire I'm thinking about her."

Claire decided Linda wasn't a friend who could be depended on. She gathered her energy and plastered a smile on her face.

"I'm getting hot again. I'd better get something cool before I start to melt."

Claire struggled to get up on her shoes gracefully. She didn't see how any woman ever learned to be comfortable in these platform atrocities.

"I can't tell if she simply doesn't know anything or if she's just too afraid to talk," she said, as they headed toward the bar again.

"This is too high up for someone in her position," Eric said. "Who else can we target?"

They wended their way to the bar, adroitly avoiding delays from one man after another. One of the executive vice presidents from international banking proved more difficult to elude.

"I haven't had a chance to get to know you," he said to Claire, sidling up to her and putting his arm around her waist. She could feel his fingers exploring her side and stomach. Her first inclination was to throw him off and split his skull with a potted plant, but she managed to control her reaction. Eric was at her side. He wouldn't let anything happen. She didn't know the man well, but he would be as likely to know something about the theft as anybody else.

"There's not a lot to know," she replied in a breathy voice. She tried to wiggle her body just like Marilyn when she walked down the aisle in the sleeper car before crawling into the upper bunk with Jack Lemon. "I'm just a girl looking for a job."

"And I'm looking for a girl like you to take a very special position in my department."

Special sounded like "peshil" when he said it.

"What does your department do?"

"We handle international banking."

And any female who comes within range, I'll bet. She

wanted to tell him his efforts to explore her body, to be sexy, were not only pathetic, he was tickling her. She found it hard not to laugh in his face.

"It sounds much too difficult for me," she said.

"Don't worry. I'll make sure you get an easy job."

"The man in personnel said he didn't know where he was going to put me."

"I'll make sure you get in my department."

"Will I have to work with computers?"

"Yes."

"I don't know much about computers."

"It's easy."

"I'm not sure. A girlfriend of mine used to work with computers here, and she got into a whole lot of trouble. Now she has no job and the police are saying they're going to put her in jail."

He was trying to slip his hand under her bra. She slapped it playfully.

"Naughty," she said, trying to remain breathy, not angry. "My girlfriend said I was to stay away from computers. She said things could disappear and turn up someplace else when you had no idea how they got there."

"Your girlfriend probably wasn't very smart."

Claire stifled a desire to push him into the water that was pooling around the melting ice sculpture.

"Everybody said she was brilliant. She told me to stay away from them, and that's what I mean to do."

The executive looked thoroughly annoyed by her continued harping on this unknown female. "Who is your girlfriend?"

"Claire Dalton," Claire answered.

That information sobered the man.

"How would you know someone like Claire?"

"She lives down the hall from me. I didn't see her very often. She works an awful lot."

"She worked too much."

"How could she do that?"

"She got into something that was none of her concern."

"Claire wouldn't do that." Claire tried to sound shocked rather than indignant, but it wasn't easy. How did a woman play a vamp when she was trying to pump information? Marilyn hadn't had to do that in the movie.

"She was nosing around in somebody else's computer," the executive said. "Never touch anybody else's computer, and you'll be fine."

"I thought people used other people's computers all the time," Eric said. "They're always breaking down in the middle of things."

"Not in our company," the executive said, irritated that Eric hadn't abandoned Claire to him.

"All this talk about computers is making me hot," Claire said to Eric. "I need something cool to drink."

"Let me get something for you," the executive said.

"Make it weak," Claire said. "I don't think my head can take anything else this evening."

"Let's get out of here before he comes back," Eric said as soon as the executive started toward the bar. He steered Claire toward the door.

"Why? We still don't know what was stolen."

"I don't like that guy."

She didn't like him, either, but he was no worse than any of the other executives after they had too much to drink and started to put the moves on the attractive women. Claire had never experienced what it was like to be blond or the center of attention, but she decided both had a lot to recommend them. Maybe red and leather would be part of her future wardrobe. Wouldn't her father love that! She ought to have Eric take a picture of her and send it to him. He'd be certain she'd gone the way of all women foolish enough to leave the protection of their homes.

"I think he knows what happened," Claire said.

"Me, too, but he's not going to tell us anything. At least we know where to begin looking."

"Where?"

"In your boss's office."

"But I didn't find anything there."

"Did you use any other computer during those last two weeks?"

"No."

"Then the file had to be on his computer."

"Then why didn't they try to buy me off, or offer to let me join?"

"I don't know, but we've got to find some way to get into that computer."

"If you think they were careful before, they're going to be paranoid now. They'll probably post a guard over it twenty-four hours a day."

"We'll figure out what to do about that later. Right now I want to get out of here."

"Why can't we stay a little longer?" She really was ready to leave. Her feet were killing her and she thought her face would crack if she had to smile one minute longer. But she had started to suspect Eric was jealous of the attention she was getting. Nobody had ever been jealous of her before.

But then whole groups of men had never paid her attention either, crowded around her, offered to bring her drinks, promised to get her assigned to their departments. Those seemed to be the times Eric was the most restless.

As incredible as it seemed, he was jealous. He had to be.

"We've found out all we can," Eric said. "We ought to go before somebody sees through your disguise."

"If my boss didn't recognize me, none of the men here would."

Her boss had arrived late, stayed a few minutes, and

left quickly. She hadn't had a chance to talk to him. He was obviously upset about something. She had even gotten the feeling he was avoiding her, though she was sure she had just imagined it. He'd huddled with one of the other executives; then both had left. She hoped the bank wasn't in financial trouble.

But she didn't work for them any longer. The future of the bank was no longer any of her concern.

"One of the women is more likely to be the one to recognize you. Your friend Linda, for instance."

Even as Eric said her name, Linda seemed to materialize out of nowhere.

"Leaving so soon?"

"It's getting too hot," Claire said, fanning herself.

Linda couldn't suppress a smile. "You're going to make some bigwigs very unhappy."

"They'll get over it," Eric said, hustling Claire out the door. "I thought you didn't want to come," he said when they were outside. "Now I have to practically drag you away."

"It's nice being admired," Claire said, not bothering to pretend. "It's never happened to me before. Now I can understand why some women go to so much trouble choosing their clothes, why others dress in such an indecent manner."

"You seemed to get over your reluctance to be seen in indecent clothes soon enough."

Yep, he was jealous. Claire had to practically press her lips together to keep from smiling.

"Once they'd seen me, there was no point in trying to hide. I'm beginning to think I used the wrong strategy. I might have gotten more promotions if I'd dressed differently."

"You'd have been expected to make several trips to a motel room for every one of them," Eric said, sounding rather impatient. "Men are very bad about putting people, especially women, into categories. Once they decide you belong in one category, it's practically impossible to get into a different one."

"You're saying as long as they think they can go to bed with me, they won't think I have the brains to do the work."

"Precisely."

"But that's stupid. I knew a brilliant woman in graduate school who slept around with just about anybody."

"I thought you never took your nose out of a book long enough to notice things like that."

"Some things you can't help but notice."

Eric had helped her into the car. He backed out and headed for the parking lot entrance.

"Well, you don't have to worry about what they'll think of you. None of them will ever see you looking like this again."

She was relieved to know that. It had been fun, but this kind of cloak-and-dagger stuff wasn't her style.

"I want you to think back over every moment you were in your boss's office," Eric said.

"We've already done that," she said with a fatalistic sigh. They were in traffic, headed back to the lake. If he were going to grill her on her movements all over again, it was going to be a long ride.

"There has to be something you've forgotten. Was the computer on when you went in? Did he exit a program quickly? Did he hide disks that were on his desk?"

"That's not the sort of thing I pay attention to. The computers are always on, even when we're not using them, and we're always exiting programs. Sometimes I have a dozen on the screen at once."

"I'm convinced there was something you weren't supposed to see. I don't suppose you nosed through any reports on his desk."

"Of course not."

"I didn't think so. You're much too honest for that."

"Don't make it sound like a crime."

"I admire you for it, but right now it would have been more useful if you'd been an incorrigible sneak."

"Well, I'm not. We'll just have to think of something else." He didn't seem to be listening. "I said—"

"I heard you."

"You didn't act like it."

"I was watching the car behind us. It's been following us for several miles."

She looked back. It was an ordinary SUV. It seemed everybody had one these days, especially people with houses at the lake. "Maybe it's going to the lake like us. There are thousands of homes out there."

"Maybe."

She could tell he wasn't certain, but when the car passed them at the first opportunity, he relaxed.

"You've been hiding in bushes too long," she said. "You think everybody is following you."

"That's because I'm frequently following somebody. That makes you suspicious of other people. Let's get back to your boss's office."

"I don't know anything else. I promise I'll think about it, but I can't stand your asking me the same questions over and over again."

"Okay. We'll let it ride for a while."

"How about letting it ride forever and concentrating on when I can go back to my apartment? People are already starting to think I'm your live-in girlfriend. Next they'll want to know when we're getting married."

"They know better."

"Okay, so they know you're a confirmed womanizer; but I'm not a loose woman, and I don't want a reputation for being one. I want to get back to my own apartment, my own things, my own clothes."

"Mildred can buy anything you need."

She spent the next twenty minutes telling him exactly why staying on his boat was not satisfactory. He spent the same twenty minutes disagreeing with everything she said.

"No wonder you only deal with your customers over the phone," she said, as they pulled into the marina parking lot. "They'd strangle you if they had to put up with you in person."

She got out of the car on her own this time. She only wobbled slightly as she started toward the boardwalk without waiting for him. "I will stay one more night," she called over her shoulder. "If the marina hasn't already hauled it away, I'll even leave my car here for another day or two." She reached the boardwalk. Her shoes tapped out a satisfactory rat-a-tat-tat on the wooden slats. The sound matched her mood. "I'm sure nobody's looking for me any longer."

"We'll talk about it after dinner," Eric said as he caught up with her. "Though I don't know why I have to go over it again. I've explained everything to you at least—"

His sentence was cut off by what she thought was the sound of a gun and the unmistakable feeling that a bullet had passed very close to her head. Before she could think or move, Eric grabbed her and threw both of them into the water.

FOURTEEN

Eric cursed himself as he felt the water close over his head. He'd been in detection long enough to know to trust his instincts, and his instinct had been that they were being followed. It didn't matter that the car had passed them awhile back. If the driver knew who they were—and he obviously did—he knew they were returning to the marina. It was only logical the would-be killer would pass them so he could be in position when they arrived. They were lucky he was such a poor shot.

And if he wanted her to survive, he'd better pay attention to the fact that they were under water and Claire didn't know how to swim.

Still holding her tight, he guided her toward the dock. If they came up under the walkway, they wouldn't be seen. They could also find their way to his boat without trying to swim underwater.

"Sssssh!" he hissed the moment they got their heads above water. "He may still be up there."

"What are we going to do?" Claire asked between gasps for air.

Eric didn't get a chance to answer. The noise of activity burst all around them. It was late enough for many couples to be in bed, but the shots must have woken everyone. Lights had come on in one houseboat after another. People started moving about, shouting, calling out to each other. Then someone activated a burglar alarm. Then another. Within moments, at least a half-dozen alarms were sending wailing, whining, screaming sounds into the night.

The quiet of the lake had been completely shattered.

"I don't think we have to do anything for the time being," Eric said. "It sounds like plenty is being done."

"I'm talking about the man who's trying to kill me," Claire said. "What are we going to do about him?"

"I don't know. Right now I want to get you safely out of the water. Let's swim down to my boat."

"I can't swim."

"Hold on to me."

People were running back and forth, everybody asking if anybody else had heard the same sounds, if it had really been gunshots, and who could possibly be shooting at whom in this place at this time of night. Eric thought several of them sounded pleased. He supposed nothing so exciting had happened to them during their rather ordinary lives.

"I wonder if Mildred is worried about us," Claire said.

"Probably, but we'll reach my boat in just a moment."

"There's a body floating in the water," someone shouted.

"Where?" another asked.

"Over there. It's a blond. You can see her hair."

"Oh, my God," some woman wailed and started to cry.

Eric turned back to look at Claire. It was almost pitch black under the walkway, but he could see that she'd lost her wig.

"I've called the police," someone said. "They'll retrieve the body."

"Come on," Eric said, "we need to get out of the water in a hurry or there's going to be total panic up there."

"Do you think he's still out there?" Claire asked.

"Not with all this commotion."

"Who knows where I am?" she asked

"Somebody at the party recognized you. That has to be it."

"Then they know where I am."

"Yes."

"I can't stay here."

"I know."

"But I don't have anywhere to go."

"We'll worry about that later. First, let's get you out of the water. Do you think you can climb up a ladder by yourself?"

"I'm not completely helpless."

Eric guided her to the ladder that was attached to the side of his houseboat. Claire climbed onto the deck without anyone's noticing. He had just joined her when Mildred turned to look at their boat, a worried look on her face. She immediately broke into a relieved smile and started toward them.

"There's nobody drowned," she called back to the crowd gathered along the walkway, watching transfixed as the wig floated toward open water. "It's just a wig."

Claire clamped her hands to her head. "I can't let everybody see me looking like this."

The tension broke, and Eric started to laugh. "I thought you were untouched by the normal female vanity, but I see I was wrong. You've just been shot at, thrown into a lake, you can't swim, you're standing here dripping wet with most of your body exposed to the night chill, and all you can worry about is your hair." He laughed again. "You're a lot stronger than you think. You'll do."

"Let me inside before the police get here," she said. "I'll be mortified."

Eric managed to extract his key from his wet pants.

"Help her find the red wig," he said to Mildred. "She won't be able to face the neighbors without it."

"Is either of you hurt?" Mildred asked, worry still creasing her face.

"No."

"What's going on?" Mildred asked.

"I don't know, but I think I finally know where to start looking. Now you'd better help Claire. Did anybody call the police?"

"At least three or four of us," Mildred said as she disappeared inside the houseboat.

"What's going on here?" a man asked as a crowd approached the boat. "Why is somebody shooting at you?"

Eric did his best to allay the fears of his neighbors, but most were retirees and didn't want this kind of excitement in their lives unless it came from television or videos. Nobody said they wanted Eric to leave, but he knew the thought was on their minds. They were sorry for whatever trouble he and Claire might be in, but they didn't want it spilling into their lives.

Sentiment took a turn in the opposite direction when Claire, accompanied by Mildred, reappeared.

"Is that the little woman they're trying to kill?" one man asked.

"Yes," Eric replied. "This is the second attempt."

"I think it's a disgrace that a nice young woman like her has to lose her wig. Somebody ought to get it for her."

"Don't worry about it," Claire said. "We were just using it for a disguise."

"We can't have a wig floating about in the lake," said another man. "I'll get it. Somebody else is liable to think it's a body." He dived into the water.

"Why are they trying to kill her?" somebody asked.

"She's been framed for a crime someone else committed," Eric explained. "If she's dead, the police won't have any reason to look around for the real perpetrator."

"That's disgraceful," said a woman. "I'll bet a man did it."

"I'm fairly certain it was a man," Eric said.

"I knew it," the woman announced, triumphantly turning on her long-suffering husband. "Only a man would do something as contemptible as that. We can't let him get away with it."

"But what can we do?" another asked.

"We can organize a neighborhood watch," Aubrey announced. He received several blank stares. "We're all retired. We have nothing to do all day except eat, sleep, and hope our wives don't have a headache every night." That remark earned a few polite chuckles. "Each couple can take an hour shift. There's enough of us so we'll only have to do it every other night."

"That's very kind of you," Claire said, "but we—"

The wail of police sirens cut her off midsentence.

Eric figured with so many calls, the police must have thought there was some sort of invasion going on. From the number of cars that roared into the parking lot a few minutes later he was certain of it. A dozen policemen poured out of cars—bulletproof vests and long-nosed guns in every direction.

"Oh, Christ."

"They're going to be mad, aren't they?" Claire asked.

"Probably."

"They'd better not be," Mildred declared. "It's their job to protect citizens. We can't help it if they can't tell a simple gunshot from the beginning of World War III."

But Eric doubted the elderly couples, woken from a sound sleep by gunshots, were too careful to differentiate between a single gunman and gang warfare.

The policemen fanned out along the side of the lake and the dock. They started entering each houseboat as they came to it, which infuriated the owners. Eric decided he'd better do something before they had a real war on their hands.

"Who's in charge here?" he asked, coming up to the first policeman.

"Stand aside," the man ordered. "You're impeding the police."

"You keep searching these boats without permission, and your whole department will be facing a dozen lawsuits by morning."

"We got several calls about a shooting war going on here."

"Only one person shot, and they shot just twice. I know because I'm one of the ones they shot at."

"One of the ones?" the policeman asked.

"They're really after Claire Dalton. Someone tried to kill her two days ago. We filed a report, remember?"

"I'd better speak to the sheriff."

The officer retreated down the walkway. After a few words with a man who didn't seem at all happy to be anywhere near the marina, he returned.

"The sheriff wants to talk to you."

They had to retreat to the far end of the dock to be able to hear over the outraged owners.

"I'm sorry for all this trouble," Eric said, "but there was only one gunman. He was firing at me and my client."

"What's your client done?" the officer asked.

"Nothing, and she's hired me to prove it. I'm a private detective."

Eric knew about the only thing policemen disliked more than private detectives was head lice.

"Where is he?"

"It's a woman. She's waiting on my boat."

The policeman's expression barely changed, but Eric could guess what he was thinking.

"She came to see me two days ago. She was leaving

when someone attacked her. I had to go into the water to keep her from drowning. I told the young officer who responded to our call to check with the Charlotte police. That's where she's accused of the crime. I thought someone there might be trying to put her out of commission so the investigation would stop."

The chief looked blank.

"I assume this wasn't done."

"I don't see all the paperwork that comes through the department."

In other words, no.

"I think I'd better talk to this young woman."

"I'd appreciate it if you could limit your questions. This woman has never had so much as a parking ticket. She's just about at her wit's end."

Claire was handling everything better than he'd expected, but he wanted to protect her as much as possible. This thing was nowhere near over. He didn't know what she might be called upon to endure in the days ahead.

The next hour was one Eric would like to forget as soon as possible. The policeman asked Claire dozens of unnecessary questions about tonight, the attack two days ago, her job, the indictment, everything. Eric tried to shield her until he realized he was doing more harm than good. In retaliation, he did absolutely nothing to help calm the boat owners now threatening to sue for invasion of privacy.

Finally, the police were ready to leave. They had found two discarded rifle shells in the parking lot. Eric figured the gunman was either too much of a novice to know to pick them up or the lights and burglar alarms had come on so quickly he hadn't had time. That probably wouldn't help the police find the gunman, but at least there was no question that this time there had been an attack.

"What are you going to do now?" Mildred asked as they retreated inside Eric's houseboat.

"You can't stay here," Aubrey said. "They know where to find you."

"I realize that," Eric said.

"I can go back to my apartment," Claire said.

"That's the one place you absolutely can't go," Eric said. "I don't know how many people are in on this, but they followed us from the party. They know you have to try to hide somewhere. They'll check your apartment first."

"What are you going to do?"

"I'm going to take her to my house."

"You have a house?" Claire asked, surprised.

"How are you going to get there?" Mildred asked. "They must know both your cars by now."

"I'll rent one," Eric said.

"Nonsense," Mildred said. "You can use our car."

"We couldn't do that," Claire said.

"I don't see why not," Aubrey said. "And we could drive your cars around. That ought to confuse them real good."

"No. That would put you in danger," Claire said.

"Not when they see it's only two old people," Aubrey replied. "We could figure out someplace to go that would confuse them, keep them off your tail for a while."

"I couldn't ask you to do that," Eric said.

"It's better then sitting here wondering if our children are waiting for us to die so they can get their hands on our money."

"I think we ought to go to the mountains," Aubrey said to Mildred. "I'll bet the dogwood and redbud are still blooming up there."

"Sounds good to me," Mildred said. "We'll leave first thing in the morning."

"I can't let you do this," Eric said.

"Shut up and give me your car keys," Mildred said. "You concentrate on keeping Claire safe."

"Work fast," Aubrey said. "They'll figure it out soon enough."

"Okay," Eric said, "but if you change your mind, don't hesitate to tell me."

"We're not only *not* changing it," Mildred said, "we're going to chase you out of here tonight. Now's the best time to leave."

"I think so, too," Aubrey said. "I'll get the keys. You can follow the policemen out of the parking lot."

"Collect everything you can carry in five minutes," Eric told Claire.

"I'll help her," Mildred said, pulling the reluctant Claire into the bedroom behind her.

"I don't think you ought to go to a cabin or anyplace like that," Eric said. "Check into a big hotel with lots of people around. I'll pay for everything."

"Forget it," Aubrey said. "I've been promising to take Mildred someplace fancy for a couple of years. Now seems like a good time to do it."

"She's ready to go," Mildred said, pushing Claire out of the bathroom. "Aubrey, haven't you given Eric the keys yet?"

"In a minute, dear." Aubrey disappeared through the sliding glass door.

"Call when you get there," Mildred said. "I won't be able to sleep until I know you're safe."

"Thanks," Claire said, tears in her eyes. "My own mother couldn't have been kinder."

"She would have if she'd been here," Mildred said. "Now the two of you get out of here. And as soon as you get this mess straightened out, you get yourselves right back here and tell me every lurid detail. Nothing this exciting has happened to me in my whole life."

"I could have done without it," Claire said.

"I'm sure you could, dear, but it'll be a great story to tell your children."

Aubrey returned with the keys. "Watch the idle," he said, handing Eric the keys. "It'll sometimes cut off on you at stoplights."

"I'll be careful. Now everybody out. I need to lock up."

"But you didn't pack anything," Claire said. "That's stupid of me," she said almost immediately. "You don't need to pack to go to your own house."

Eric locked up and they headed for the parking lot.

"Don't forget to call," Mildred reminded them.

"I won't," Eric said, but his attention was focused on trying to make sure there wasn't anybody waiting for them in the parking lot. They reached the car without incident.

"Do you think he's gone?" Claire asked when they were on the road.

"Probably. I can't see anybody hanging around with all those police here."

"Do you think he'll stop now?"

He wanted to tell her the gunman would probably give up and go away, but he knew that wasn't true. He might leave after trying once and failing. But after a second try—one in which he'd been willing to commit cold-blooded murder—he obviously didn't mean to give up.

"No, I don't. This must be even bigger than they told the police. Somebody is very determined to get you out of the way so it will never come to light."

"But who could it be?"

"Somebody at the party."

"That's ridiculous."

He turned to look at her briefly before looking back at the road. She looked badly frightened. He wished he could do something to make her feel better, but he couldn't. She was being hunted, and the sooner she realized it, the safer she would be.

"Claire, I think we can safely assume whoever came after you the other night thought you were dead. Security says nobody's gone near your car. My friend watching your apartment says nobody's tried to get in. Whoever followed us from the party knew where we were going. That indicates it was the same man who followed you here before and pushed you into the water, or the man who hired him."

"What did he look like?" Claire asked. "I can tell you if he looked like anybody in the company."

"I couldn't see him in the dark, only his outline. Medium height, medium build. That could fit nearly anybody, including your boss. Tonight's attacker was probably an amateur, or he wouldn't have missed. That makes it even more likely it was your boss. You didn't talk to him at the party, did you?"

"No."

"Why does that sound like you're really saying *yes?*"

"He was in a group of men. He seemed worried about something. He wouldn't even look at me."

"Damn!" Eric said.

"What?"

"He recognized you. That has to be it. He had to guess you were at the party trying to get information. He might even have seen you talking to Linda."

"No, he left almost immediately afterwards."

"We don't know when he got there. We have no idea what he may have seen. But it's obvious that having seen you, he had to get out of there and contact his hit man. Or get set up to do it himself."

"Mr. Deter wouldn't do—"

"Claire, get over this fixation that the man who gave you so many promotions couldn't possibly want you dead. The two have nothing to do with each other. He gave you the promotions because you were good at your job. He wants you dead because he thinks you know something that can be extremely dangerous to him."

"But I don't."

"He obviously thinks you do. We're going to have to go over everything again, in more detail this time."

Claire groaned. "Why, if we know what happened?"

"I think they lied. I think they told the police you sold secret information so they wouldn't have to say what is *really* going on. But we're not going to worry about that tonight. Getting you safely to the house will be enough for one evening."

They talked about different things for the rest of the trip—the clothes she needed and whether he had anything in the house she could eat.

He pulled his car into a driveway, around the back of a detached garage, and came to a stop under the spreading branches of an oak that must have been at least seventy-five years old.

"Is this where you live?" Claire asked, pointing to a huge house that must have had room for a family of ten. It had obviously been built a long time ago for a very wealthy owner.

"No. A friend lives here. I didn't want to park at my house."

"Do you think somebody followed us?"

"No, but it's possible they can figure out we took Aubrey's car. I don't want to give them any help finding us." He didn't think this kind of extra care was necessary, but it was better to be safe than sorry.

"Where is your house?" Claire asked as they collected her bag.

"A few houses down. We can cut through."

Eric's house was in an old residential section that had a thick canopy of trees planted at least a half a century ago. It was nearly as black as midnight under the trees. He was so familiar with the arrangement of houses and yards he never gave it a thought until Claire balked.

"Are you afraid of the dark?" he asked.

"No. I'm afraid of what might be hiding in the dark."

"There's nothing here but a few dogs. Don't worry. They all know me."

"They don't know me."

Eric laughed, reached out, and took her hand. "Come on. I thought you were raised on a farm, that you were familiar with animals."

"I was familiar with *our* animals. I never went roaming around in the dark."

Eric could feel the tension in Claire's hand. He supposed she had a right to feel nervous. Someone had shot at her, and she was being forced to walk through a strange neighborhood in the dark.

"One of my favorite pastimes when I was growing up was climbing out the window and roaming the neighborhood with my buddies."

"What did you do?"

"Nothing much. The exciting part was being out without our parents knowing."

"Did you have lots of friends?"

"No, but I had two very good ones."

"Where are they now?"

"I parked my car behind the garage of one, and we're walking through the backyard of the other."

"You mean you grew up around here?"

"In that house over there," he said, indicating the second house down on the right.

"It's bigger than the others," she said.

"Now you understand why I like living on the houseboat."

A black Labrador bounded up to them with a loud *woof* that nearly sent Claire climbing up Eric's body.

"How're you doing, old girl?" Eric said dropping down and roughing up the dog. "I want you to meet Claire. Let her smell you," he said when Claire just stood there.

Claire extended her hand tentatively. The dog sniffed.

"Now she knows you. You can come through this yard anytime you want."

"Which I devoutly hope will be never," Claire said. "Can't we go on to your house? All this dark is giving me the creeps."

"Where's your sense of adventure?"

"It got drowned."

Eric stood, headed toward his house. "I could see how that would take the edge off, but don't let it throw you." He didn't know how she could keep from getting rattled, but she had to keep her head.

They passed through another yard without incident.

"We're going in the back door," Eric said as they approached the house. "I'm not going to turn on a light, so you'll have to stay right behind me."

"How can I see in the dark?"

"You won't have to. I know every foot of that house."

Eric could never enter this house without being swamped by so many different emotions. That was why he spent most of his time on the houseboat. He supposed the sensible thing to do would be to sell the old mausoleum and buy a place that wasn't haunted by memories. He suspected the memories would stay, even though he sold the house, until he faced up to his father and all that stood between them.

He led Claire through to the front of the house.

"There's just enough light to make out the stairs," he said. "Hold on to me. They're stone. Sometimes it's slick."

He remembered playing on the stairs, on the landing above, watching the parties below even though he'd been told to stay in his room. He remembered the loneliness of the big house when his parents were away. He'd climbed out at night for companionship. The adventure was only secondary.

"You can take your pick of bedrooms," Eric said.

"There are seven in the house. I don't want anybody to know we're here, so don't turn on the light."

"I have to. I can't find my way around a house I've never been in."

"Absolutely no light."

"In that case, I'm sleeping with you."

FIFTEEN

Eric stopped so abruptly Claire ran into him.

She wanted to *sleep* with him? If she had any notion what thoughts that gave rise to, she'd never have mentioned it.

"That's not necessary," he said, trying hard to keep his voice steady. "I've got seven bedrooms."

"I don't care if you've got a hundred. I'm not sleeping by myself in a strange house in a strange room when I can't turn on a light. You may think it's great fun to go gallivanting about in the dark, but it scares me half to death."

"But you're inside."

"This house is like a hotel, and you've led me around in the dark as if I were a blind woman. I don't know where I am. I couldn't even find my way out of here. I'm not staying by myself."

"None of the rooms has two beds."

"You can sleep on the floor."

"That's ridiculous. I've already spent two nights on the couch. I don't intend to do it again."

There was a silence. He wished he could see her expression, but he could barely make out her outline in the dark.

"Do you have a king-size bed?"

"In the main guest suite."

"Then we can sleep in there. A king-size bed is so big it'll be like sleeping in separate beds."

She hadn't moved, but he could tell from the way she hadn't loosened her grip on the back of his shirt she was still frightened.

"I don't think it's a good idea."

"Of course it's not a good idea," she snapped. "Nothing that's happened to me in the last several days is a good idea, especially having someone try to kill me. But they did. And now you want me to sleep in a strange house where I can't even find the bathroom."

He didn't *want* her to sleep in a separate room. In fact, driving back from the party he'd tried to think of a way to talk her into letting him share her bed. He'd told himself it wouldn't be fair to take advantage of her situation. Now she was demanding he let her sleep in his bed. His libido was racing out of control.

"I've got a flashlight in the garage. If I get that—"

"I'm not sleeping in a room by myself, not even if you give me a hundred flashlights."

Eric sighed. He'd tried his best to talk her out of it. He would do his best to control himself, but he couldn't be responsible if the almost inevitable happened. A man could only do so much.

"Okay. Follow me."

He knew the house so well he could visualize where he was at every step, but he imagined it could be frightening for someone who'd never been here before. He'd always liked the dark. When things had been the worst after his mother's death, he had been able to hide in the dark. It had closed around him like a cloak, protecting him.

"Why would your parents need such a big house for just three people?" Claire asked.

"My mother's father built it. How big was your house?"

"Nothing like this. I had three sisters. We all slept in the same bed."

"I'm surprised you ever got any rest."

"You learn."

He supposed you could. He was going to get a chance to see if he could learn tonight.

"This is the guest room," he said. "Once we're inside, stay by the door until I close the curtains."

The curtains were already closed.

"I guess the maid thought the sun would fade the carpet."

"You have a maid for a house you don't even live in?"

"I do live here occasionally."

"I didn't know you were so rich. I'm surprised you bother to work."

"I told you. I had a mission."

"I forgot. What do we do now?"

"We get ready for bed."

"How?"

"I'll show you the bathroom. You can turn the light on once you close the door."

"Thank goodness. I thought I was going to have to brush my teeth in the dark."

"It would be easier than shaving." He led her to the bathroom. "Let me know when you're done."

She went inside and closed the door. Almost immediately he saw the sliver of light appear under the door. He went over to the bed and dropped down on it. What had he gotten himself into? He couldn't allow himself to seduce Claire, even if she were willing. He'd be taking advantage of her when her defenses were down. He'd gone to law school to help defenseless women. If he slept with Claire tonight, he'd be just as bad as the men he'd prosecuted all those years. He didn't know how he was going to do it, but he had to keep his hands to himself, because he wanted his relationship with Claire to continue after she was no longer in danger of going to jail.

Now that was a thought out of the blue. When had

that entered his mind, and where had it been hiding until now? How did a man get so interested in a woman in such a short period of time, especially when he was doing his best *not* to become interested?

It had happened too quickly. It had to be one of his infatuations again, falling in love with a woman in trouble. He'd fall out of love as soon as she didn't need him anymore.

But he felt certain this time it was different. He didn't know how, and he didn't know why, but he'd figure it out. He just needed some time to think. He was a smart man. He'd managed to outwit lawyers, doctors, business tycoons, even one man who qualified as a crime boss. If he could do all of that, he ought to be able to figure out the difference between love and infatuation.

But somehow it was easier to see things in somebody else than it was in himself. It felt a lot like an infatuation—fast, intense, and physical. Yet this time he was thinking of his future. He'd always thought about his clients' futures. Part of helping them was getting them settled into a new life. It must be an accident that he had included himself in the plans this time. He wouldn't be able to tell for sure until the case was over and he could get away by himself. Then he'd know.

In the meantime, he had to get through tonight, and probably several nights to come. He didn't know if he and Claire could keep their presence in the house a secret, but he knew they couldn't afford to advertise it by using the lights. It wouldn't be too difficult for the killer to find out who owned his boat or to learn he had a house in town. But as long as no one appeared to be staying here, he hoped they would be safe.

The light went out in the bathroom, and the door opened.

"You'll have to come get me," Claire said. "I can't see my hand in front of my face."

He got up and crossed to the bathroom. "It'll be a little better once your eyes get readjusted to the dark."

"I couldn't see anything before."

He wasn't going to argue with her. She'd be able to see her way around the house tomorrow. Until then he'd lead her wherever she needed to go. "Are you hungry?"

"A little bit, but I'd rather wait until morning. I don't want to go rambling about in this house in the dark."

He guided her over to the bed and she sat down.

"I could bring it to you."

"You're not going to leave me here. If you go anywhere, I'm going with you. Are you very hungry?"

"No." He was, but he could wait. She'd been upset enough for one day.

"Good. It's your turn in the bathroom, but don't be long, please. I hate to sound like such a scaredy cat, but I am."

He made his way to the bathroom. He closed the door, turned on the light, and looked at himself in the mirror.

"You've got yourself in a real kettle of fish this time, old son. This is a lot more than taking pictures of husbands cheating on the side. You've taken on the job of defending that poor woman *and* finding out who framed her. You've gone completely out of your depth. This is a game of murder. You must be in love. You've never done anything this foolish before."

Not only that. He had to spend the night in the same bed with Claire and not touch her. He didn't know if he could do it.

Claire felt she was stepping into the jaws of a very hungry lion, but she couldn't do anything about it. She would not spend the night alone. She'd have a nervous breakdown before morning. It had only really sunk into her brain during the drive from the lake that someone was determined to kill her, that he wanted her dead so badly he'd tried to kill her twice. Neither her parents nor college had prepared her for anything like this. She didn't know how to cope with the panic inside her that threatened to turn into hysteria. Only Eric's presence had enabled her to enter a strange house in the dark.

Only his presence would enable her to go to sleep in it.

But his presence might be the very reason she couldn't sleep at all.

She'd never slept in the same room with a man, much less the same bed. She and her sisters had been practically forbidden to have any contact with a man that wasn't part of their immediate family. Now, here she was, just as naive and inexperienced as if she'd stayed at home, and she was spending the night in the same bed with a man. There was no question of her sleeping alone. She wouldn't do that. She *couldn't* do that.

But somewhere deep inside her, some part of her that had never made its existence known until now wanted him to touch her. She didn't know what she wanted to happen, but she knew she didn't want *nothing* to happen.

Yet, what would she do if he *did* anything?

She didn't know, but she did want Eric to look at her with pleasure. She wanted him to desire her.

That shocked her. She'd never felt that way about a man before. She didn't know why it should have happened now. Eric Sterling wasn't her type, if she had a type. She'd always assumed she'd meet some super executive, they'd somehow know they were meant for each other, and they'd go to a kind of orderly, definitely nonsexual corporate heaven together. Apparently Mother Nature had something entirely different in mind for her.

And at that moment, he stepped out of the bathroom.

"I'm on the side away from the door," Claire said quickly. She pushed her overnight bag under the bed and quickly got under the covers. She lay there stiff and straight. She felt the mattress give under Eric's weight as he sat down on the bed and got under the covers. There had to be at least six feet between them, maybe more, but she felt that they were inches apart.

"I'm sorry the disguise didn't work," Eric said. "I was certain nobody would know you."

"Nobody did."

"Except the man who wants to kill you."

"Yeah, except him."

Silence.

"What are you going to do tomorrow?" she asked.

"Nose around and see what I can find out about your boss. Maybe he's in debt or in trouble. Sometimes you can turn up all kinds of things."

"What am I supposed to do?"

"Try to remember what you did that could have put all this terrible mess into motion."

"But I've told you—"

"I know, but there's something you've forgotten."

Silence.

"You're not going to be here all day?"

"Probably not."

Silence.

"Don't go near the windows."

"I could figure that out."

More silence.

"Well, good night."

"Good night."

She lay there, every muscle taut, every nerve ending swollen with sensitivity. Her skin felt almost too tender to have the sheets touch her. She felt alive from top to bottom, a seething mass of feeling.

She'd never felt like this before, but she knew the cause of her condition lay just a few feet from her. His touch would cause some of the tension to vanish, but she was certain it would be replaced by something a thousand times worse.

Or better.

She didn't know. Her parents had taught her only one thing—fear. Instinct told her something quite different—fulfillment. But she didn't understand fulfillment that could come from a man, unless it was in the form of a promotion.

But promotions were a thing of the past. Her career was a thing of the past. She had to start over, reevaluate. Things weren't adding up the way they used to.

"Are you asleep?"

That was a stupid question. How was she supposed to drop off to sleep in less than thirty seconds in a strange house with a man in her bed? "Almost."

"I didn't mean to throw you into the lake again. It was the only way I could think of to protect you from those bullets."

"That's okay. It wasn't your fault."

It wasn't his fault she had ended up in the same bed with him. Neither was it his fault she desperately wanted him to touch her, to show in some way he found her attractive. It angered her that this simple need should make her feel trashy. She owed that to her parents' teaching, and she deeply resented it. What could be wrong with wanting to be desired by an attractive man?

If she didn't start thinking about something else, she was likely to give in to temptation and touch him. The idea shocked her, but it was impossible to ignore. She'd never been attracted to a man the way she was attracted to Eric.

"Are you still frightened?"

She lied again. "No."

"I don't believe you."

"I'm not, really."

He reached over, touched her arm, and she practically jumped straight up out of the bed.

"I was right," he said. "You're petrified."

"Not really," she said, forcing herself to lie down, to relax. "I'm just nervous."

"Because of me?"

She might as well stop lying. He obviously knew the answers to his questions. "Yes."

"I'm not going to hurt you."

"I know that."

"I'm not going to try to make love to you."

"I didn't think you would." Did her voice sound as tight and quavery as his? Was it possible he wanted to touch her as much as she wanted him to?

"But I want to. I want to very much."

Claire would never have believed any words could have had a greater impact on her than learning she had been fired and that the police were coming to arrest her, but Eric's simple sentence had the power to make that seem almost unimportant.

"Why would you want to . . . do that?" Her voice nearly failed her. Her body was so tight, her muscles so beyond her control, she shook as if she were shivering from cold.

"As Mildred told you, I have a weakness for lovely women."

"I'm not lovely."

"I think you are. The men at the party this evening thought so, too."

"They like hair and black leather. That's not me."

"It could be if you'd let it."

She instinctively turned toward him. "Is that the kind of woman you want?"

"I want the kind of woman you could be if you hadn't been scared to death by your parents, if you hadn't sacrificed yourself on the altar of success. I want the kind of woman who is aware of her sexuality and is proud of it, who's willing to share it."

"I've never had any . . . sexuality." The very word made her wince.

He laughed softly. "You have it. You just have never let yourself experience it. Once you stop being afraid of it, you'll soon figure out what to do about it. And if you have any questions, there'll be more than enough volunteers to help you."

"Like you?"

"Like me."

Claire hadn't thought it was possible for her body to respond anymore fully to Eric's presence, but she was wrong. She felt almost as though she were about to explode. Her entire body was tuned to a fever pitch of anticipation. She desperately wanted something to happen. At the same time she was wildly afraid something would.

"Thank you," she managed to say.

"For what?"

"For thinking me attractive. I know you're just trying to be nice, but I like it. Nobody else ever has."

"Then you've been working with blind men."

"Do you really find me attractive?" She shouldn't have asked such a question. She should have let well enough alone.

"Do you find that so impossible to believe?"

"Yes."

"I'm ashamed of my own sex. I can't believe they have been so blind."

"Maybe you're just different. Maybe you're the only one who could find me attractive."

"Up until now you've been sending signals that said *Back off! Keep your distance.* Tonight you sent out different signals, and you got a different response."

She'd never thought of it like that. She guessed she'd been too busy trying to succeed to think of it at all. But she remembered times when thoughts of men, the feeling of loneliness, the sense that something important was missing—one or all of these thoughts—had threatened to force themselves into the front of her consciousness. She'd responded by working more, later, and harder. Now she didn't want to run anymore. She wanted answers, but she didn't know where to begin.

Suddenly the bed shifted and the covers rustled. Then, much to her consternation, she felt Eric's lips on hers in a brief, tender kiss.

"Go to sleep, Cinderella. We're going to find a way to take you to the ball yet."

He moved back to his side of the bed and was quiet. Claire expected he'd fall asleep within the next minute. She knew she'd be lying awake for hours.

One kiss had turned her world upside down all over again.

"My contact couldn't get a copy of your indictment. He got a look at it, but I can't see that it'll help much. You're supposed to have sold investment strategy to the New Chinese World Bank for a half-million dollars. They deny it, but your bank has convinced the police they're lying. The money trail looks solid."

"I would never sell anything to a communist country."

"I'm sure you wouldn't, but it doesn't matter. I think it's just a cover-up to hide what's really going on."

"What's that?"

"I still don't know."

"Didn't you find anything that could help?" Claire asked.

They were sitting in a small, windowless room eating a pizza. Claire had found this room, which appeared to have been a playroom, when she'd made a tour of the house. When it started to grow dark and Eric still hadn't returned, she'd retreated there. Light and the noise of the television helped to give her the illusion of safety, of not being alone.

He hadn't gotten back until nearly ten o'clock. Despite his orders to do nothing that would let anyone know someone was in the house, she'd been on the verge of calling Mildred. She probably would have if she'd known the number.

"Nothing really," Eric said. "He's been buying real estate recently, but not so much his salary and profit from his shares in the company couldn't explain. He might have property in other states or other names, but that will take more time to uncover. He doesn't have any debts. In fact, he seems like a model citizen."

"I told you he couldn't have had anything to do with framing me."

"It can't be anybody else, Claire. I don't know how, when, or why; but unless you've forgotten to tell me something, you haven't been close to anybody else in weeks. You've either been in your office or at home. The only person you've even talked to beyond your boss is your secretary, and I can't imagine how she could implicate you in such a scheme."

"She couldn't."

"So, we concentrate on your boss. I'm bushed. We'd better get to bed. I've got to come up with a new way to attack this problem by tomorrow.

Just mentioning the word *bed* revived all the tensions that had bedeviled Claire most of the day. Trying to forget about Eric and what he'd said the previous evening had been part of the reason she'd gone over the house room by room. That had served its purpose for a short while. She had never seen such a home, not even those of the top executives in her company. Their houses were all modern, with lots of glass, strange angles, and weird art. And they were nearly all on a lake or a golf course.

This house looked like something out of the Victorian era but with a modern touch. It was huge without being heavy, decorated with meticulous care down to the smallest detail without being overdone. Claire decided Eric's mother's preference for French styles probably accounted for that. Paintings in massive frames hung all over the house. Oriental and Aubusson carpets were scattered over parquet floors that looked as if they'd never been walked on. Chandeliers, marble floors and columns, silk drapes, and solid-silver ornaments caused Claire to feel she'd stepped onto a movie set. She wondered what event or set of circumstances could have been awful enough to cause Eric to turn his back on such an inheritance.

But that hadn't occupied her thoughts for very long. She'd spent most of the day remembering what Eric had said the night before, wondering if he'd really meant it, wondering what would have happened if she had had the courage to be equally honest with him. Now she was in the same situation again. She would have a chance to repeat her answers . . . or change them to something else. The mere possibility of such an eventuality had kept her in a ferment all day, had made the hours pass with agonizing slowness. Now she had a second chance.

"Are you calm enough to sleep by yourself tonight?" Eric asked.

"No."

She could have said yes. She *should* have said yes, but she hadn't.

"Are you sure?"

This was her last chance to put herself out of the reach of temptation. "Yes."

She could almost feel him release the tension in his body.

"You get ready for bed first. It won't take me long."

* * *

Claire had been in bed at least fifteen minutes and Eric still hadn't come out of the bathroom. She didn't know why she should be surprised he had decided to take a shower. Just because she showered in the morning didn't mean everyone did.

Maybe he was hoping if he took long enough, she'd be asleep when he came to bed. Then he wouldn't have to keep telling her she was pretty and he wanted to make love to her. She couldn't have gone to sleep if she'd wanted to. But the shower had stopped running some time ago. What could he be doing?

The light under the door finally went out; the bathroom door opened, and she heard the sound of Eric's bare feet as he padded across the oak floor, then across the large rug on his side of the room. She waited expectantly for the sound of the covers being drawn back, for the bed to move when he lowered his weight to the mattress. He got into bed and lay still.

She waited.

"Are you asleep?" he asked softly.

She knew this was her last chance. She didn't have to lie; she didn't have to do anything except lie there, silent, unmoving, and he would turn over and go to sleep.

"No." One tiny word, and the die was cast.

"Are you still frightened?"

"No."

She wished she could see his face, his eyes, his expression. It was so difficult waiting in the dark wondering, fearing he wouldn't want to touch her. Afraid he would.

"Are you frightened of me?"

"No." Only of the unknown inside herself.

He reached over and took her hand. "You know I would never hurt you, don't you?"

"Yes."

"I want to kiss you."

"Please." She had steeled herself to let him kiss her. She had never expected she would actually ask him to.

The kiss was gentle and sweet. He barely touched her lips. Then he kissed her again, and again. Each kiss was like a caress, a comfort rather than a threat, an invitation to let go of her fears, to welcome the excitement coursing through her body, to move into his embrace rather than lie stiff and wary.

She turned toward him, took his face in her hands, and kissed him back, gently at first, then hungrily as the fears that had bound her soul for so long loosened and fell away. This was more wonderful than she could have imagined. It was impossible to be afraid when she felt for the first time she was actually free.

She moved closer, felt Eric's arms go around her. For a fraction of a second she expected to feel trapped; instead, she felt comforted. Safe. Protected. It was such a wonderful sensation, something she'd never felt before, something she'd never expected to like. She'd been looking for this, but in all the wrong places.

She pressed herself against Eric, burrowed into his embrace like a child seeking the comfort and shelter of its parent's arms. She couldn't get enough of this feeling of comfort, of security, of not having to be afraid, of not having to struggle against the world. His embrace represented peace, sanctuary, safety, and she didn't ever want to leave.

But it didn't take her long to discover her sanctuary was a man alive with unexplored feelings, feelings she couldn't label but which her body seemed to understand perfectly.

Eric had come to bed without a shirt. She wore a nightgown that covered her from head to foot. She always had. He wasn't wearing pajamas, either. She felt his bare legs against her ankles. This frightened her and caused heat to flood her body. Her safe haven was not without risks.

Would he ravage her body? She didn't believe that. Would he persuade her to give in to him against her will? She didn't believe that, either. Then what was the risk?

That she would give in because she wanted to.

But was that a risk? Everything she'd discovered so far had been a blessing, a release from a kind of self-imposed prison.

"Kiss me," she said. "Kiss me as if I'm the most beautiful woman in the world and you love me desperately."

She didn't know where that request came from. She'd never wanted to be the most beautiful woman in the world; nor had she wanted to be the object of a great passion. She no longer knew herself. Someone with an entirely different set of desires and ambitions had emerged and swept the old Claire Dalton aside.

When Eric kissed her, it was the new Claire who responded by kissing him back as passionately. It was the new Claire who turned into his embrace, molding her body to his. It was the new Claire who discovered the evidence of his desire for her and didn't cringe or flinch. It was the new Claire who welcomed his hands as they moved along her back, her shoulders, her bottom, pulling her to him, nestling her against his erection.

Eric suddenly froze. She didn't understand how he could stop. Her body was aflame with desire. She wanted him to keep touching her until she exploded.

"What—"

"Sssshh!"

The hiss was imperative. She instantly recognized the urgency caused by danger.

"What is it?" she asked, almost afraid to know.

"There's somebody in the house."

SIXTEEN

A chill went through her with lightning speed.

"Maybe it's one of your friends."

"They're both away right now. Get dressed. We have to get out of here. Now."

Claire hadn't heard any noise, but she didn't question that someone was in the house. She didn't question that he was trying to kill her. After the last few days, anything was possible.

"Pull on your clothes over your nightgown and grab everything you can in five seconds."

Eric was dressed before she stumbled into her clothes. He went to the bathroom and started throwing things into his bag. For once Claire was grateful that growing up sharing a room with three sisters had taught her to keep everything she owned carefully organized. She only had to pick up her overnight bag and she was ready to leave. She started toward the door.

"Not that way," Eric hissed. "They're downstairs in the front hall."

"They?" She hadn't expected more than one.

"I heard talking. That means at least two people."

"How are we going to get out? This room opens on the main landing."

"Follow me."

They entered a large room which had been turned into a walk-in closet. Eric cut on the light.

"Push those shirts back, and you'll see a door. It leads to the servants' hallway."

Claire pushed aside the shirts and opened the door. She stared into a black hole.

"Stay there," Eric said. He cut off the light and crossed over to her. "Hold on to me and be as quiet as you can."

He led her into a hallway with only one tiny window to relieve the gloom.

"Why does this house have a secret hallway?"

"When it was built, servants weren't allowed to use the main stairways. This hallway extends the length of this floor to give access to all the bedrooms. There's one just like it upstairs."

"How do you know so much about it?"

"Little boys like to explore forbidden places. Here are the stairs. They're narrow and steep. Hold on to the railing."

She was alarmed to discover Eric was leading her up rather than down.

"How are we going to get out of here by going up?"

"I'm afraid they'll hear us if we go downstairs. There's a fire escape leading from the attic. It's nothing more than a ladder on the outside wall, but I think we can get away without their knowing they just missed catching us in bed."

The thought of her dead body being found wrapped in an amorous embrace caused Claire to miss a step.

"Be careful or they'll hear you."

They came out on a second hallway and started up another set of stairs. The air was cold and stale.

"Does anybody still use these stairs?" she asked.

"Not since I grew up."

She didn't want to think of the critters, large and small, that might have taken up residence in this dark stairwell over the last two decades. Whatever they were, she was

certain they could see in the dark and were displeased
to have her and Eric disturb their privacy. She didn't feel
a lot better when they reached the attic. Enough light
came in through dormer windows to show it was a minefield of boxes, discarded and broken furniture, and stacks
of what were probably newspapers and magazines going
back seventy-five years.

"Let's pray the window isn't swollen shut and the
hinges don't squeak," Eric said.

Claire was more worried about the view from the window. The ground seemed a hundred feet below. "Do we
have to crawl out this window?" she asked.

"It's a snap," Eric said. "I used to do it all the time.
It was my favorite escape route."

She'd have taken the stairs or she wouldn't have escaped. Only they weren't playing a game now. It wouldn't
be an angry parent who would catch them.

Eric got the window open and crawled out onto a narrow ledge.

"Once I get on the ladder, climb out," he said. "Hook
your overnight bag over your arm. It'll make too much
noise if you drop it."

Claire didn't think she could make herself climb out
on the ledge. Then she heard what sounded like someone
stumbling into some furniture. The curses that followed
were unmistakable. She climbed through the window and
onto the fire escape. She'd never been so high, and she
wasn't certain the old mortar would hold against the
weight of two adults, but to stay inside would mean certain death.

It surprised her how quickly she reached the ground.
Eric took her hand, and they raced across the open lawn
into the safety of deep shadows under the trees.

"What are we going to do now?" she asked.

"Get out of town. I don't know who's after you, but

they're a lot better at this game than I suspected. I can't risk keeping you here any longer."

But they didn't go in the direction where he'd left Aubrey's car.

"Where are you going?"

"I'm going to take Cameron's car. He's not here, so he won't need it."

He led her through a maze of backyards. This time the Labrador didn't betray their presence by barking. They reached a garage like the ones built fifty years ago—free-standing, white clapboard, with room for four cars. It looked almost like a carriage house. Considering the age of this neighborhood, it might have been.

"Cameron keeps extra keys to everything in the garage," Eric told her. "His wife loses at least one set a year."

They climbed into an SUV. Eric started the engine and backed out without cutting on the headlights. Once on the road, he turned on the lights. A moment later Claire realized they were driving by his house. He picked up the phone in the car and dialed.

"Who're you calling?" she asked.

"The police."

"I'm calling to report a break-in," he said when some-one apparently answered. "There's someone in the house at 4432 Biltmore. The owner is away. You'd better come quickly before they clean the place out. There are four entrances on the main floor. You need to station someone at each of them. I'm a neighbor."

He hung up.

"Do you think they'll catch them?"

"Probably not, but maybe it'll slow them down."

He sped up and wove his way quickly through the sleep-ing neighborhood. He pulled to a stop in front of a bank and pulled up to the ATM machine.

"What are we doing here?"

"We need money. You don't have any, do you?"

"No." She hardly ever used money. She preferred to pay everything by credit card.

"Neither do I. I don't know what connections your nemesis has, but he will find it difficult to trace cash."

Eric got his money and returned to the car quickly. Very soon they were on the Inner City Expressway headed for the interstate going north.

"Where are we going?" she asked.

"Toward the mountains for tonight. Tomorrow I'll figure out what to do next."

Claire was silent while they drove along I-85 then 64 West. It seemed that instead of getting closer to the answer of what happened, they were getting farther away and into more danger all the time. She was beginning to feel as if she were in quicksand. Unfortunately she'd dragged Eric in with her. She looked over at his profile. He looked very serious, as if he were in deep thought; but they hadn't learned anything except that somebody was determined to make sure she didn't tell anything she might know.

Only she didn't know anything. Or if she did, she didn't know what it could be.

"I'm sorry I forced you to take my case," she said.

"Why?" He glanced at her before returning his gaze to the road ahead. They were in country where deer often ran into the road at this time of night.

"They must know who you are, that you're helping me. They have to assume I've told you what I know."

"Probably."

"Then they'll need to kill you as well as me to keep their secret."

"That seems logical."

"Doesn't that bother you?" She couldn't understand how he could take things so calmly.

"I'm not exactly thrilled to be on a hit list, but I'm

more concerned with trying to figure out how to corner your boss."

"You still think it's Mr. Deter?"

"It's the only possibility. It's definitely not organized crime. They wouldn't have missed the first time. Even those men in the house weren't professionals or they wouldn't have talked. Mr. Deter obviously has contacts all over the city—he couldn't be getting information so quickly without them—but fortunately for us, he doesn't have access to professional hit men."

She supposed it was stupid, but she'd have felt better knowing a stranger was after her rather than someone she'd known and trusted for so long.

"Keep thinking about what happened these last two weeks," Eric said. "Something happened, apparently something so small and insignificant you didn't notice or remember it, but it made Mr. Deter think he had to get rid of you. He's gone to a lot of trouble and expense. You must have scared him very badly."

They turned off Highway 64 onto a narrow, winding mountain road.

"Do you have a cabin up here?" she asked.

"I do have a mountain home, but I wouldn't go anywhere near it. I'm looking for a motel I remember at one of the small lakes. It's not really prime tourist season yet. I'm hoping they have a vacancy."

To Claire who rarely left the city, and then only to go to someplace like Lake Norman or Myrtle Beach, Eric had taken her into the backwoods of North Carolina. They followed the twisting road and the stream that ran next to it for about ten miles until the overhead canopy suddenly opened up and they circled the rim of a small mountain lake. It was beautiful. Moonlight reflected off the mirror-smooth surface.

"There's the motel," Eric said, indicating a sign that

blinked *vacancy*. He pulled into a parking space. "I'll probably have to wake up the owner."

"I'll come with you."

"I'd rather you stayed here. The fewer people who see you, the better."

Claire had never thought of herself as a fugitive, and she didn't like the feeling. Despite the moonlight and the crickets and frogs, the night seemed unusually dark and sinister. She could hardly resist the temptation to look over her shoulder from time to time. Once, when a car passed along the road, she slid down in the seat. By the time Eric returned, she was as jumpy as a rabbit.

"They only have one room. It has one queen bed."

"So?"

"We can drive on to another motel."

She looked at the dashboard clock. It was past two o'clock. "It's too late. We can stay here."

Eric drove around and parked in the back. They walked back around the motel to enter their room.

"I don't want anybody to see the car," he said. "I don't think your boss can find us, but I'm not taking any chances."

The room was basic—a bed, one chair, a lamp, and a TV on the dresser where they could put their clothes. The bathroom was small but adequate. The closet was small but too large for the few things they'd brought.

"I can sleep in the chair," Eric offered.

"No," she said, looking directly into his eyes. "You'll sleep in the bed with me."

His look was just as direct. "You know I can't be that close and not touch you, not want to make love to you."

"I know."

She knew what her words meant. She didn't know how she'd found the courage to utter them. She'd never wanted any man to make love to her. But she'd never before met a man who instilled in her—or awakened—

the need to be near him, to share something at once spiritual and physical.

She saw Eric as a protector, as someone who shared her belief in her innocence. But over the course of the last few days he'd become more than that. Claire didn't understand how her feelings for this man could have erupted so suddenly or grown so quickly, but she wasn't in the mood to question any longer. She accepted the change; she wanted to know where it would lead. She had the distinct feeling it could be somewhere very wonderful.

It didn't take her long to get ready for bed. It took Eric less time. He didn't hesitate when he got into bed. He reached out to her immediately. She turned into his arms.

"Have you ever been with a man before?"

"No."

She felt him flinch, heard his breath catch, then resume at a slightly faster pace.

"Maybe this isn't the time—"

"I trust you," she said. "I want the first time to be with you."

She didn't realize until she heard her own words that she wanted every time for the rest of her life to be with Eric.

His kiss was as tender as before, but there was a different feeling about it, an urgency, a controlled tension that fought against whatever held it in check. She didn't wonder at the certain feeling he was close to exploding. She didn't need to know what lay behind such a feeling. She was content to nestle in his arms, to kiss him and be kissed by him. She loved the feeling. She was certain she could never get enough of it. The sense of being safe, protected, warm, cared for, of being attractive, desired—all of it was new and wonderful. It filled the need in her.

For the moment.

Eric's hands began to move over her body as they had done earlier, drawing her close to him, forcing her to become aware of the outward sign of his need for her. A tiny frisson of fear coursed through her. She was inexperienced but not ignorant. You couldn't be raised on a farm and not know the male and female anatomy and understand how it worked, but that knowledge had never for her been so immediate or personal.

She fought an impulse to pull away. Eric wouldn't hurt her, wouldn't force her.

Without warning, Eric deepened his kiss until Claire thought he might devour her. Rather than retreating, Claire felt herself responding, attacking his mouth. He reacted by opening his mouth and forcing his tongue between her lips. Surprise caused her to open to him. She recovered quickly, let her tongue meet his in a sinuous dance.

The effect on her body of this feast of the senses was to make her unable to remain still. She pushed her body more tightly against Eric, ground her hips against him until she was firmly lodged between his legs. The need to be closer to him grew more urgent.

She'd never been held by a man, never been close, never let a man's body touch her own. The feelings were a revelation. Despite what she'd been taught, regardless of what she'd felt when propositioned by other men, she knew this was right, that the right man could make everything as wonderful for a woman as the wrong man could make it horrible, disgusting, and scary.

She trusted Eric.

He moved his hand between them and covered her breast. The shocked surprise caused a quick intake of breath, caused her body to shudder. She'd never thought of her breasts as sensitive or sexual. She'd been very wrong.

His hands massaged her breast through the fabric of her nightgown until her nipples grew as hard as pebbles and achingly sensitive. The sensations were increased fourfold when he slipped the nightgown off her shoulder and she felt his hot hand on her bare skin. Her nerve endings came alive with a degree of sensitivity she'd never imagined possible. But none of this compared to the eruption of feeling when his mouth found its way to her nipple.

Claire practically rose off the bed. She'd never felt anything so absolutely wonderful in her whole life. She felt that her entire being had suddenly been distilled into one small part of her anatomy; that every sensation, every feeling, emanated from there; that the rest of her existed only as it related to her breast and the feeling of Eric's warm, moist lips as he suckled her inflamed nipple. Nothing else mattered. Nothing else existed.

Until his hand moved down her side, under her nightgown, and across her abdomen. Now she felt a second fire ignite in the pit of her belly. But this was a different kind of fire, a different kind of feeling. While her breast sent sparks exploding all through her like a fire igniting the nearby dry tinder, the flame in her belly burned slowly with a warm glow that started to expand like slow-moving liquid. Sparks and hot liquid. It made no sense, but together they were reducing her to a mindless, seething mass of sensation.

"Let me take off your nightgown," Eric whispered.

It seemed like magic that she could lift and maneuver her body without losing contact with his lips or his hands, almost as magical as everything else that was happening to her. The feel of her bare skin against the rough sheets, against the warm, smooth skin of his chest, of his hand cupping her buttocks and pressing her firmly against him caused the fire in her belly to grow warmer, the circle of liquid radiance to spread out a little farther. It seemed to turn everything it touched into a pool of moist heat.

The feel of his erection against her abdomen intensified that feeling.

She shocked herself by realizing she wanted to touch him. Fear of what he might say discouraged her, that and the havoc caused to her nervous system by what his hands and lips were doing to her breasts. She couldn't focus her mind for more than a split second on anything that didn't have at its center what he was doing to her body.

Then his hand moved between them once more, massaging the softness of her belly before moving between her legs.

She couldn't help it. Her muscles clamped down.

"Relax," he whispered. "Open up for me."

She tried, but her body wouldn't respond.

"I won't do anything that will hurt you."

"I know."

She did know.

"That's good," he whispered. "Now a little more."

Her muscles suddenly gave way. She lay fully opened to him.

"Has anybody ever touched you?" he asked.

"No."

"This won't hurt. If you let yourself relax, you'll enjoy it."

She couldn't imagine being able to relax. She felt as though every part of her body was stretched to the breaking point. Eric's hand moved over her lower abdomen, along her thighs, along the inside of her legs, soothing, warming, helping her to relax. She followed every move, barely breathing, waiting for something cataclysmic to happen. When it did, it wasn't at all what she expected.

She felt his fingers part her flesh and delve into the

moist heat that had pooled between her thighs. She felt
slick and wet, hot and open, the prisoner of needs that
welled up with frightening speed from somewhere deep
inside of her and swallowed her whole. Now, rather than
be anxious about what Eric would do to her, she couldn't
wait. She pushed against him, trying to drive him deeper
inside, hoping he could find the need that was torturing
her.

Then he touched something inside, and she felt like
a Roman rocket flung far into space just before it exploded. He touched it again, and exquisite shudders
shook her body from head to foot. She couldn't decide
whether this was the most exquisite pain or pleasure,
but she knew she'd never experienced anything with
such intensity, such power. Eric didn't stop. He continued to rub that spot until she thought she must cry
out.

Then when she felt she could hold back no longer, the
tension broke and flowed from her like a dammed flood.
As the waves grew weaker and her breathing returned to
a more normal pace, she was aware of Eric's movement
beside her. She heard what sounded like paper being
torn. She started.

"Protection," he whispered.

She hadn't thought of that. She was glad he had. He
moved above her, and she felt herself tense.

"This will be hardly any different from what it was before," he said.

But the sight of him looming over her and the knowledge she must take him into her body combined to banish the remaining wisps of euphoria.

He straddled her, lowered his head, and let the mois-
tened tip of his tongue play in the valley between her
breasts. Then he made circles around each nipple,
nipped with his teeth, took each into his warm mouth
and sucked gently. At the same time he found once more

the nub of extreme sensitivity that had carried her to such heights of ecstasy. Between the exploding effects of the dual assault on her body, she hardly noticed when he replaced his hand with his penis.

She felt the pressure as something large and hot pressed against her. Then before she could become worried and uneasy, her body opened and he entered her.

Claire gasped with surprise. He felt huge, as though she were so full she might burst from the effort to encompass him. He drove a little deeper, and a little deeper, until she was certain she could encompass no more.

He started to move inside her in a slow, steady rhythm. He continued his attentions to her breasts, but the pool of liquid heat in her loins continued to grow and spread until it blocked out everything else. The need that had enveloped her earlier rose up again and gripped her entire body. She felt helpless before the onslaught of the clashing, merging, exploding sensations that tossed her body about like hurricane-force winds.

She felt herself moving in rhythm with Eric, then moving to meet him, to drive him deeper and deeper inside as she strove to satisfy the need that clawed at her like a wild thing.

She heard someone cry out and was surprised to find it was herself. She couldn't stop. She gripped Eric's body, digging her nails into his back. Then as she felt another cry rise up in her throat, she felt her breath desert her, her muscles lock, her mind grow dim. Before she lost consciousness, the dam broke and the tension flowed from her in a torrent that left her feeling weak, emptied and filled at the same time, without need. She was hardly conscious of Eric as he experienced a release that caused him to erupt with a hoarse cry. They fell apart, utterly exhausted.

* * *

Claire lay awake listening to the sound of Eric's steady breathing. She had been awakened by a bad dream. She was glad to be awake, to think back on the wonderful events of a few hours before rather than the dark dream that still skirted around the edge of conscious thought.

Eric's lovemaking was still a cause for unbelieving wonder. She'd never believed such ecstasy was possible between a man and a woman. Nothing else she'd ever achieved or experienced came close to the impact this night had had on her. And she knew why.

She was in love with Eric Sterling.

It seemed almost too incredible to be possible, but she had no doubt in her mind. She loved him and wanted to spend the rest of her life with him. She didn't know how he felt about her, but she knew in her heart that no man could make her feel the way Eric had unless he loved her, too. They hadn't known each other long, but the circumstances of the last few days had made their bonding as intense as it was sudden.

Remembering that brought the truth of her situation tumbling down on her like a bucket of ice water. She had been arrested for a crime. She was out on bail. She would soon be indicted, tried, and sent to jail. It made no difference what they felt for each other.

Why couldn't she remember what it was she'd seen or done in Mr. Deter's office that set off this whole thing? It couldn't have anything to do with her dream. She'd been working at home, surrounded by competitors trying to snatch a disk from her hand—the disk that held the secrets of the new investment strategy she was developing. They offered her fabulous sums for it.

She tried to tell them she hadn't developed the strategy yet because she hadn't begun the project, but they wouldn't believe her. She told them the disk was one she'd picked up from Mr. Deter's desk by mistake.

Claire froze, her mind locked on that one tiny fact.

She turned and started shaking Eric. "Wake up! I just remembered what I did."

SEVENTEEN

"Tell me once again exactly what you did," Eric said. "The details may be important."

They were on their way back to Charlotte. If he were right, and Eric thought he was, they'd found the clue they needed. Now they had to collect the proof, and that was in Charlotte. So was the man who was determined to kill Claire, but that couldn't be helped. They had no choice but to go back.

"When my computer went down, I picked up my work and moved to my boss's office. He won't let his secretary or anyone else touch his desk, so the mess stays several inches deep. I don't know how he finds anything."

"I had a professor like that," Eric said. "He would dig down through six inches of paper and come up with exactly what he was looking for."

"I tried to find a clear spot on Mr. Deter's desk, but there wasn't one, so I put my work down on top of his stuff. I had just really gotten back to work when the whole system went down. I suppose it was the frustration that caused me to grab up one of Mr. Deter's disks without noticing."

"What did you do then?"

"I stuffed everything into my briefcase, went home, and finished my work."

"Did you touch anything else in the office?"

"No."

"Did you go in there again?"

"Not until the next morning."

"Okay, what did you do at home?"

"I booted up my computer and finished my work."

"When did you notice the extra disk?"

"When I was putting everything back into my briefcase."

"Did you put it in your computer?"

"No. I knew as soon as I picked it up that it wasn't mine."

"Do you remember what was written on it?"

"No. It was very late; I was very tired, and I wanted to be in the office early the next morning. I tossed it into my briefcase and went to bed."

"Okay. What did you do the next morning? And this is the important part. I need to know everything you can possibly remember about what you did, what you said, how Mr. Deter reacted."

"I didn't pay much attention. I had a presentation coming up in half an hour. I was concentrating on that."

"Take your time. Try to remember."

Pairs of lights came toward them through the fog like eyes of some prehistoric monster. Eric wasn't prey to superstitions, but knowing someone out there was trying to kill them gave him a creepy feeling.

"I don't remember saying anything unusual," Claire said. "About eight-thirty, I asked Mr. Deter's secretary if he'd come in yet. She said he had, but he seemed to be in a bad mood. I said I wouldn't take more than twenty seconds of his time. She buzzed him on the intercom, and he said for me to come in."

"How did he sound?"

"Irritated or impatient. I'm not sure. As I said, I was concentrating on my presentation."

"So what happened?"

"I went in, told him about the computers going down, that I'd tried to work at his desk but the entire system had gone down. I told him I'd picked up a disk by mistake. I handed it to him and left."

"Did he say anything to you?"

"No."

"He didn't ask whether you'd discovered your error before or after you loaded it onto your computer?"

"No."

"Are you sure he didn't say anything?"

"Yes. He seemed preoccupied; he was barely listening to me."

"Did that change at any time while you were in the room?"

"I guess it did. I mean, he still didn't say anything, but he was paying attention to me when I left."

"How do you know?"

"I told him I had discovered something last night that was going to make me rich. I told him I had to run because I had a presentation in half an hour, but I wanted to talk to him later. He started toward me and stumbled over his chair because he wasn't looking where he was going."

"What happened then?"

"I asked if he were all right. He said he was; so I left."

"What did you mean by what you said?"

"I'd worked out a new investment strategy that could make our department at least ten percent more effective."

"But you didn't tell him that?"

"No. It would have taken too long."

"When did you see him again?"

"I expected to see him at the meeting, but he wasn't there. I didn't see him the rest of the day. His secretary said he had locked himself in his office to get some very important work completed before a deadline. I was a little surprised because I didn't know about any deadline; but it fit in with his not being at the meeting, so I forgot about it."

"Did anything unusual happen after that?"

"No. He was preoccupied for a few days—again I put it down to that deadline I didn't know about—but I do remember his secretary saying she wondered if something had gone wrong at home."

"Why would she say that?"

"She said she'd never seen him look so worried. She wondered if his kids were in trouble again. He has two boys who've been kicked out of three or four private schools in the last few years. He's really fond of those kids and doesn't like to admit they're practically hooligans. She even wondered if his job were in jeopardy or if the department were in trouble. He'd had several private meetings with members of the big brass."

Eric felt a little better. There were no overt indications that Deter was upset about what Claire might have seen or that he was planning his frame-up, but Claire's impressions could be interpreted to mean that. He hoped he was right. If not, he might as well admit he'd never solve this case.

"Do you remember what was written on that disk?"

"No. As soon as I saw it, I knew it wasn't one of mine."

"You don't remember anything?"

"I have to go through a lot of information, handle a lot of projects, and I pick up new ones every time I get a promotion. I learned a long time ago to put out of my mind any information that didn't apply to my immediate work or job description."

"You sound like a computer deleting files."

"Exactly. My long-term memory is the filing cabinet or storage room."

Eric wished he could delete a few files that had been haunting him for years.

"The only solution is to break into your boss's computer and hope we can find what he was trying to hide."

"I don't remember the name of the file."

"I'm hoping you will remember it before we reach Charlotte. The first thing, however, is how to get into the office. I think I can pick the locks, but we have to figure out how to get around security."

"I have keys."

"Didn't they ask for them back when they fired you?"

"Yes, but I have duplicates in my apartment. I always had two extra sets made in case I lost one. Men expect female executives to lose their keys and have to call for security to let them in their offices. I made up my mind that would never happen to me."

"Now the problem is how to get them out of your apartment."

"I can just go in and get them."

"I'm sure your apartment is being watched."

"Anybody could go in and get them. They're on a hook in the kitchen."

"Of course Aubrey and I will get the keys," Mildred said. "I was hoping you wouldn't leave us out of the fun."

Eric had asked Aubrey and Mildred to meet him at the airport. He couldn't risk going back to the marina.

"It hasn't been much fun," Claire said. Her gaze cut to Eric. She didn't want him to think she included him in that statement. "But I have enjoyed getting to know you and Aubrey—and Eric, of course."

"I should think so," Aubrey said with a wink. "I haven't seen a woman yet who didn't like getting to know Eric."

"Or him getting to know them," Mildred added.

"If you two don't stop, Claire will think I'm a confirmed womanizer."

"Aren't you?" Mildred asked.

"No."

"I suppose you're going to tell me you've been waiting for the right woman to come along."

"Why not? That's one hell of a way to pass the time," Aubrey observed dryly.

"One more remark like that out of you, Aubrey Strickland," Mildred snapped, "and you'll spend the rest of the month on the couch."

"Thanks," Eric said, "but you'd better let me take the flack."

"Glad to," Aubrey said. "You've got nobody to account to."

"Unless he's found the right woman," Mildred said, eyeing Claire.

Claire couldn't prevent a blush from coloring her cheeks. She didn't know how Mildred would interpret that, but she was certain guilt would be high on her list.

"All things are possible," Eric said without looking at Claire, "but the first thing we have to do is get into that office."

"Give us an hour," Aubrey said. "If we're not back by then, send for the police."

"Are you sure we can dodge security?" Eric asked. They were going up from the parking lot through a back entrance. Claire was wearing her red wig and enough makeup to disguise three people, but he wouldn't be able to take an easy breath until they were safely out of the building.

"One of the really big bigwigs told me about it when he was trying to convince me we could sneak up to his office for a little private sex and be back before anyone knew we were gone."

"Nice people you worked for."

"They're no different from any other big executives. All men think power equates to privilege, especially when it comes to women."

Eric couldn't argue with that.

"Why did you have to have an office on the thirty-fourth floor?" he asked.

"In this company, the higher the floor, the more stature the position."

"It's a good thing you weren't president."

"If I had been, I wouldn't be in this mess."

They passed the twenty-fifth floor. Claire was out of breath. She wanted to stop and take a breather, but he hurried her on. Every minute they were in the building, they were in danger.

"What are you going to do when this is over?" he asked.

"I don't know. I've been too worried about staying out of jail to think of anything else. I have to go home," she said after a pause. "There are a lot of things I have to settle there that I've put off for years. Now seems like a good time. After that, I'll have to think about a different career. Nobody in banking will want me."

"I don't know. Depending on what we uncover, you might be a heroine. If so, you can probably get your old job back. They might even give you your boss's job. After all, nobody knows what's going on in his office better than you."

Claire grimaced.

Eric was pleased Claire didn't appear overjoyed at the prospect of going back to her career. He didn't want to have to share her with a career that had taken everything she had to give and still wanted more. He liked Claire a great deal. She deserved more than an important title, a big salary, a private secretary, and a job that consumed her entire life. She deserved a husband who could help rid her of the pernicious cant her parents had preached at her for so many years. She deserved a family, a home, and children.

Odd that they should be in similar situations.

They reached the thirty-fourth floor. "Let me check the halls," Eric said. "Stay here until I call you."

He eased the door open and looked out. The lights were on low, but he didn't see anyone in the hall. He listened intently but heard no sound.

"I don't see anybody," he said, as he motioned for Claire to follow him. "Lead the way."

They were down the hall and in Mr. Deter's outer office in less than a minute. The office was dark. He clicked on his flashlight and followed as Claire unlocked the door to her boss's office.

"Rank has its rewards," Eric said as he entered an office nearly the size of his houseboat. One whole wall was glass. Light from the city below flooded the room. "I'll fire up the computer," he said. "And for pete's sake, try to remember what was written on that disk."

"Let me do it," Claire said. "You don't know our programs or passwords." She sat down at Mr. Deter's desk. "The file name is bound to be listed on the computer," Claire said. "Maybe I'll recognize it when I see it."

Eric waited impatiently while Claire booted the computer and waited for the screens to come up. "Why is it so slow?"

"This is fast," Claire said. "You're just impatient."

"That's because at this very minute your boss's goons might be on their way here to pitch us off the roof."

"If you want me to concentrate, stop scaring me."

He was losing his cool, his edge. He didn't do a lot of breaking and entering—it wasn't his style—and he'd never done any with a woman, wouldn't have considered doing it with a woman he cared for if it hadn't been absolutely necessary.

And he did care for Claire. Very much. Every moment in this building, every moment danger hung over their heads, showed him just how much he cared.

"Found anything yet?"

"No. There are hundreds of directories, files, and subfiles. It could take hours even if I knew what I was looking for."

His instinct told him they didn't have hours. He had the feeling an hour would be too long. Unfortunately, his instincts were almost never wrong.

"Go look out the window," Claire said. "Find something to do. Looking over my shoulder bothers me."

He prowled the office, opening doors to closets, the bathroom, the storage room, looking into every corner, even behind filing cabinets; but it didn't take his mind off the problem that had just confronted him.

He was in love with Claire. He didn't want to lose her after this was over, but he couldn't tell her that he loved her, couldn't ask her to stay with him as long as he was still running away from his past. If she could face hers, he would find the courage to face his.

He knew what he'd have to do. He'd always known. He just didn't want to admit it.

"I've found it," Claire said. "I remembered the name as soon as I saw it."

He left the storage closet he'd been rummaging around in and hurried back to the desk. "Open it."

"Damn! I thought so. You have to know the password."

This was infuriating. The information he needed was just inches away, and some damned machine wouldn't let them have it because they didn't know the password. "Can't you make something up?"

"I'll have to, but I can only guess. Don't stand over my shoulder. I can't think."

He couldn't do anything but wait. Considering how many years he'd spent doing that, he was doing a very poor job now. The minutes rolled by, and the computer refused everything Claire typed in.

"What was the name of the file?" he asked.

"Elevator to the skies."

"That's peculiar."

"It doesn't make any sense to me, either."

"Do you think that's a clue to the password?"

"I don't know how it could be."

"Try something. Elevator, escalator. Plane. Helicopter. Rocket. Spaceship." He rattled off every word he could think of that had anything to do with upward motion, but nothing worked.

"Maybe it's a person's name."

They ran through everybody from industry giants to movie stars to half the leaders of the western world.

"We're not going to figure it out," Claire said. "We could be here for days, even weeks, and not figure it out."

"What we need is one of those code busters that goes through every possible permutation of letters and numbers in a split second."

"I wish I had a brain like that," Claire said. "I'd have gone straight to the top."

Eric felt as if he'd been hit with a huge fist. "You do have a brain like that," he said. "And you were going straight to the top."

"What are you talking about?"

"The password. It's your name, Claire. That's why he was so certain you knew what was on that disk. It would have gone against human nature not to open a file with your name on it."

"But what could have been in it?"

"Evaluations. Promotions. Anything. Go ahead, type in your name."

The letters came up on the screen.

CLAIRE

The program opened. They were in.

"It looks like a stock report," Eric said, "or a record of stocks and their prices."

Claire didn't answer. She was staring at the screen.

"What is it?" he asked.

"Numbers of shares in companies we bought," she said. "The prices look about right for what they were selling at before we bought them."

"They went up afterwards?"

"Of course. We have a remarkable record of buying companies and turning them around."

"Then I think what you've got there is a record of insider trading. Your boss was buying up stock before it could go up, selling later, and making an indecent profit."

"But this could represent hundreds of millions," Claire said.

"I never thought your boss was the only one involved. They've used too many contacts for it to be just one person." He handed her a disk. "Download everything so we can get out of here. I've got a prickly feeling along the back of my spine that says somebody's onto us."

"It'll take several minutes and more than one disk."

He handed her a box containing about two dozen disks. "I found these in that closet. That ought to be enough."

"Let's hope so."

Claire put a disk into the computer, selected several files, and started the download. It seemed to take forever. She put a second disk in and repeated the process.

"How long is this going to take?" Eric asked.

"I figure at least a dozen disks."

Something told him they didn't have that much time, but he knew if they left now, they'd never get back in. And if they did, the information would be gone.

"I'll check the hallway."

Claire nodded without taking her eyes off the screen. Eric looked around the office to make sure they hadn't displaced anything. He didn't want anybody to know they'd been there. He wanted the information to be here when the police showed up. He passed into the outer office, leaving the door open. He crossed the office, soundlessly opened the door, and stepped into the hall. He'd taken only one step when he noticed the elevator numbers were flashing.

They stopped on number thirty-four. Someone was coming up to this floor. He jumped back into the room, leaving the door cracked just enough to see down the hall. A security officer with a portable phone stepped out of the elevator.

"I'm on your floor now, sir. It'll just take a minute to check your office."

Eric eased the door shut, sprinted across the office, and closed the inner door.

"A security guard is on his way to this office," he hissed. "We've got to go now."

"I've finished," Claire said. "I just have to cut off the computer."

"We don't have time."

"If I don't, they'll know we've been here."

The screen was still blinking, sending messages to do this, do that. Eric could hear the guard's keys in the lock to the outer door. "We've got to go now."

"One second more," Claire said.

"We don't have one second more," he hissed and jerked her out of the chair just as she hit the last button and the screen died. "Into the storage closet," he hissed as they scooped up the disks. Eric managed to close the door just as the guard put his key into the lock of Deter's office. They stood perfectly still.

A sliver of light under the door told them the guard had cut on the light. Eric hoped they hadn't left anything lying around. For a minute that seemed like an eternity they heard nothing.

"I don't see signs of anybody being here, Mr. Deter," the guard said. "No, the computer's not on. Yes, sir. I'll check all the other rooms, but there's nobody here."

"How are we going to get out?" Claire asked. "He'll see us the minute he opens the doors."

"Follow me," Eric whispered, "and don't bump into anything." He cut on the flashlight and led her to a door on another wall. "This opens into the outer office. I discovered it while you were on the computer."

He cut off the flashlight and eased open the door. Light from the hallway entered the door to the outer office the guard had left standing open. He'd also left the door to Mr. Deter's office open. There was a good chance he would see them; but if they stayed, they'd surely be caught. They tiptoed across the room, eased out into the hall, and walked as fast as they could to the stairs.

"Thank goodness, we're safe," Claire said the moment the stairwell door closed behind them.

"We're not safe yet," Eric warned. "They may have someone watching the parking lot."

Going down the stairs was easier. They seemed endless, but they finally made it outside and into their car. Eric didn't draw a deep breath until they were out of the parking deck and several blocks away.

"Where do we go now?" Claire asked.

"To Kinko's to print all this stuff out. I want at least two hard copies."

"Then where do we go?"

"To the police station."

Claire sighed. "And after that?"

"I know where there's a great little cabin in the woods. I doubt we'd be bothered for at least a week."

EPILOGUE

"He'd been buying stock at depressed prices in companies we were about to take over," Claire explained to Mildred and Aubrey. "Then he'd sell the stock after the price had gone up."

"He was buying for other people, too," Eric said. "The scandal has just about wiped out management. They'll have to hire at least a half-dozen new people."

They were seated around the table in the dining room of Eric's house in Charlotte. The dishes from their meal had been pushed aside while Eric, Mildred, and Aubrey enjoyed a brandy. Claire had opted for coffee. She was too nervous to take more than a swallow or two. Her whole future hung in the balance, and she didn't know yet which way the pendulum would swing.

She knew she had to go home. There were some things that had to be said. But she wouldn't stay. The differences between her and her family were too great.

"I guess this was your biggest case yet," Aubrey said to Eric. "Quite a way to go out."

"I couldn't have done it without Claire."

"Are you sure Claire's been cleared of all charges?" Mildred asked.

"Yes," Eric said.

"Is she clear enough to get a job?"

"Clear enough that the bank wants her to take over her boss's position."

"Are you going to take it?" Mildred asked Claire.

"I'm thinking about it."

Claire squirmed under Mildred's gaze. She knew what the older woman wanted to know, but Claire couldn't tell her what she didn't know herself. She was relieved when Mildred turned her gaze on Eric.

"What are you going to do now?" she asked him.

"What I should have done years ago," Eric replied, "go see my father. I finally figured out there are two sides to any story, and I never let him tell his. Besides, he is the only father I'm ever going to have. I used to think he was very unsatisfactory, but I haven't been a very satisfactory son. Maybe we've both learned something."

"And then?"

"There's a company to be run, and he's close to retirement."

"Are you thinking about taking over from him?"

"I don't know. But if I do, I'll need a brilliant co-executive to help me, one who knows all there is to know about computers and investing."

Eric turned his gaze toward Claire, and her heart started to beat faster. She knew she didn't want to take that job in the bank; she wanted a different life altogether now, but what she did depended on Eric. "Is that all you want?" she asked.

His gaze seemed to intensify.

"She'll need to be available nights and weekends. I've got a lot of catching up to do."

"And after you've caught up?"

"I hope her job description will include more than computers."

"Such as?"

Mildred made a sound that could only be described as a snort. "You've been consorting with hussies so long,

Eric Sterling, you don't know how to talk to a decent woman. He's trying to propose to you, dearie, and doing a very poor job of it."

Claire's gaze never left Eric. "Is that what you're doing?"

"Couldn't you tell?"

"Of course not," Mildred said. "If you want to ask a girl to marry you, you don't ramble on about computers. You ask her straight out."

Aubrey stood up. "Let's you and me carry the dishes to the kitchen," he said to his wife. "They'll get along a lot better without you coaching from the sidelines."

Mildred looked doubtful, but she stood. "I'm giving you five minutes," she told Eric. "Think you can manage it?"

Eric's gaze never left Claire. "I'll do my best."

Mildred made that sound again. "I hope you're better at talking to your father than you are at talking to your future wife."

"Is that what I am?" Claire asked as Mildred, still grumbling, followed her husband from the room.

"If you want to be."

"Do you want me to be?"

"Yes."

"Then why can't you say it?"

"I don't want to have to take what's left over after your job."

"And I don't want to be left with the remnants of your life your company doesn't use up. Remember, I've been there."

A slow smile spread over Eric's face. "I propose a partnership. Each of us first with everything else way in the rear."

Claire smiled in return. "Practically out of sight."

Eric reached across the table. She put her hand in his. "I love you," she said.

"I love you, too."

"Are you sure? I'm not beautiful or voluptuous."

Eric sighed as if a tremendous weight had just been lifted off his shoulders. "The minute I get this table from between us, I'm going to do my best to convince you that you're both."

Not even Eric's kisses could convince Claire she was voluptuous, but they did convince her that Eric was rather fond of her—just the way she was.

BOOK YOUR PLACE ON OUR WEBSITE AND MAKE THE READING CONNECTION!

We've created a customized website just for our very special readers, where you can get the inside scoop on everything that's going on with Zebra, Pinnacle and Kensington books.

When you come online, you'll have the exciting opportunity to:

- View covers of upcoming books
- Read sample chapters
- Learn about our future publishing schedule (listed by publication month *and author*)
- Find out when your favorite authors will be visiting a city near you
- Search for and order backlist books from our online catalog
- Check out author bios and background information
- Send e-mail to your favorite authors
- Meet the Kensington staff online
- Join us in weekly chats with authors, readers and other guests
- Get writing guidelines
- AND MUCH MORE!

**Visit our website at
http://www.zebrabooks.com**

COMING IN APRIL FROM
ZEBRA BOUQUET ROMANCES

#41 MEN OF SUGAR MOUNTAIN: ONE TOUCH
by Vivian Leiber

__(0-8217-6577-9, $3.99) Ten years ago, one of three local *girls* had borne a son. All three called the child their own, never revealing which of them was the birth mother—or which irresistible Skylar brother was the father. Now, one by one, their paths will cross with the Skylar man they once loved . . . and the secret can't remain hidden forever.

#42 IT ONLY TAKES A MOMENT by Suzanne McMinn

__(0-8217-6578-7, $3.99) Prince Ferrand doesn't like going into hiding but when his life is in danger, it's his royal duty. He's not even sure he can trust the woman who's letting him take refuge at her cabin. But even he has to admit that her beauty is making him forget he's a prince . . . and remember he's a man.

#43 CHARMED AND DANGEROUS by Lynda Simmons

__(0-8217-6579-5, $3.99) One minute Maxine Henley was handed a love charm at a fair, the next, her fiancé was breaking off their engagement—over the phone! Her one consolation was Sam, her best buddy from way back. But since when did *he* become so charming?

#44 THE COWBOY AND THE HEIRESS by Anna DeForest

__(0-8217-6580-9, $3.99) Fleeing life in a gilded cage of wealth, Beth Richards immediately found herself drawn to handsome cowboy Lang Nelson. But a dark secret in her past made her shy away from Lang's passionate touch. And though she knew she'd covered her tracks enough to hide out forever, her own heart was starting to give her away . . .

Call toll free **1-888-345-BOOK** to order by phone or use this coupon to order by mail.

Name _____

Address_____

City_____ State _____ Zip _____

Please send me the books I have checked above.

I am enclosing $_____

Plus postage and handling* $_____

Sales tax (in NY and TN) $_____

Total amount enclosed $_____

*Add $2.50 for the first book and $.50 for each additional book.

Send check or money order (no cash or CODs) to: **Kensington Publishing Corp. Dept. C.O., 850 Third Avenue, New York, NY 10022**

Prices and numbers subject to change without notice. Valid only in the U.S.
All books will be available 4/1/00. All orders subject to availability.

Visit our website at **www.kensingtonbooks.com.**

Put a Little Romance in Your Life With
Fern Michaels

__Dear Emily	0-8217-5676-1	$6.99US/$8.50CAN
__Sara's Song	0-8217-5856-X	$6.99US/$8.50CAN
__Wish List	0-8217-5228-6	$6.99US/$7.99CAN
__Vegas Rich	0-8217-5594-3	$6.99US/$8.50CAN
__Vegas Heat	0-8217-5758-X	$6.99US/$8.50CAN
__Vegas Sunrise	1-55817-5983-3	$6.99US/$8.50CAN
__Whitefire	0-8217-5638-9	$6.99US/$8.50CAN

Call toll free **1-888-345-BOOK** to order by phone or use this coupon to order by mail.

Name_____

Address_____

City _____ State _____Zip_____

Please send me the books I have checked above.

I am enclosing $_____

Plus postage and handling* $_____

Sales tax (in New York and Tennessee) $_____

Total amount enclosed $_____

*Add $2.50 for the first book and $.50 for each additional book.

Send check or money order (no cash or CODs) to:

Kensington Publishing Corp., 850 Third Avenue, New York, NY 10022

Prices and Numbers subject to change without notice.

All orders subject to availability.

Check out our website at **www.kensingtonbooks.com**